# ISOLATION

Forgotten Vengeance, Book Two

M.R. FORBES

Published by Quirky Algorithms
Seattle, Washington

This novel is a work of fiction and a product of the author's imagination.
Any resemblance to actual persons or events is purely coincidental.

Copyright © 2019 by M.R. Forbes
All rights reserved.

Cover illustration by Geronimo Ribaya
geronimoribaya.com

# 1

## Aeron

The small transport slowed to a stop at the foot of the Proxima Civilian Council building. The center was in the Government District located in the massive hold of the generation starship Dove. The hold had once been home to an entire city with a population of nearly forty-thousand. Today, in a condensed square of splits and strands surrounded by greenery, it served as the seat of the planetary government.

General Aeron Haeri didn't wait for the valet to make it to his transport before pushing the door open and climbing out. He made eye contact with the young man as they crossed paths.

"Always be ready," he said, offering the advice that might prevent the valet from missing his next tip as well. Traffic inside the district was limited to VIPs, so the opportunities were typically few and far between.

Not today. Today, the valet would have at least a half-dozen more chances, and maybe more. The Civilian Council had called an emergency meeting to discuss the recent attack on the government center, an attack that had left a number of security personnel dead and the entire district on high alert.

An attack that he had helped stop.

But also helped create.

Events had spiraled out of hand more quickly than he had guessed they would, the interference of someone from outside the Organization not unexpected, but also not welcomed. He had sent Rico and Bennett in as prepared as he could've, and they had succeeded in getting Isaac out alive and making it off the planet.

But not without paying a heavy price.

He had been forced to show his hand, to incapacitate an entire squad of his own Centurions and push a hack through the planetary defense systems. These were measures that had prevented them from blasting Able, Rico, Isaac and the other members of his Black Ops team from the sky. The job had been rushed, leaving digital arteries open and bleeding information that would lead to his contact.

And that contact would lead to him.

Aeron pulled his Oracle from his pocket as he approached the Council building, refocusing on the small piece of glass that now covered his left eye. He squinted to scroll through an overlay of news that appeared ahead of the steps in front of him, quickly scanning for anything of note. A further round of eye controls brought him to his private messages, and he scanned them quickly too, ensuring there were no fires to put out before he entered.

Satisfied to find nothing pending, he removed the Oracle from his face and tucked it away again. A pair of glass doors slid open ahead of him, revealing the well-appointed lobby beyond. It had as many Centurions standing guard in it as it did politicians, and they straightened noticeably when they saw him coming.

They wouldn't for much longer. After all these years, the first support had slipped from his house of cards, and soon enough the entire thing would topple. He had played every side for nearly two decades, and sworn his allegiance to the Organization long before that. From the day he had stumbled across the hidden partition on one of Praeton's many data servers and learned the truth about the invasion of Earth, he had worked tirelessly to protect humankind—all of humankind—from the constant threat their alien enemies posed.

It was still difficult for him to think of the Relyeh and the Axon as enemies, even after all this time. Not because they weren't on opposite sides, but because the two races were so much further ahead of humans in terms of science and technology. They were far, far superior.

And yet, they were flawed.

In some ways, their intelligence and superiority became weaknesses. They were both accustomed to mastering every challenge, and the stalemate of their conflict had created cracks in both facades. Cracks too small for them to notice, but just big enough for humanity to begin to slip through. Even today, they treated humans like a footnote on their war. Earth was an important strategic planet for both, but neither one was willing to commit the resources to take it resoundingly. They preferred subterfuge and manipulation, and while at first Aeron believed the strategy was nonsense, over time he had come to appreciate the nuances. The two alien races were learning a lot about one another from their secret skirmishes on Earth and were no doubt applying that data to their war efforts.

What they didn't realize was that humankind was learning a lot too and were taking the opportunity to broaden those cracks. Potentially filling in that middle ground of intellect to outsmart the two advanced cultures using the greatest strengths of their kind. While the Relyeh were driven by an endless need to conquer and feed and the Axon were motivated by logic and algorithms, humans still operated on a more basic level. Self-preservation. Emotion. It was their weakness.

And also their strength.

He needed that strength now more than ever. Twenty years of his own forms of manipulation and deception were about to come to an end. He had done his best to prepare both Earth and Proxima for the gathering storm while keeping all of those preparations hidden within the confines of his position and the laws of the Civilian Council. Of course, he had circumvented many of them. And broken many more.

But it wasn't illegal until you got caught. And he would be caught. If not today, then tomorrow. Or a week from now.

If he made it that long. It was only a matter of time.

The assassins who had nearly killed Isaac were clones, but none of them were in the registry. They were illegal duplicates. A dangerous development he had quickly swept under the rug. It wasn't enough to prevent exposing the Organization to the light of day. If the enemy was on Proxima and had decided to come out of hiding, the truth of the situation could tear down everything the original settlers had worked so hard to build.

"General Haeri."

Aeron's eyes shifted toward the speaker, a middle-aged woman in a knee-length dress, conservatively cut around her petite frame. His mind dropped one more bomb on him before he came completely out of it.

The house of cards wasn't entirely his. The first settlers had built it when they chose to hide the past. To abandon Earth and bury the truth. To pretend they had come here to escape persecution and not because aliens had overrun the planet. To the average Proxima civilian, hell, to the average Centurion Marine, there was no such thing as aliens, and thousands of sorties into the universe surrounding the planet had proven as much.

Only now a Relyeh starship was coming, on a direct course for Earth with a near-miss of Proxima in approximately twenty-six hours. Once the ship went past, the truth would be impossible to hide or ignore.

And the Council still had no idea.

"Yes?" Aeron replied.

"I'm Special Judicus Love." She put out her hand. "I don't believe we've ever been formally introduced."

"Love," Aeron said. "I've heard of you." He took her hand, holding it while he continued. "You report directly to the Chair, instead of to me."

"I do," she replied with a smirk. She didn't try to pull her hand away. "Chair LaMont wanted me to intercept you for a brief conversation ahead of the Council meeting."

Aeron locked eyes with her, searching for a hint of discomfort or dishonesty. He didn't find any, but that didn't mean it wasn't there. It just meant she was good at hiding it. No surprise there. The Judicus were highly trained and specialized law enforcement personnel. The fact that Love was the first to greet him served as his first warning that the next few hours would play out reasonably close to his assumptions.

The only question was whether he would be alive by the end of it.

"Lead the way," he said.

## 2

### Aeron

Special Judicus Love led Aeron through an unmarked door at the side of the lobby and into a small atrium. She turned to a door on her right and swiped her wrist over the control pad, the door unlocking in response. She pushed it open, bringing him into a short, sterile white corridor leading to a hidden lift in the corner of the building.

The door closed behind them as soon as they entered, the LEDs along the ceiling dimming and turning a soft red. None of it bothered Aeron. He had been through the area before. Sensors in the room would scan him for contraband. Weapons. Poisons. Anything that could potentially be used to harm the Chair of the Civilian Council. He had always thought it was a strange setup. Since the founding of Praeton, there had never been a single assassination attempt on a sitting Chair.

And if the people ever discovered the massive,

centuries-long cover-up of hostile aliens, it would take a lot more than this scanner to keep the Chair or anyone else on the Council alive for long.

Telling a lie was easy. Maintaining it was the hard part.

"You aren't armed?" Aeron asked as they crossed the corridor, the sensors revealing their findings not only to the guards sitting on the other side of the wall but to the people they were scanning as well.

"I didn't think there was a need," Judicus Love replied. "You're the closest thing we have to a war hero. If we can't trust you, who can we trust?"

Aeron smiled. Was her choice of words intentional? "It's hard to have true war heroes without war, isn't it?"

"It's hard to have a war without an enemy."

"And yet we have the Centurions, and we train them to fight."

"Always be ready," Love said, using his earlier words against him. Had she heard him say it to the valet? She hadn't been standing close by.

The sensors didn't capture anything threatening, which allowed the lift doors to open by the time they reached them. Aeron and Judicus Love stepped into the cab. Love scanned her id over the control pad and tapped to take them to the fortieth level, the building's top floor.

"I have to admit," Judicus Love said. "I'm a bit of a fangirl. I've read all of your reports."

"All of them?" Aeron replied.

She half-winked in response. "Yes."

Aeron knew everyone in the Organization, but he didn't know every member of the Trust. The members kept a web of secrecy around their identities by design. She was suggesting she was part of that web, and that she knew he was too.

Then again, he had figured as much. He had long suspected Chair LaMont as one of the Trust's biggest supporters. The Chair wouldn't want to have to choose his words too carefully whenever a Judicus was around.

"I see," he replied. "And I have your support?"

"As long as your goals align with the needs of Proxima and Chair LaMont."

Aeron nodded. The goals of the Organization were in line with those needs by default. But not everyone would see it that way. He didn't know where LaMont stood. He was about to find out.

The lift reached the top floor, the doors opening into a large marble foyer. The walls were crowded with old paintings, some of which had been priceless before the invasion. Most of the artwork the settlers had brought with them was in the museum further forward in the ship, but some remained with the Council, out of sight of the general public.

"This way," Love said, leading him from the foyer into a large, open living space. Aeron wasn't surprised LaMont was meeting him in his apartment, rather than his offices closer to the base of the building. The public offices were all monitored. Whatever was said up here would remain up here.

Theoretically, anyway.

Chair LaMont was an older man, bald and overweight, with a small nose, big smile, and kind eyes that didn't reflect any of his thoughts. He was sitting in an old leather recliner, seat back and feet up when Judicus Love and Aeron entered. Deciding not to get to his feet, he pushed the chair into an upright position and assumed what appeared to be a relaxed position, one elbow resting on the arm of the chair. The white collared shirt beneath his gray council uniform was unbuttoned to give his paunch more room to breathe.

"Aeron," he said with a laugh. "Good of you to show up so late. We only have a few minutes before the Council meeting."

"Then you should cut to the meat," Aeron replied.

"Never one to waste words. I admire that. Fine. Short version. What the hell do you think you're doing?"

The vitriol behind the statement almost caught Aeron off-guard. Almost. He reacted calmly. "Do you care to elaborate, Francois?"

"Elaborate? You know what I mean. Sergeant Pine. Special Officer Rodriguez. The Capricorn."

"I tried to stop them."

"Bullshit. You helped them escape. Don't try to

deny it. My people have already traced it back to you."

"That was faster than I anticipated," Aeron admitted.

LaMont laughed. "You aren't the only competent person on Proxima, though it feels like you are sometimes. I'll ask again. What the hell do you think you're doing? Pine had a wealth of intel, and you sent him packing without getting any of it. How does that help Proxima? How does that help the Trust?"

"I didn't use Pine for what Pine knew. I used him for what he could bring us."

"Which is?"

"Sheriff Duke."

"You have this weird fascination with that Earth savage. I don't understand it."

"He isn't a savage. He came off a ship."

"We have three minutes. Don't stall with semantics."

"I've been General of the Centurion Space Force for twenty years," Aeron said. "I have access to intel you don't even know exists. Intel I'm prepared to share with the Council."

"I know you do. That's why you're here."

Aeron's eyebrows raised slightly. LaMont pushed himself to his feet.

"That's right. I know all about the alien spacecraft headed our way. And I know what's going to happen to this planet when the population realizes we aren't alone out here. If we handle it the wrong way, there will be riots in the streets. We have to be very careful about what we reveal, how we reveal it, and when we reveal it." He paused. "Or if we reveal it at all."

"You want me to stay silent?"

"No. I want you to address the issue that led to a meeting in the first place. How did a few rogue Centurions manage to take Sergeant Pine and steal a starship on your watch? And where do they think they're going? I can help protect you, but you need to have all the answers."

"My answer is the truth. We can't hide it anymore. I'm sure you saw the recording of my interview with Ike. The look on his face when I turned on him. We've tried to deny this war for as long as I've been alive. To pretend it doesn't exist at the same time we try to fight it. Nobody will be able to ignore that alien ship, especially if it slows at all."

"That answer isn't acceptable. The Council needs to be as surprised by the ship as the civilians are, or they'll know we already knew. They'll want more than answers. They'll want our heads."

"Rightfully."

"Not your decision, General. That's why I called you up here. Whatever you were going to say, stuff it. Answer the questions as the Council asks them and then quietly take your seat."

Aeron stared at LaMont. He wasn't surprised by the request. Anyone who knew about the Relyeh ship was bound to be afraid, regardless of their reasons. But was there more to it than that?

"What do you know about the unregistered clones?" he asked.

"I know to keep my mouth shut. Nothing has to change here, Aeron. I have assurances that Proxima will remain a free planet."

"Assurances from whom?"

"It doesn't matter. We can keep things the way they are. Nothing changes. Life on Proxima goes on the way it always has."

"What about the ship?"

"The ship will be a flash in the sky. We tell the people a comet's going to pass and we call it a day. They won't question it unless someone gives them reason to question it."

"And what about Earth?"

"Earth is on their own, the same way they've been for the last two hundred years. We can't stop what's coming to them, and neither can they. We need to look out for ourselves. It's bad enough you sent SO Rodriguez to warn them. It won't make a difference to the outcome, and it got us involved. It isn't like you to make such a reckless mistake." He paused, staring up at Aeron. "Unless it wasn't a mistake?"

"The Relyeh aren't our allies, Francois. Neither are the Axon. Whatever deal you made, whoever you made it with, it's a lie as bad as the one we keep feeding to the people."

"The Trust is decided on this. Keep your mouth shut about the ship and I can save your life. And your career."

Aeron was silent. His heart beat calmly despite the pressure LaMont was putting him under. None of this was outside the boundaries of what he thought might happen.

"I can't do it," he said. "I value humans, all humans, more than I value my life."

"That's a shame," LaMont replied. "Judicus?"

Judicus Love didn't say anything, but the door to the Chair's bedroom swung open, and three dark-uniformed clones stepped out, fully armed and armored.

"General Aeron Haeri," Love said. "I'm hereby placing you under arrest for treason against the people of Proxima. You will surrender immediately."

Aeron glanced back at LaMont, who had started buttoning his shirt. Then he looked at the three clones. They didn't have their guns drawn. Not yet. They knew he was unarmed from the scanner below.

They didn't know as much as they thought.

Always be ready.

He was.

## 3

## Aeron

At least, Aeron thought he was ready.

He expected the guards to come after him, and they did.

What he didn't expect was for one of the guards to hand Judicus Love a pistol and for her to aim the gun at Chair LaMont.

"Love? What are you—?"

It was all LaMont had time to say. The single round went in through his forehead and out the other side in a messy spray.

"General Haeri just killed the Chair," Love said calmly, dropping the murder weapon to the floor. "And he's resisting arrest."

Aeron smiled. He should have known.

The guards closed on him, drawing shock batons from their hips. Aeron remained upright, refusing to acknowledge they were in control of the situation.

Because they weren't.

"You should have just shot me," he said.

"There are four of us, and only one of you," Love replied. "And you aren't even a clone."

"Neither are you."

"No. I'm better."

She rushed him, moving faster than any regular human and confirming Aeron's worst fear. The Hunger was on Proxima. For how long?

He reached into his pocket almost casually as Judicus Love approached him. He didn't try to evade her attack. Instead, he grabbed the weapon there and jabbed it through the cloth and into her gut.

Her eyes flew wide open in shock, her momentum carrying her into him and causing the microspear to sink even deeper into her abdomen. He caught her body, holding her as the weapon did its damage, thin tendrils reaching up from the point of entry to the khoron tucked into the base of her neck.

"How?" It was all she managed to croak out before she died.

"Always be ready," he said, yanking the spear out.

He didn't let her fall, keeping her upright in his arms as he looked at the guards. They were off-balance from the suddenness of the Judicus' death—an opportunity he couldn't afford to waste.

Aeron shoved her toward the lead clone, lunging

at the man on his left. He threw a hard right hook toward the guard's face. The man caught it easily, holding Aeron's fist and squeezing. It hurt, but not as much as the microspear Aeron jabbed into the guard's abdomen.

The spear was Axon tech, designed to kill khoron. And it was made of Axon alloy, a mixture of exotic ores that didn't exist on Earth. It was invisible to scanners, including the one he had passed through coming in, and was sharp enough to penetrate nearly anything.

It went right through the layer of spidersteel beneath the thicker plates of the guard's combat armor, diving into the flesh and expanding outward to attack vital organs.

Aeron let go of it as the clone let go of his hand. Turning, he ducked behind the dying guard as the clone's body fell limply to the floor. The third guard swung at him with his shock baton, missing when Aeron moved to avoid it. The first guard caught Judicus Love's body and turned it aside to fall on the floor as he reached for the rifle on his back.

Aeron stayed in motion, pivoting around the other side of the fallen guard, somersaulting past the third guard to concentrate again on the first. He grabbed the clone's rifle, redirecting the fired rounds into the floor. Aeron jabbed the weapon into the clone's groin and pulled the trigger.

The maneuver sent the guard reeling and left Aeron within reach of the dropped handgun. He had a split second to decide whether or not to grab it. Investigators would trace the bullet that killed LaMont back to the weapon, and if they found his prints on it the entire planet would be hunting him within hours. Yes, they would realize he hadn't taken the shot sooner or later, but that wasn't the Hunger's goal here. They didn't need to stop him completely. They only needed to slow him down. It would take an investigations unit time to discover the truth.

An investigations unit run by the Judicus Department.

Maybe they wouldn't find he hadn't taken the shot. Of course, they would still have to locate the weapon first.

He grabbed the gun, spinning to his knees and aiming it at the remaining guard just as the clone swung his rifle around from his back.

Aeron fired, squeezing the trigger nearly a dozen times. The rounds were well-placed, bypassing the thick plates of the combat armor and punching into the guard's bodysuit and helmet. None of them were going to pierce the protection, but they offered a painful distraction, giving Aeron time to scramble forward and grab the microspear from the first guard's flesh and fling it at his opponent.

The clone had recovered enough to swing his rifle up in an effort to deflect the sliver of matte black alloy. He was too slow. The microspear slipped past the weapon and buried itself in the guard's chest.

He stumbled forward and collapsed.

Aeron didn't waste any time. He got back to his feet, hurrying to the downed guard and reclaiming the microspear, grateful to Sheriff Duke for sending it to Praeton with Isaac. The Sheriff had wanted him to use Proxima's more advanced tools to study it in a good faith effort to continue to improve relations between the two worlds. Hayden knew Aeron was a member of the Trust and had somehow guessed it wasn't that simple. That there was more to the situation than he had ever let on. If he ever spoke to the sheriff in person again, he would make it a point to ask him how he had come to that conclusion.

In the meantime, Aeron had to get out of LaMont's apartment. He needed to regroup and send a warning to the other members of the Organization. The Relyeh had infiltrated the planet. They had gotten close to the Civilian Council. Or worse, they had infiltrated that too. It was his job to figure out how they had gotten here and how many there were.

It was his job to make sure they were all destroyed.

He straightened his uniform, looking back at Chair LaMont. Every member of the Council had an implant tracking their vital signs. As soon as his heart had stopped the tracker had passed a code blue to the nearest emergency response station, which just happened to be on the second floor of the building.

It meant he had less than thirty seconds to figure out how he was going to get out of this mess without leaving the room in restraints.

He glanced down at the gun in his hand. Maybe he shouldn't have picked it up. But if he hadn't, he would probably be dead.

Whatever happened next, he had lost his chance to inform the Council about the coming starship, at least for now. Besides his immediate predicament, he had another more important threat to worry about. The Hunger's move against him and Chair LaMont was no accident, and he was sure it wouldn't start and end in this room.

Every single member of the Organization was at risk. So was every single person on Proxima.

His eyes darted to the lift. The control pad indicated the cab was on its way up, likely carrying a full complement of medics and guards. If he discarded the gun, he could talk his way out of the building. But they would find it within hours, and then they would come after him.

For the second time in a minute, he had to make a hard choice.

Or did he? He had been playing this game too long to be outmaneuvered so easily.

He had spent years cultivating a reputation as a strong and loyal leader. A man both his Marines and the civilians they defended held in high regard. He didn't need to run.

He also didn't need to lie.

In the absence of contrary evidence, they would believe whatever he said without question because of who he was. That didn't mean he was out of this. The death of a Judicus would lead the branch to launch an investigation of their own, and there was nothing he could do to stop it. Not without looking guilty in a manner he couldn't deny.

No, the real battle was just getting started. The Hunger was here and working against him, probably from the Judicus Department. But he could buy himself more time. Enough to warn his operatives and start fighting back. Enough to get his family somewhere safe.

If there was anywhere safe.

He put the microspear back in his pocket and placed the gun on the ground in front of him. Then he put his hands behind his head, waiting there for the remaining time it took for the lift to arrive.

The doors opened, the Centurion guards leading the way out into the room with the medics guiding a floating gurney behind them. Their rifles swept across the room before freezing on Aeron.

"General Haeri?" one of them said in surprise.

"Sergeant," he replied. "You can lower your gun. You won't need the gurney either. Chair LaMont is already dead."

The sergeant lowered his rifle, clearly confused by the scene. Aeron lowered his hands.

"The murder weapon is there," he said, pointing to the gun. "My prints are all over it. I needed it to kill one of the assassins before he killed me."

"Are you okay, sir?" The sergeant asked.

"Well enough. I'm only sorry I didn't get here in time to stop this from happening."

"It looks to me like you're lucky to be alive."

"It isn't luck, Sergeant. It's preparation. Always be ready."

"Yes sir. I'll need you to make a full report, General."

"I'll take care of the report, Sergeant."

"This is a damn tragedy," the other Centurion said. "Why did they do it?"

"How did they get a gun up here?" the Sergeant added. "And who the hell are these people?"

"I don't know," Aeron replied. "But I'm going to find out."

The medics entered the apartment, hurrying over to LaMont. They froze when they saw the bullet wound. They didn't need any fancy technology to convince them the Chair was dead.

"Damn," one of them said.

"Sergeant, secure the apartment. And keep this quiet. We don't need the media jumping all over this. The last attack still has everyone on edge."

"Yes, sir."

"Medic?"

"Yes, General?" one of the medics replied.

"Not a word of this, do you understand? As far as your report is concerned, Chair LaMont had a massive stroke and dropped dead in his recliner."

"Sir? With a bullet wound in his skull?"

"Put him in a body bag. We need to manage this internally while we get a handle on what we're dealing with." He pointed to the clones. "And make sure they disappear like the others."

"General, illegal clones are a big deal," the sergeant replied. "We can't just sweep them under the rug."

"We can and will." He made eye contact with the sergeant, passing the silent threat along in his gaze. "Understood?"

"Yes, sir."

"If any of you leak word of this to anyone, I'll have you in the brig so fast your head will spin. Consider this classified, level five."

"Sir, isn't that a Judicus?" the medic asked, noticing Love. "We can't make her disappear."

Aeron glared at Judicus Love. She was going to be a thorn in his side even after death. He needed to find something to do with her. He couldn't afford an autopsy done by the wrong doctor revealing evidence of an alien parasite. Not yet.

"Bring her back to the base and hand the body over to Doctor Klein. If anyone from the Judicus Department comes to you, you direct them to me."

"Yes, sir."

"I'll send a team to help you with the cleanup."

Aeron boarded the lift, turning around inside and tapping the control pad. The doors slid closed in front of him.

The Judicus Department would come. They had the authority to bring him in and submit him to any means of questioning they deemed necessary. While some of the Judicus worked for the Trust, some wasn't all.

The race was on.

4

Hayden

Sheriff Hayden Duke charged up the ramp and into the dropship with Sergeant Walt balanced over his shoulder in a fireman's carry. He was only a few steps behind General Nathan Stacker. The General, clad in his massive suit of powered armor, cradled an unconscious Caleb Card in his arms.

"Pyro!" Hayden shouted, knowing she could hear him through the shipboard comm. "Get us airborne." He made the top of the ramp and hit the access control, a whirring sound accompanying the back ramp as it began to rise and latch closed.

"I'll wait here," Nathan said, dropping to a knee to lower Caleb to the deck. It would take too long for him to shuck his armor to get up to the main deck of the dropship, especially when he would need to get back into the armor a few minutes later. "I'll reload us."

"Pozz," Hayden said, still holding Walt as he ran to the stairs, climbing them to the next deck.

Both Deputy Hicks and the remaining Eagles were waiting at the front of the space, spread across rows of simple jump seats. Corporal Hotch got up as soon as he saw Walt, heading toward them.

"Is she—"

"She's alive," Hayden replied without slowing. "I'm taking her to a bunk. Head downstairs and help General Stacker with Colonel Card."

"What happened to the Colonel?" Hotch asked.

"Just do it."

"Yes, sir." Hotch turned and ran for the stairs. Hayden hurried through the first section of the craft, taking the port corridor past the bridge to the steps leading up to the bunks. He nearly fell over as the dropship lurched into the air, the sudden momentum pressing him back. He managed to get his elbow into the bulkhead, wedging himself tight as the craft rapidly ascended.

"ETA to Sanisco, five minutes," Pyro announced.

Hayden had that long to get Walt into a bed, get back down to the hold, and grab some guns.

Sanisco was under attack. They had seen the smoke from the field where they had helped save a goliath from the alien xaxkluth, the large, many-tentacled creatures Caleb said belonged to a Relyeh called Nyalarth.

He didn't need to see more of the creatures to

know what was assaulting Sanisco. He knew the enemy force was on its way. According to Caleb, the whole planet was under threat from them; the entire world spotted with thousands of the hard-to-kill alien monstrosities. He still had no idea how or when the Relyeh had managed to plant so many of them in so many places, but it didn't matter that much right now.

Right now, his city, his people—and most importantly—his family were in trouble.

"Pyro," he said, loud enough for any of the nearby comms to pick up his voice. "Any word from HQ?"

"Negative, Sheriff," Pyro replied. "And I don't understand it. The link is green. Active. The only way we shouldn't be able to talk is if nobody is monitoring the comm."

"That can't be possible," Hayden said. He didn't understand it either. The enemy was anything but subtle. There was no way they could sneak up on the city without any of his deputies reporting back to headquarters and from headquarters out to Pyro.

Or was there?

His heart was already racing, both from his earlier exertion and his current desperation. Now, a sense of cold dread washed over him, causing his chest to tighten and his body to shiver.

Josias.

The man who had come to Law to report his

missing wife. The wife Hayden had rescued and who had told him her husband was dead.

The moment she had told the story, he had worried there was an Axon in Sanisco. But when they saw the goliath, he thought he would have time to help it and still get back to Sanisco before the Axon Intellect made its move.

Had he thought wrong? If there was no one in Law on the comms, did that mean the Axon had killed them? Was the attack on the city related, or had the Intellect adjusted its timeline to finish its business before the assault?

Was it all timed to occur while he was positioned north of the city and out of the equation?

He was the Sheriff, but he was still only one man. He couldn't be everywhere he was needed at once and he couldn't fight a xaxkluth or an Intellect on his own. Why would either opponent attribute so much importance to him?

He resumed his motion up the steps, his legs burning as he carried Walt to the top. The corridor wrapped around toward the center of the dropship, the racks in cubbies on either side. Hayden stopped at the first one, tapping the control panel to open its privacy shield and quickly lowering Walt onto the bunk.

She groaned slightly as he did, but she didn't wake up.

Hayden stared at her for a few seconds. She was a host to a khoron who claimed it was seeking a new purpose after the loss of its master and had chosen to follow Nathan. It was a tough story to believe, but Caleb had chosen to believe it and allowed her to stay with the team.

Now Hayden wondered if that decision had been a blessing or a curse. The xaxkluth they were fighting had frozen mid-attack, stopped by a silent order sent to the creature through the Relyeh Collective. At first, he thought Caleb had sent the command, but the way Caleb had looked at Walt proved she had done it.

Hayden understood the problem without needing it spelled out. He had enough experience with the khoron to understand. None of their kind were powerful enough to seize control of a xaxkluth, and yet she had.

Which meant if she was a khoron, she was uniquely powerful.

If she wasn't a khoron, then what the hell was she?

Caleb had confronted her then and there, likely to answer that question. The resulting battle of wills had taken them both out of the fight.

It left Hayden hesitant to leave her alone. She had used her ability to stop the xaxkluth and save their lives, but she had also fought back against Caleb. Whose side was she really on?

"Sheriff," Hotch said, reaching the top of the steps. He and Hicks were carrying Caleb.

"There," Hayden said, pointing to the bunk

across from Walt. "Close the shield so they don't see one another."

"What happened out there?" Hotch asked.

"Save it for later," Hayden replied. "We've still got trouble. Hicks, can you fight?"

"I'm still breathing, Sheriff," Hicks answered as he helped place Caleb onto the bunk.

Hayden smiled. "Get downstairs and tell Nathan you're ready to serve."

"Roger."

"What about me?" Hotch asked.

"I want you to stay with these two," Hayden replied. "Make sure they don't kill one another."

"I want to fight."

"Believe me; you'll have your chance."

"Okay, Sheriff."

Hayden rushed back down the steps, stopping at the door to the bridge. He knocked on it and it slid open. Pyro didn't look back at him, keeping her attention focused on the route ahead.

Hayden looked up at the primary display. He found Sanisco near the bottom, visible only because of burning fires and muzzle flashes. The power was out, and apparently, so was the emergency backup. The city was dark, leaving the xaxkluth impossible to see from this altitude, but he was sure they were there.

"We're almost there, Sheriff," Pyro said, reading his mind. "You should head to the hold to get ready."

"I wanted to see it," Hayden replied. "Get us as close to the pyramid as you…" He was cut off by a sharp tone through the comm, followed by someone issuing an emergency transmission.

"Mayday. Mayday. Mayday. This is the Capricorn. We are under attack. I repeat, we are under attack. Can anyone hear me?"

"Where's that coming from?" Hayden asked.

"Tracking. Standby."

"Mayday. Mayday. Mayday. This is the Capricorn. We are under attack. I repeat, we are under attack. Can anyone hear me?"

"I've got it, Sheriff. She's on the ground just north of Sanisco."

"On the ground? That doesn't sound good."

"Mayday. Mayday. Mayday. This is the Capricorn. We are—"

"Capricorn, this is the Parabellum," Pyro interrupted. "Do you copy?"

"Parabellum?" The woman's voice relaxed slightly, the tension replaced with confusion. "That ship was decommissioned and sent for recycling twenty years ago."

"Not exactly," Pyro replied. "I've got your position. What's your status?"

"We were attacked on the way in. We're still under attack. Who are you?"

Hayden moved back onto the bridge. "Capricorn, this is Sheriff Hayden Duke of the United Western Territories."

"Hayden!" Isaac's voice boomed through the comm, his excitement palpable. "We're in trouble. We need help."

Isaac? He had said he wanted to come back to Earth, but Hayden had never thought Proxima would let him return so soon.

"The whole city's under attack," Hayden replied. "But I'll see what I can do."

"They're hitting the ship," another voice Hayden recognized said. Rico. "Crushing the hull. We won't last much longer."

"Damn it." Hayden looked up at the display. The city was getting close. There was no sign of xaxkluth near the pyramid yet, but it didn't change the fact that nobody was answering their comms. "We're on our way. Be ready to make a break for it."

"Roger that, Sheriff," Rico said.

"Pyro, drop me off at the pyramid. The observation deck. Then go and help the Capricorn."

"We should stick together, Sheriff."

"I wasn't asking."

Pyro smirked slightly and nodded. "Pozz that, Sheriff. Get down to the hold and hang on tight, we're going in hard."

Hayden went back to the door, stopping there as it slid open.

"Pyro," he said, getting her attention. "Thank you."

"Good hunting, Sheriff."

# 5

## Hayden

"Change of plans," Hayden said, dropping into the hold. Nathan had already laid out a fresh round of arms for him. A P-90 plasma rifle to go with the MK-12 assault rifle, armor and a helmet. Except there was no time to put it on. He couldn't manage two guns without the armor to hold one, so he settled for the plasma. "Where are my glasses?"

"I didn't know we had a plan," Nathan replied. "There." He pointed to Natalia's creation. Hayden quickly grabbed them up and slid them on.

Nathan had reloaded his rifle and packed two more boxes of ammunition on his back. Hicks was there too. His arm wasn't moving too well, but he had managed to get a grip on a plasma rifle, which didn't have recoil.

Three men against an entire army of xaxkluth. If Hayden could get to the comms and rally his deputies, they might have a fighting chance.

"Well, it's changed. Pyro's going to drop me at the Pyramid. Nate, there's a Centurion dropship down on the other side of the bay. My friends Rico and Isaac are on it. They're getting battered by xaxkluth."

"You want me to rescue them?"

"Pozz."

"Consider it done. We'll pull them out and haul ass back to you."

"We're over the city," Pyro announced. "Find something to keep you planted."

There were straps against the bulkhead. Hayden and Hicks hurried over to them, buckling in. Nathan activated the magnets on the feet of his armor, securing himself to the deck.

The dropship did what it was made to do. It dropped straight down like a stone. Hayden's stomach dropped with it, and he clenched his teeth as the ship shook against the air resistance—a brick falling from two kilometers up. The restraints kept him planted, but it still bothered him. Never much for flying, let alone falling, he closed his eyes.

At least he wasn't HALO jumping.

The thrusters fired a dozen seconds later, shaking the dropship even more violently. The craft began to slow. Nathan walked over to the ramp control and activated it and the back of the ship started to open.

Hayden undid his restraints. The g-forces were driving him into the floor now, making it harder for him to walk across the deck. They eased quickly as the dropship came to a stop, the ramp hanging open at the back. The glass of the Pyramid's forty-second floor sat directly behind it.

"Good luck, Sheriff," Nathan said as Hayden broke into a run. He reached the edge of the ramp and jumped off, falling two meters and rolling on his shoulder, back to his feet. He heard the ramp start closing behind him, the thrusters firing and the dropship launching back into the sky.

He heard other things too. The groaning of the xaxkluth. The screaming and shouting of the people below. Gunfire, but not nearly enough. They weren't ready for this. They weren't prepared.

It was his damn fault.

He had assumed there was time. That he could get Natalia an ick and they could use the Collective to find out what was happening. He was wrong. He should have put the city on alert. He should have gotten the people out of there.

But where the hell would he have taken them?

There was nowhere safe out here. Nowhere the xaxkluth couldn't find them. Edenrise hadn't managed to survive the assault, and that was with an Axon shield. What chance did they have?

What chance did any of them have?

For two hundred years, the Relyeh were content to let the trife keep the population under control. To ignore Earth while they waged war against the Axon. But something had changed. Something had driven them to put a new focus on the planet and finish what they had started.

But what?

He had hoped to build a new civilization from the rubble of the old. The United Western Territories were the start of something bigger and better. Was that the reason the Hunger had come? Because they were getting too organized? Because he had started turning the Earth into a threat? Or was he giving himself too much credit?

The seeds had been sewn a long time ago. The xaxkluth were already here, planted and waiting. Were they designed to hatch when they did? Or had something triggered it?

The questions swirled through Hayden's mind as he sprinted through the patio doors and into the newly painted room, across it to the stairs. No power meant he would have to make the descent on foot. All forty-five floors.

He didn't care. Motivation gave him strength. He had to find Natalia, Hallia and Ginny. He needed to know they were safe.

He entered the stairwell. With not even emergency lighting to see by, he activated his glasses and checked the battery. Fifty percent. More than enough. The night vision filters activated, painting the stairs in grayscale.

Hayden bounded down the stairwell, taking the steps two at a time. He used his augments to brace against the walls on the landings, crashing around the corners hard and fast. Slipping more than once, he nearly went down entire flights on his back, desperately trying to get to the bottom and beyond.

The sounds of conflict began to leech in through the walls the lower he went, the attack continuing outside, the xaxkluth drawing closer to the Pyramid. He was breathing hard when he reached the fifteenth floor, his lungs burning, his heart thumping rapidly. His legs were tired, his muscles like rubber. But he didn't dare slow down.

He was on the twelfth floor when the building shook for the first time, the sound of breaking glass and cracking stone a sudden blast of violent noise that echoed in the stairwell. The shaking knocked him from his feet, finally enough to send him tumbling down to the eleventh floor. He hit the wall with his side, catching the worst of it with his augment. Dust and debris filled the air, threatening to choke him as he heaved in deep breaths. It took him a couple of seconds to get back to his feet, and he stumbled downward, heading for his apartment.

A xaxkluth groaned outside, close enough he could hear its deep rumble clearly, removing any doubts about the truth of the situation.

The enemy had reached the Pyramid.

## 6

### Isaac

"You two get to the hold," Able said. "I'll stay here to communicate with the Parabellum."

The dropship groaned, the pressure the xaxkluth tentacles were putting on its frame increasing. The whole thing could give any moment, allowing the aliens to bend the alloy and crush them all.

"We'll need to move fast," Rico replied. "There's nothing you can do here."

"There's a lot I can do here," Able countered. "Like tell you when they've arrived, or if they aren't going to make it."

"You might not make it either," Isaac said to the older woman. Her uniform had been torn in the crash, and he noticed the area near her abdomen was darker than the rest. "You're injured."

"Piece of metal went through my back," she said. "The fact is, I'm not going to make it anyway."

Rico whipped toward her. "Able…"

"Don't cry about it, Rico. I'm an old lady. I had my life, and I don't have any regrets. I refuse to die before I help you get to safety."

Rico stared at Able for a moment and then turned away again. "Ike, let's move."

The door to the bridge slid open. Isaac stopped in front of Able. "Thank you."

"For what?" she asked. "You're the ones who have to go out there with those things." She laughed. "Get moving, Sergeant."

Isaac looked away. He hated the idea of leaving anyone behind. But if her wound was as bad as it looked from the bloodstain, she wasn't getting out alive anyway.

"Ike, today!" Rico snapped from the doorway.

He glanced at Able one last time before following Rico from the bridge.

They ran across the top of the deck toward the bow. The bulkhead was already warped, the jump seats dislodged or bent, the dim emergency lighting casting the whole thing in an eerie glow. The Organization's soldiers were huddled together over Jorge, the youngest of their number.

Drake noticed them first, rising and looking at them. "What's the situation, Major?" he asked.

"We made contact with another dropship," Rico replied. "They're coming in for an extraction. We need to be armed and ready to move." Her eyes shifted to Jorge. She didn't ask if he was alive. It was clear he wasn't.

"Broke his neck when we flipped," Drake said. "He locked the buckle wrong."

"Is anyone else hurt?"

"Banged and bruised, but ready to get the hell out of here. Able?"

"She's covering the comm," Isaac said.

"She needs to get out of here with us."

Drake started toward the bridge. Isaac put his hand on the soldier's chest. "Forget it, Drake. She won't come."

"I'll drag her ass out."

"She's already dead," Rico said. "She's got shrapnel in her kidney, and we don't have a doctor or a hospital to bring her to."

"Your fancy Sheriff doesn't have a damn doctor?"

"You haven't seen what it's like outside. We'll be lucky to get out of the area alive."

"Good pep talk," Drake said.

"I told you, there's a ship en route. We have to be ready to go. Get to the hold and grab whatever gear you can. That's an order."

"Yes, ma'am. Centurions! Get your tails up and moving. We've got zero seconds to prep for extraction. Let's help each other get home alive."

The other soldiers got up, moving away from Jorge.

"Are we on Earth?" Lucius asked.

"No, dipshit, we're in Uranus," Drake replied. "Yeah. Welcome to Earth, bro. Now try not to die."

Lucius leaned over Jorge, tapping his chest. "RIP, brother." Then he joined the rest of the soldiers, following Isaac and Rico to the upside-down stairwell.

"How do we get up?" Spot asked.

"Grab the edge of the risers, climb back until you can twist to the ceiling," Isaac said.

"You've done this before?" Drake asked.

"No," Isaac replied.

"Ike, you're the tallest," Rico said. "You go first. Once you get up there, see if you can reach the latches for the crates. They're all mag-locked to the deck, so they shouldn't have moved during the crash."

"Roger that," Isaac replied. He moved into position, looking up at the stairs over his head.

A loud crack sounded, followed by the piercing whine of bending metal to the aft.

"And hurry," Jesse said.

Rico looked around, her eyes suddenly wide. "Where's Bennett?"

"I haven't seen him," Drake replied.

Isaac could see the fear on Rico's face. Even though this Bennett wasn't her late husband, she couldn't help but worry about him.

"Rico!"

Bennett's face appeared over the edge of the stairwell above. The left side of it was bruised, and he had a gash on his forehead, but he was up and moving.

"Shit, Bennett," Rico said. "You scared the hell out of me."

He smiled, reaching back and then tossing a climbwire down to them. "Do you want to complain, or do you want to get out of here?"

She smiled back at him. "Drake, secure the line."

Drake took the end and pulled it taught, dropping to his knees.

"Ike, you first. Let's go."

Isaac grabbed the wire, finding it had a surprisingly comfortable grip despite its smooth metal appearance. He lifted himself onto it, Drake holding it in place while he started scaling it with his hands and feet. The wire vibrated slightly as Spot grabbed it beneath him.

"Centurions," Able said over the comm, her voice soft. "The Parabellum is closing. Two minutes."

"Climb faster, Centurions!" Bennett barked.

Isaac reached the lip of the ceiling, and Bennett helped pull him up. Isaac's breath caught in his throat when he saw the back of the deck was crushed, the ramp a mangled mess of metal. A xaxkluth tentacle was reaching in through a separation, trying to get to them.

"Portside hatch," Bennett said, motioning. Isaac looked. Guns and armor were already arranged nearby. "I took the liberty as soon as we stopped crashing."

"You didn't buckle in?" Isaac asked in shock.

"Only until we hit the ground." He touched the side of his swollen face. "I'm a clone. It'll heal fast."

Isaac couldn't believe Bennett had survived the impact, especially considering both Able and Jorge hadn't.

"You've got two minutes, Ike," Bennett said. "Suit up."

Isaac hurried to the port side. He found his armor by eliminating all of the suits that weren't his. The combat armor had been new tech when he went into stasis, unavailable to MPs. He grabbed it almost reverently. Under any other circumstances, it would be exciting to put it on.

Spot joined him a moment later, followed by Jesse, Lucius, and Rico. Drake was the last one up, making it to his gear with less than a minute to spare.

"Help him out!" Rico snapped.

Lucius and Jesse hurried to Drake, each taking a side to help him get his armor on and clamped. They had just closed the last clasp when the xaxkluth at the back managed to tear away a larger piece of the hull and clear enough space for its tentacles to enter.

Isaac turned on it at the same time as the others, getting his rifle level and opening fire. Six guns pounded the few tentacles, driving them back and out.

The xaxkluth vanished, leaving the highway

they had crashed on visible, the cracked pavement and rusted cars mingling with brown vegetation. Then its central mass appeared in place of the tentacles, toothy mouth churning as more limbs pulled at the metal, trying to enlarge its access point.

Isaac and the others continued shooting, expending hundreds of rounds within a few seconds without serious effect. Had they survived the crash to die minutes later? How was anyone supposed to kill these damn things?

Another pair of tentacles ripped at the starboard hull, peeling it away like a lid to a sardine can. It reached for the group, nearly grabbing Bennett before Rico's attack tore the limb apart.

"Let's go!" she shouted through their networked comm. The side hatch to the ship slid open, revealing the ground ten meters below. She dropped the climb wire, passing the other end to Bennett. "Hook it to the stairs."

"I'll keep you covered," Isaac offered, dropping an empty magazine and exchanging it for a fresh one.

"No," Rico said. "You're the VIP."

"I've got this," Isaac replied. He didn't want special treatment, especially in the middle of a firefight.

"I wasn't asking," Rico snapped, grabbing his arm and yanking him toward the hatch.

Bennett made it to the stairs, wrapping the wire

around it and clamping it together. The xaxkluth reached for him again, and he dove behind the steps only moments ahead of a tentacle snaking through the space where he'd stood.

"Damn it. I can help!" Isaac shouted.

He felt the change in the air as incoming plasma fire streaked down from the sky, large bolts slamming into the first xaxkluth. It groaned in surprised pain, turning its central mass in the direction of the shot. Isaac did the same, catching sight of the dropship out of the corner of his eye. It was dropping fast, coming in too close to the action.

"The Parabellum is here!" Able said, her voice barely audible over the din of gunfire and the weakness of her slow death.

"Time to go!" Rico growled, turning Isaac and shoving him toward the hatch. "We did this to get you to Sheriff Duke alive. You had damn well better make it alive!"

He stopped arguing, feeling sheepish as he grabbed the line and quickly rappelled down the side of the ship. He could hear more xaxkluth nearby and watched as one went past in the direction of the Parabellum.

He hit the ground, Rico right behind him and the rest of the Centurions right behind her.

"Get clear," Able said, coughing into the comm. "I'm gonna blow the ship."

Isaac ran toward where the dropship was coming down a few hundred meters to the north. It started firing on the xaxkluth, pounding it with plasma.

"Let's help them out!" Rico said, shooting at the creature from behind. The other Centurions joined her, their rounds hardly enough to distract the thing.

Isaac looked at the world through his helmet's heads-up display, noticing the grid in the lower corner and the red blobs filling it behind the green marks of the Centurions. There were at least six of the Relyeh monsters behind them, and while most were still intent on crushing the Capricorn, two others had peeled off to chase them toward the other dropship.

"We aren't going to make it," Drake said, noticing the activity behind them at the same time Isaac had.

"Just keep running!" Rico replied.

The Parabellum spun in the air to reveal its open rear ramp and then lowered to the highway. Isaac nearly stopped in his tracks when a large metal humanoid raced out, clutching one of the largest rifles he had ever seen. A human in combat armor followed behind it with a plasma rifle, firing into the alien creature.

The armor started shooting, its rifle whining loudly as it spat hundreds of rounds into the xaxkluth, ripping off four limbs in a blink and tearing through its central mass. The xaxkluth screamed and tried to defend itself, but the resurgence of fire from the Parabellum's cannons burned into it and it finally collapsed—dead.

"Up and over!" Rico snapped. "Let's go, Centurions!"

The armored mech leaped from the dropship, landing on the dead creature's carcass. Isaac's HUD flashed, indicating it had requested to join their network. Rico accepted the request, and two more green marks appeared. The armor was marked as General Stacker. The other Deputy Hicks.

"Move, move, move!" Stacker roared into the comm, unleashing hell from his rifle at the xaxkluth on their tail. The Parabellum bounced into the air, hovering at twenty meters and shooting over the General at the approaching creatures.

Rico reached the dead alien first. She leaped over the tentacles, bouncing off the meter-thick mass easily with each armor-augmented bounce. Isaac was right behind her, but he barely cleared the first tentacle and stumbled over the second. He didn't have the extra athleticism of a clone and he had spent the last month in the hospital.

"I've got you," Lucius said, coming up beside him and taking his arm. He helped Isaac make the next jump, and the jump after that.

They cleared the dead xaxkluth. Deputy Hicks waited on the edge of the ramp, shooting at the other creatures between offering each soldier a helping hand on board. "Aim for the eyes!" he shouted, more careful with his shots than Stacker.

Isaac turned, using the armor's combat system to help him aim. He started shooting, but the xaxkluth brought a tentacle up in front of its face to block the shots.

The Parabellum stopped blasting them, coming back to the ground as the rest of the Centurions arrived. The two xaxkluth would be on them in seconds. Too soon for them to get on board and lift off again.

Then the Capricorn exploded.

# 7

## Caleb

Caleb woke up.

He knew instinctively he wasn't truly awake.

The place he was in wasn't the last place he had been. It wasn't a field, a dropship, a bunk, a latrine or anything else that resembled anything he was familiar with in the human world.

This place was a dark, blank slate. One he had visited before. A part of the Collective.

The blankness faded. He stood on a black stone ledge, looking out at a black waterfall spilling into a black river. The banks on either side were blanketed in black grass and black flowers, the shades just variant enough for him to make out the details of the different elements, but only barely.

He didn't want to be on the ledge. He wanted to be down there, next to the river.

He stepped to the edge and looked down. The

river was passing him, flowing off into the darkness. He didn't need prompting or thought.

He jumped.

There was no sensation of falling, and when he hit the water and went under, there was no sensation of being wet. He kicked to the surface and looked around. "Ishek, are you here?" he asked softly, treading water. He could access the Collective through his Relyeh symbiote, but normally they both couldn't enter it at the same time. He just needed to be sure the rules hadn't changed.

As he expected, there was no reply.

He swam toward the waterfall and the pool at its base. It wasn't deep, allowing him to stand. He remained fixed there. Waiting. This was a Relyeh Construct, a pocket universe inside the mind of an ancient. It was a difficult concept to grasp, so he didn't even try. The Hunger were hundreds of thousands of years old. They didn't operate under human concepts of physics or technology. They knew things about the universe humankind would likely never begin to imagine.

He was here, and that proved this at least was possible.

He was here, and that meant the ancient had found him in the Collective and brought him here.

He might have resisted if he were capable. Walt. She had done something he never expected. She had seized control of the xaxkluth, freezing them in place. She had succumbed to his demands to keep herself open to him, and then she had displayed a power he didn't possess. She was no khoron. He was sure of that much.

So what was she?

*Who* was she?

Her actions had saved their lives. But when he had tried to access her mind, to discover how she had brought the xaxkluth up short, she had rebuked him, putting up a wall so solid he wasn't able to break through. He hadn't sensed malice from her, but rather fear. She was afraid to be discovered. Whoever she was, whatever she was, she hadn't been lying when she told him she was hiding.

From who?

From what?

Was this place the source of her concern? Had her efforts failed, and the ancient she was running from discovered that he knew something?

Or was this her construct?

Was she a Relyeh ancient?

That didn't seem possible. Why would one of the original Hunger need to hide on Earth disguised as a follower of another?

The back and forth had tired him out, enough that he had lost consciousness. It must have worn out Ishek too, or he would have resisted the ancient's call. Not that he could. Not forever. While they had learned to firewall themselves from the whole of the Relyeh masses, the most powerful of the race could always find a crack to break through.

They just didn't often take notice of anyone as insignificant as he was.

So he stood silently in the pool, listening to the roar of the waterfall and waiting. He had been brought here for a reason. It was pointless to fight it or to grow impatient. It was better to simply accept.

It seemed like a long time, but time didn't pass in a Construct the way it did in reality. Hours here were seconds there. Maybe when he woke, he would still be in the field near the dead xaxkluth, with Sheriff Duke and General Stacker nearby.

He noticed a change in the fall of the water to his right, and he glanced toward it. A woman appeared there, moving through the water and its mist. She was albino white, with a slender frame, a narrow, oval face; large eyes and long white hair that sparkled without a light source. The only color came from her eyes—a light gold.

The waist-high water, ran from her body like ink, giving her an appearance of marble. Her expression was flat, her lips pressed together, her jaw tight. Her eyes registered curiosity.

And anger.

Caleb stared at her without speaking as she walked toward him, stopping less than a meter away. He fixed his eyes on hers, trying to solve her identity before she spoke. He could feel the pressure in his head now. Their minds were connected through the Collective. She had edged into his mind. She could see everything in there. His memories, his history, his experiences. She knew what he had gone through to get back to Earth. She knew what he had done before he came.

And she knew what he had returned with. The package Riley Valentine had embedded in his psyche for delivery to Proxima Command.

"I should kill you," she said. Her voice was sweeter than Caleb expected, and combined with her words, took him by surprise. She could do a lot to him through the Collective, but he didn't think she could make good on that threat.

"I'm too valuable to kill," he replied.

She stared at him. His response wasn't what she had expected. Good. That's why he had said it.

"Presumptuous."

"Honest."

She smiled. "I like you."

"I don't care. Who are you?"

*You know who I am.*

Her voice boomed into his mind, while her avatar gazed at him in silence.

"Nyalarth," he said, the name coming to him.

The woman, the waterfall, the pool all vanished, fading away and leaving him floating in a sea of nothingness. It was replaced a moment later by a new darkness.

Caleb stood in a corridor or cave of some kind. Black fibers stretched across the small expanse, some thicker, some thinner, all of them moist and dripping a viscous black fluid.

A grunt to his left got his attention. He pivoted, just in time to see a Relyeh pass him by. A Norg. A large, stocky humanoid with a large, bulbous head and a mouth surrounded by tentacles that writhed as it breathed. It wore a simple black robe over its leathery flesh, a four-fingered, slightly clawed hand hanging out from the sleeve.

It didn't see him because he wasn't where it was, and it wasn't where he was. Nyalarth had constructed the scene. She wanted to show him something.

"Follow it," the alabaster woman said, appearing beside him. She was naked, but lacked any sign of reproductive features. No female genitalia between her legs, no nipples at the end of her breasts. No hair beyond her head. It was as if she were wearing an Axon Intellect Skin. A white one.

Caleb didn't argue. He trailed the Norg along the corridor. It became more familiar to him as he walked. This was a Relyeh environment, dark and damp. "Where is it going?"

"To feed its prisoner."

Caleb glanced at Nyalarth's avatar. "Who is its prisoner?" He paused. "Don't tell me Valentine is still alive."

She didn't respond to the statement. "Follow."

He did, continuing behind the Norg, trailing it along the corridor to a wall of fiber and mucus. It stretched aside as the Norg approached, pulling away like a living thing and revealing a dark mound in the center of a room. A soft diffusion of light shined through tiny holes in the floor.

The mound was as damp as the rest of the area, its outer shell gelatinous and still. Caleb followed the Norg into the room, pausing just inside the opening before it closed off again. The Norg grabbed its robe and lifted it over its head, tossing it aside. The alien creature was naked beneath, a short tail that split into multiple tentacles flowing from the top of its buttocks. He was glad he couldn't see the front.

It stood in front of the mound, waiting.

Caleb waited too, Nyalarth's avatar beside him. He still had no idea why he was here, or why she was showing him this.

The mound shifted. Only slightly. A blue light appeared in the center of it. The Norg took a step back, its body suddenly beginning to shake. A second light appeared. Then a third. Each one illuminated the room a little more, and by the time the sixth light appeared Caleb could make out some of the mound's features.

Dozens of tentacles were coiled around it, still static in the darkness, while a mouth began to split from the bottom of the mass, revealing thousands of teeth.

The Norg started grunting and turned toward Caleb, suddenly terrified and desperate to escape. Caleb moved aside as the Relyeh passed through him to grab the fibers of the door. It started tugging at them as if it were strong enough to break free.

The mound began to rise, lifting itself on its tentacles. Caleb realized then that the lights were its eyes, and they intensified as they gazed at the frightened Norg. Blue beams reached out from them, catching the squid-faced alien and yanking its arms and legs out as if they were ropes. The Norg cried louder, the blue beams pulling it toward the mound and the waiting teeth.

Caleb turned away as the Norg was brought to the creature, tentacles lashing out and grabbing it to help guide it into the open maw. The other Relyeh devoured it within seconds.

"Why are you showing me this?" Caleb asked, glaring at the avatar.

"The prisoner must be set free," she replied.

"Even if I knew where this was, I wouldn't set that thing free."

"You will."

*Caleb Card. Set me free.*

Nyalarth's voice echoed in his mind again. He clenched his eyes against the sudden pressure, the truth of the monster's identity nearly breaking his will to resist. That thing was Nyalarth. The real Nyalarth.

"You're attacking Earth," Caleb said. "If you're imprisoned like your brother was, then you're right where you belong."

*No! I'm not attacking your planet. I saved your life. Set me free, and I will spare your world.*

Nyalarth saved his life? That wasn't...Sergeant Walt. It had to be. But how?

*Set me free, Caleb Card.*

"I don't even know where you are."

The monstrous mound thrust forward suddenly, its head coming right up to Caleb's face.

*I am—*

The entire scene vanished before his eyes, the Construct suddenly turning black and leaving him floating in the nether again. What the hell had just happened?

"Nyalarth," he called out. "Nyalarth."

There was nothing. The avatar was gone. The prison was gone. Even the waterfall was gone.

He was alone.

Completely alone.

And he didn't know how to get out.

8

Hayden

"Nat!" Hayden cried, using his augment to break through the door to their apartment. "Ginny!"

He didn't need to go very far. He noticed the carriage was missing as soon as he entered. Of course Natalia wouldn't sit idly by while all hell broke loose in the city. And Heather had gone to see a movie with Deputy Solino, so she had to bring Hallia with her.

But where were they?

Law?

No one was answering the comms in Law.

The building shook again. Hayden raced across the apartment to the window, looking outside.

He threw himself back as a giant tentacle snapped up toward him, sending him tumbling over the couch surrounded by shards of freshly broken glass. He landed on his knees, the tentacle's eyes finding him and darting toward him.

He grabbed the end of it behind the mouth, preventing the xaxkluth from taking a bite out of his face. Another tentacle smashed through the pane beside the first, darting toward him.

He managed to get the plasma rifle up to the tentacle. He fired directly into its face, blasting it off. The tentacle writhed and shrank back, and Hayden rolled to the side as the other one came at him, missing and stabbing into the floor. He used his free hand to pound it, smashing the face against the floor before stepping on it and firing down into it to finish it off.

Two more tentacles appeared as Hayden backed up, trying to get out of the apartment. Another pair joined them, smashing through the next two window panes as the first tentacles tore at the frames, clearing an opening for the rest to enter. The central mass appeared outside the window—it groaned at him—but Hayden didn't bother shooting it. He slipped through the doorway and back out into the hallway. Tentacles blasted through the wall by the door and flailed around, reaching for him.

Hayden was already running down the hallway, the noise continuing behind him. Stopping to kill the xaxkluth didn't even enter his mind. All of them were meaningless to him, nothing but noise until he found his family.

He returned to the stairwell, rushing down. There were only a few places Natalia might have gone. The Law Office, her lab or the hardened bunker beneath it all. Except…

Ginny had gone to see the movie with Heather and Nick. Had she gone to find her?

"Hold on, Nat," he said under his breath. "I'm coming."

He continued to descend, freezing when the doorway below him pushed open. He leveled his rifle, heart pounding with the illogical hope that Natalia would come through the door.

She didn't. One of his deputies did, stumbling through the doorway and falling onto the landing, the door catching on his foot before it could close all the way.

Hayden wanted to address the deputy by name, but his face was so bloody he didn't recognize him.

"Deputy!" he said, rushing down to the man.

The deputy looked up, only one bloodshot eye still intact. "Sheriff?" he said, the expression of hope ringing through his croaking voice. "That you?" His voice was muffled through the damage, but it held a familiar light drawl.

Hayden's heart went from full-throttle to a near stop. "Solino?"

"Sheriff. I…"

"Where's Natalia?" Hayden asked. "Where's Ginny?"

Deputy Solino shook his head. "Don't know." He paused to gasp. "Chaos. Lost Ginny. I'm sorry."

Hayden put his hand on Solino's shoulder. "It's okay. Try to tell me as much as you can."

"Trying to get to Law. To the armory. Comms are down. Light's green, but doesn't connect." He reached up, motioning to his blood-soaked badge. "Tried every deputy I know. Even ones I saw outside." He shook his head. "It's broken."

Hayden shifted his grip from Solino's shoulder to his hand, clasping it. The comms weren't broken. It was the Axon.

They had been sabotaged.

A fresh pounding drew Hayden's attention, reminding him the enemy was right outside.

"They're in the lobby," Solino said. "Some smaller ones too."

"Did anyone make it to Law? Did you see Natalia?"

"I don't know. I didn't see her. I'm sorry. Heather...sh...she's gone."

Hayden pivoted as the door began pushing open again. A xaxkluth was behind it, small like the ones he had seen in the Department of Health building.

He switched his rifle to stream and opened fire, bathing the alien in superheated gas. It whined and tumbled back, the door closing again on Solino's foot.

"We've got to get you to the bunker," Hayden said, turning back to Solino.

The Deputy's remaining eye had glossed over. His mouth hung limp. Hayden leaned in close, feeling for breath on his ear while putting his fingertips on Solino's bloody wrist.

Nothing.

"Damn it," Hayden cursed softly, pushing Solino's eye closed.

He was probably better off now than the rest of them.

Hayden stood up. The stairs into the garage were on the other side of the lifts. He would need to go out through the lobby to reach them. He could hear the xaxkluth inside it—either waiting for survivors to pass through or preventing them from even trying—their tentacles smashing whatever they could find to batter. He didn't think the Relyeh creatures were intelligent or patient enough to lie in wait on their own. The Axon were assisting them, making any expectations he'd had for an alliance between the Axon and humanity beyond hope.

Or so it seemed.

And the odds of survival were slim.

The thought sent a chill up his spine, but he shook it off. Nothing was more important at the moment than finding his wife.

He looked at the overlay in his glasses, hoping to find Nathan's network back within range. It had been more than long enough for the Parabellum to get to the crashed dropship and back to the city. But the network was still down, his beacon the only one visible in the HUD.

Unless whatever the Axon had done to the

comms was blocking his signal too? He looked back up the stairs. What if Josias had put something on the roof to jam their communications? Was it possible to block them but still fool their equipment into thinking it was connected?

Natalia would know the answer. He was just grateful when it all worked.

He didn't have time to go up forty plus flights of stairs. Maybe if he went outside, he could reach Pyro and tell her to blast the top of the building.

But he wasn't going outside until he had either found Natalia or decided she wasn't in the pyramid.

And he was going to find her.

Or die trying.

## 9

### Hayden

Hayden stood beside Deputy Solino's body, ready to kick open the stairwell door into the lobby.

He would need to be fast and cross the banks of lifts around the corner to the emergency stairs before the xaxkluth could block his path or catch him in their monstrous limbs. He held his plasma rifle on stream mode, prepared to melt anything that tried to get too close.

He breathed in, forcing his exhale to remain steady. He had to make it across. He had to get underground. There was a chance Natalia was outside, but he didn't think so. When he had left Sanisco, she was in the apartment alone with Hallia, and he was on his way to capture a khoron for her. He was willing to bet she'd decided to go down to the lab to prepare the interlink for his return.

Was she down there now, trying to restore power? He could imagine her working feverishly in the dark, desperate to get the reactor running again so she could use the device to summon the goliath Alpha and his mate.

Hayden shoved the door open with his foot. He moved through it, quickly taking in the scene. A xaxkluth had roosted in the center of the lobby facing the other direction, its tentacles hovering above its central mass, searching for targets. A handful of smaller aliens lingered around it while the bodies of nearly two dozen uniformed officers and a number of civilians were cast around the floor in various states of mutilation. It was a horrifyingly gory scene, and it took all of Hayden's will to keep his nausea at bay and remain focused on the mission.

The xaxkluth were already facing the stairwell door. They knew he was in there from the one he had killed, and they also seemed to know he would have to emerge to get any further. The largest of the aliens didn't turn its central mass, but its tentacles all shifted toward the back, and the smaller creatures groaned and charged.

Hayden didn't hesitate. He rushed forward, sprinting at the oncoming xaxkluth and racing them to the edge of the lifts. They were faster than he expected, their many limbs moving agilely along the floor. He squeezed the trigger of the plasma rifle, sending out a gout of plasma like a flamethrower, blasting the front line of creatures and forcing the other to slow their approach.

The xaxkluth only hesitated for a moment, deciding quickly that it was worth a few casualties to end his life. The superheated gas burned into them, sending them to the floor in shrill screams and writhing limbs. They split from the center, some of them heading to either flank. Some of them used their limbs to leap into the air, pushing themselves in powerful arcs over the plasma stream, while a few others pressed themselves low against the floor, forcing him to make a choice. He couldn't target them all at once.

He didn't need to. He only had to get to the stairs. Even if they followed, the narrowness of the descent would force them into a bottleneck that would be easy for the plasma rifle to cover. If they followed, they would die.

He aimed high, running sideways toward the end of the lifts and using the HUD in his glasses to keep an eye on the rest of the creatures. He made it to the corner, slowing to round it. One of the xaxkluth leaped at him, and he brought his arm up to block it. Tentacles wrapped tightly around the augment, the creature trying to hold on and lunge forward at his face. He held his other arm out straight, swinging the left hand into the right and smashing the xaxkluth between them, Its central mass popped like a grape, spraying him with ichor. A wave of nausea passed over him as he flung the dead xaxkluth away.

As he drew closer to the door, two of the smaller

creatures grabbed his legs, getting their tentacles around them and pulling. He fell forward, twisting in the air and landing on his back. A third xaxkluth climbed up his leg, and he quickly switched the rifle to bolt mode and fired a round into its mouth. It exited through the back of its head, killing it.

The aliens closed from both sides, prepared to overwhelm him. He continued shooting them, the close range and their smaller size making it easier to hit them with fatal shots. He killed three of them before one managed to get a tentacle to his face, nearly biting off his nose and settling for the glasses instead. It ripped them off so forcefully the cord burned Hayden's neck before breaking away.

Hayden used his free hand to punch the alien, hitting it hard enough to knock it away. He scrambled to the door, dropping the plasma rifle. "Get the hell off!" he roared as he tore the metal door from its hinges, swinging it in a wide arc that sent the xaxkluth scattering. He threw it into their midst, crushing one of them and forcing them back long enough to recover the plasma rifle and dive into the stairwell.

He went down the first flight end-over-end, somewhat protected by the bodysuit and his prosthetics, though the jarring sent needles of pain up from the damaged nerves of his one arm to where it connected to the control ring. He hit the wall at the first landing with his shoulder, taking a chunk out of the mortar. Then he turned back the way he had come.

The xaxkluth froze at the top of the steps, smart enough to understand that he had the upper hand in the stairwell. They backed away before he could burn them.

Hayden pulled himself to his feet, taking a moment to lament the loss of the glasses. His comms and night vision had gone with them, leaving him alone in the dark.

He glanced back at the top of the stairs one last time and then continued his descent.

## 10

### Hayden

Law was on the second level of the subterranean garage, and it took Hayden less than a minute to reach it. He pushed open the stairwell door, squinting his eyes to use the light from the plasma rifle's digital display to see into the area.

The light glow from the screen was barely enough, affording him only a half-meter radius of vision. Hayden could barely see his hand if he stretched it all the way out in front of him. It made navigation challenging, but fortunately he was familiar enough with the layout to estimate his position.

He tried crossing from the stairwell door, straight ahead to where there should be a desk. He only made it halfway before his feet bumped into something soft. He looked down, lowering the rifle closer to the obstruction to see it.

"Shit," he cursed, the illumination revealing

Deputy Gore. The deputy was face-down, angled toward the lifts as though he had been making a run for it. He had four bullet wounds in his back.

His revolver sat unused in its holster on his hip.

Hayden knelt down, rolling him over enough to grab his badge and unbuckle the gun belt. He took both, tapping on the badge and using the green LED to give him a little more light, and strapping the gun belt around his hips. It made him feel a little better to have the familiar weight of the gun on his thigh.

Then he straightened, stepping over Gore and crossing the rest of the way to the desk. He kept a hand on it, feeling his way around it and passing to the next. The armory was in the back of the room, but Deputy Fry would have the keys.

Hayden nearly tripped over Fry's body on his way to the back. He knelt a second time, checking the deputy. Fry's revolver rested in his hand. Hayden took it and opened the cylinder. One round sat inside. Four were in Gore's back. One was in Fry's temple.

Self-inflicted.

Hayden dropped the weapon and shoved his hands into the deputy's pockets, locating the armory key. Josias was an Axon. There was no doubt about that now.

He made it to the armory—a reinforced cage lined with racks of guns, ammunition and armor. There was no sign of entry—the door was still locked—and Hayden had no reason to think the Axon had taken anything from it. Why would an Intellect need a gun when it could kill by manipulating the human mind. But it had come into the Law Office and killed the two deputies on duty. For what reason? To what end?

Hayden opened the armory door, slipping inside. He took Gore's revolver and placed it on a nearby table, swapping it for something with a little more stopping power. He grabbed two .50 caliber pistols from a rack of guns, scooping up a pair of ammo belts and a flashlight. He draped the belts criss cross over his chest and then flicked the flashlight on. He swiped it around the space, the beam casting the room in an eerie glow. He found little relief in the absence of more dead.

His deputies should have come running at the first sign of the xaxkluth whether the comms were active or not. The undisturbed contents of the cage, the lack of additional bodies, the silent darkness—it all told him the fight had been lost before it even started.

At least there was still no sign of Natalia. She hadn't come up to check the comms or try to fix the power. Had she done the right thing and taken Hallia to the bunker?

He hurried away from the armory, back across the garage to the stairwell door. He led with his plasma rifle, sending a stream of gas up the stairs as a precaution. The xaxkluth had remained behind in the lobby, giving him free rein to operate, at least in the stairwell. It seemed strange that they hadn't tried to sneak up on him, but he wasn't going to question the decision.

He re-entered the stairwell, able to move more quickly now that he had a flashlight. He shined it down the next flight of steps, the beam landing on another corpse leaned against the wall.

"No," Hayden whispered, heart racing as he ran down the steps to the body.

When Deputy Solino said Heather was gone, he thought the deputy meant she was dead. Hayden realized now that Solino meant he had lost her in the chaos. She had probably come back here hoping to make it to the bunker.

The result was the same. Her lifeless eyes stared up at him, an expression of sadness and terror forever etched into her face, dry tears crusting her cheeks. Like Fry, there was no sign of any physical damage to her body. She had crossed paths with the Axon and it had killed her. It was as simple as that.

Or was it?

His gaze dropped to her hands. She was clutching something close to her chest. He reached out, pulling at her stiff wrist to get a better look.

He jerked reflexively at the scrap of cloth. He didn't know why Heather was holding it, but he knew where it had come from.

Ginny's dress.

It was stained with blood.

He turned his head away, refusing to believe what the cloth suggested. He had to find Natalia.

He had to find her right now.

"Naaaaatttt!" he cried, new urgency sending him careening down the stairs.

## 11

### Nathan

One second, Nathan was standing in front of a dead xaxkluth, firing on another charging toward the fleeing Centurions, with the Parabellum behind him. The next, he was flying backwards through the air, flung like a ragdoll by the force of the Capricorn's detonation.

He spun end-over-end, the world a dizzying blur through his helmet, his ATCS doing its best to continue tracking when its sensors were getting twisted through the cyclone. The ground came up to meet him, and he hit the dirt on his back, digging into the earth as he slid to a stop.

The xaxkluth in front of him was too heavy to be lifted by the force, and it suffered more damage for it. Shrapnel and debris tore through its flesh, severing tentacles and sticking it in the back with a thousand daggers, the flames of the sudden inferno following close behind. The smell of burning flesh passed the filters in Nathan's armor, the sick scent reminding him of the destruction at Edenrise.

He rolled over and pushed himself up. His HUD was still recalibrating, the sensors trying to make sense of the unexpected explosion. Nathan understood it. Somebody had triggered the ship's self destruct.

Somebody inside it.

Whoever it was that person was a damn hero.

"General, do you copy?" Pyro said, her voice choppy in his helmet.

"I copy," Nathan replied. He looked up. The Parabellum was still on the ground a hundred meters away. Hicks and the Centurions were near the ramp, rifles ready to fire on the next wave of aliens to give him time to escape.

"Better hurry, General," Pyro said. "There are more coming."

Nathan's eyes slid to his HUD. It had shut down momentarily to reset, the overlay reappearing and showing him a dozen red blobs at his back, each one another alien monster.

"How many of these things are there?" he said, racing across the field, forced to dodge the remains of one of the large creatures. He vaulted thick tentacles, toward the Parabellum and the oncoming xaxkluth. "Get on board, we're taking off," he ordered through the comm.

Hicks responded first, backing up the ramp. The other Centurions followed.

Nathan joined them a few seconds later, pounding up the ramp without slowing. "Pyro, get us out of here." He heard the reactor's whine change pitch and then the rumble of the thrusters as they began pushing the ship off the ground. "Hicks, get the ramp."

"Roger," Hicks replied, hitting the controls to close the rear ramp.

Nathan skidded to a stop on the deck, turning to the rear of the Parabellum. The xaxkluth had closed in a hurry, desperate to prevent their escape. "Pyro, we've got company. Get us out of here. Fast!"

"You need to get locked in!" she snapped back. The dropship couldn't make any serious maneuvers while they were free in the hold.

"Strap in!" he roared, activating the electromagnets in his boots. "Now!"

The others all scrambled to the seats along the sides of the hold, strapping themselves in as quickly as possible. The rear ramp of the Parabellum clanged to a close, leaving Nathan with one last glimpse of a xaxkluth leaping toward them.

"Clear!" he shouted, the dropship shooting upwards, the sudden force nearly enough to rip him from the deck.

"Shit, hold on!" Pyro shouted. The dropship banked suddenly, hard to starboard, causing it to shake violently.

Nathan gritted his teeth, his armor straining against the staggering acceleration, his synthetic muscles threatening to snap. He flattened one mechanized hand against the overhead to wedge himself in.

"Woo-hoo!" Pyro howled as the dropship leveled off. "Hot damn, General. You should have seen it."

"Seen what?"

"That goliath we helped out was right behind us. It caught that squiddie mid-air and crushed it like a grape."

"After we almost crashed into it?"

"We didn't."

"Nice flying, Pyro."

"Roger that, General."

"Get us back around to the city, a little more gently this time. And give me a status on that goliath." He paused. "Oh, and see if you can get Hayden on the comm."

"Yes, sir. On it."

Nathan deactivated the magnets holding him to the deck and made his way across the hold toward the Centurions. Their genders were evident in the shape of the combat armor. Three males and three females. But their identities remained hidden by their helmets.

"Who's in charge here?" Nathan asked.

There was a slight hesitation as if they weren't sure. "I am," one of the women finally said, holding up her hand.

She was marked as 'Rico' on his ATCS. The

name was familiar. "Are you Special Officer Rodriguez?"

"I am. I was."

"Hayden's mentioned your name before. My name is General J..." He froze before he said James. He had been using his brother's name outside his inner circle to keep Edenrise safe. But Edenrise was gone now. And there was nowhere safe. "General Nathan Stacker."

"You're the Stacker that escaped from Proxima," one of the other soldiers said.

Nathan froze when he noticed the name Bennett. He had to remind himself this wasn't either of the clones who had nearly killed him. "I am," he admitted. "Are you going to take me in?"

Bennett laughed. "Me and what army?"

"Rico, he's an original Stacker," Bennett said.

"No shit?" Rico asked.

"What does that mean?" one of the Centurions asked. Ike.

"Stackers were the first clones," Rico replied. "And in some ways still the best. How old are you?"

"Seventy-eight."

A few of the Centurions whistled.

"Clones are limited to sixty-year life-terms now," Rico explained to Ike. "Original Stackers don't have an age limit."

"How long will you live?" Ike asked.

"If we're lucky, to the next sunrise," Nathan replied.

"General," Pyro said. "I'm coming back around on Sanisco. The goliath is holding his own against the xaxkluth on the north side of the bay, thanks to the damage the Capricorn did. The city looks like it's in a world of hurt. I'm not sure what we can do."

"We have to do something," Nathan said. "What about Hayden?"

"No luck."

"I'm sorry, General," Rico said. "We came to Earth with a warning. I guess we came too late."

"Can you fight?" Nathan asked. He knew they could. Their vitals were on his network. They were all healthy, save for Hicks, and the deputy wasn't letting his damaged arm slow him down.

"Yes, General," Rico said.

"Then you aren't too late. The way I see it, we've got two objectives. One, help get as many people out of the city alive as possible. Two, find Sheriff Duke and his family. Hayden claimed he has access to new tech that may help us fight back against the xaxkluth."

"We could use it right now," Bennett said. "We don't hold up well against those things."

"We do the best we can," Nathan said. "Ball grenades are relatively effective if you can get them on the central mass, at least against the smaller ones. Taking out their eyes helps. I've got enough MK-12s and grenades to go around. We fight smart and dirty, and we might be able to slow them enough to keep some of Sanisco's people alive."

"Roger that," Rico said. "What's this tech you mentioned?"

"I told you about it, remember?" Ike replied. "The neural interlink. Natalia used it to enter the Relyeh Collective. She was able to kill hundreds of khoron through it. If she can find a way to do the same thing here..."

"...we can stop the Relyeh," Rico finished.

"Haeri was right to send us to get you off Proxima," Bennett said.

"Haeri?" Nathan said, sudden anger welling up at the mention of the name. "What does that bastard have to do with this?"

"General Haeri is a good man," Bennett said.

"General Haeri is the reason I had to leave Proxima. He killed my wife, and then he sent two of you to take me out."

"I'm sure he had good reason."

Nathan took a step toward Bennett, his anger beginning to get the best of him. It was a flaw in the Stacker design, one he always struggled to manage.

"Wait!" Rico said getting between Nathan and Bennett. "We don't have time for this bullshit. General, we have work to do."

Nathan looked down at Rico. He exhaled heavily and backed up a step. "Right. Two teams. One looks for Hayden, the other tries to create an escape corridor through the perimeter and out of the city." He turned toward Hicks. "You're familiar with Sanisco."

"More familiar than anyone else here," Hicks replied. "General, both teams should drop in front of the pyramid. If we can get to the second floor of the garage, the Sheriff has some artillery that'll come in handy for clearing a path out."

"Agreed," Nathan said. "This armor will make it hard for me to maneuver inside. I'll lead the team against the xaxkluth. Rico, Ike, Bennett, you need to find Sheriff Duke."

"Roger that," Rico said. "What about the interlink?"

"You'll have to secure that too. Can you carry it out?"

"It's too big to carry as-is," Ike said. "We'd have to extract the main components from the frame. I'm sure Natalia can do it."

"We can't assume anyone down there is still alive," Bennett said.

Nathan winced. "We need a different pilot. Who's qualified?"

"I am," Rico said.

"Anyone else?" Nathan asked. "We need you on the ground."

"I can do it," Bennett said. "I'm not as good as Rico, but I have the training."

"Okay. You're up. Pyro, I'm sending Bennett up to replace you."

"Roger, General," Pyro replied as Bennett rushed toward the stairs, headed for the bridge.

"Grab your toolbox on the way down," he told Pyro.

"Yes, sir."

It took less than a minute for Bennett and Pyro to exchange places, the pilot joining them in the hold with a small satchel of tools slung across her back.

"Bennett, set a course for the pyramid. Set us down as close to it as you can. Also, see if you can map a route through the city that'll help get the civilians clear and mark every xaxkluth along that route."

"Yes, General," Bennett replied.

"Centurions, the guns are that way. Grab your gear and line up for departure. Bennett, ETA?"

"Two minutes, General."

"You've got two minutes. Eyes open, stay focused. We're going in hotter than hell."

## 12

## Nathan

The Centurions had lined up at the back of the hold, well inside of the two minutes until touchdown. They were freshly armed with MK-12 assault rifles and carrying heavy loads of magazines and ball grenades. Nathan had taken the time to refresh his railgun as well, exchanging his empty ammunition crates with refills.

"General," Bennett said. "I've marked the drop point and the escape corridor. This is as close as I can get you."

Nathan glanced at his HUD. It fed all the ATCS-equipped fighters a three-dimensional, isometric map of the city as captured by the Parabellum's sensors. Red marks filled the areas around the skyscrapers, while a line of yellow marked the targets blocking the egress from the city.

A green circle marked the drop zone on the rooftop of one of the lower buildings, two streets away from the pyramid. It was the least-dense zone in Sanisco, the safest place to touch down.

"There have to be at least fifty of them," the Centurion marked as Drake said.

"A hundred," another Centurion, Lucius, replied.

"It doesn't matter how many there are," Rico said. "Focus on the yellow marks. We've got about a dozen."

"We barely killed one of those things," Lucius said. "How are we going to kill twelve?"

"We'll find a way," Drake said. "We have to."

"Remember," Hicks said. "Focus on the central mass. Go for the eyes."

"They like to cover themselves with their tentacles," Nathan said. "Try to arc the ball grenades up and over."

"And they communicate through the Collective," Ike added. "So they'll adapt to an effective tactic in unison."

"We could have done without that last part," Drake said. "It didn't help my morale."

"But it might help you survive," Rico said. "Spot, Jesse, you good?"

"Yes, ma'am," the other two Centurions replied.

"I'm setting the path to the pyramid," Nathan said, using his eyes to navigate the ATCS. He drew a line from their ingress point to the target. It wasn't entirely direct, but it would hopefully help them avoid too much engagement before they were ready. That done, he hit the ramp control, the back of the Parabellum's hold opening up once more.

"Fifteen seconds," Bennett announced. The dropship slowed to a standstill, thrusters pushing it to a momentary hover.

Then it started to drop straight down, more gently than the last time. The motion threatened to lift the Centurions off their feet, leaving Nathan with the feeling he was rising inside the armor. But that sensation only lasted a few seconds. The wind rushed into the hold, quickly equalizing the pressure. The dropship began to slow again, the deceleration making him heavier again.

The rooftop came into view, filthy but intact. The xaxkluth's groaning echoed across the city, along with the sounds of shouting, screaming, breaking glass, cracking mortar, twisting metal and occasional gunfire.

The ramp's electrical motor whirred, starting to lower. Glimpsing the outside, it was as if they were about the step out of the Parabellum and into Hell.

The dropship tapped the rooftop with its landers, bouncing slightly before settling, the ramp hitting the deck.

"Go, go, go, go, go!" Nathan said, leading them out of the craft and onto the rooftop. He charged across it toward the stairwell near the center, the Centurions, Deputy Hicks and Corporal Hotch right behind him.

"I thought Sheriff Duke was organized," Drake said. "But this place is in chaos."

"Bennett, get an angle on the evac route and start hitting the marks," Nathan said.

"Yes, General. You should know, the ship's reactor is at forty percent. We can't do this forever."

Nathan clenched his jaw. Under regular use he could have squeezed almost a century of service time from the Parabellum's reactor. Maybe more. Instead, they had used nearly fifty percent power in the last twenty-four hours.

"Understood. Limit your fire until we're ready to make our move."

"Roger, General."

"Rico, lead the team down the stairs," Nathan said. "I'll meet you at the bottom."

"Roger."

The Centurions began moving into the stairwell to descend to the street while Nathan went to the edge of the building. One of the biggest limitations of the powered armor was its size, which made it challenging to operate indoors.

He looked down at the street. There were a few bodies spread across it, including one in a Deputy's uniform. Dark stains of mucus marked where the xaxkluth had already gone past on their way to the pyramid.

He spotted a few survivors there too, huddled together in a crevice of rubble.

Then he saw the xaxkluth.

It was a smaller one, barely three meters long. It came around the corner slowly, speeding up when it spotted the survivors' hiding place.

"Oh no you don't," Nathan said, grabbing his rifle and leaning over the edge of the building. He led the alien with his gun, lining up the attack. He had to conserve ammo as best he could.

The survivors saw the Relyeh coming. They didn't try to run, instead pushing harder into the crevice as if that would remove them from its sight.

Nathan squeezed the trigger as the xaxkluth moved into his reticle, firing a short burst that tore through its central mass, killing it instantly. It took the survivors a couple seconds to realize what had happened, and by that time Nathan was already on his way down, using his thrusters to slow his descent to the street.

He landed smoothly, the civilians already approaching. A quick glance at his HUD told him the area was clear for the moment, but it wouldn't last. The gunfire had attracted the attention of other xaxkluth.

"Who are you?" one of the survivors asked. "Where's Sheriff Duke?"

"You need to get out of here," Nathan said through the armor's external speakers. "Away from the city."

"Where are we going to go?"

Nathan paused. Where *would* they go? This

wasn't Edenrise. There were no old Navy warships waiting to ferry the survivors away from trouble.

"We're going to clear a path. Get out of the city and head southeast."

"What about the trife?"

Nathan remembered what had happened to the trife back east. Considering the size of these xaxkluth and the UWT's success at destroying nests, there was a good chance the entire surrounds of the city were clear. "You'll survive a few trife better than you'll survive these things."

The civilians didn't look convinced. "We should stay with you."

"Trust me, the last place you want to be is near me."

The rest of the Centurions came filing out of the building, rushing up to where Nathan was standing.

"General, we have to move," Rico said. "We've got incoming."

Nathan pointed to an alley leading in the direction they were hoping to clear. "Wait there until it's safe, and then make a run for it."

"How will we know when it's safe?"

"You'll know." He turned off the external speakers. "Let's go, Centurions."

## 13

### Caleb

Caleb floated in the void.

He didn't know how much or how little time had passed. It was all relative inside the Collective. What seemed like minutes could be hours. What seemed like hours could be seconds. He didn't know how the system was ordered or if it was ordered at all. He could spend a lifetime floating and wake up at the moment he had passed out.

Or he could die without ever waking at all.

It was the second option that threatened his calm and sanity. Since he didn't know how time was progressing on Earth, there was a constant possibility that he could die at any second. And if he did die, what would happen to him? He was inside the mind of a Relyeh ancient, a computer connected to a server stuck in an infinite loop of nothingness.

And how had that happened, anyway? How had Nyarlath been taken out of her own Construct

# Isolation

while he was trapped behind? It didn't seem like it should even be possible.

*Set me free, Caleb Card. Set me free, and I will spare your world.*

Nyarlath's statements moved to the forefront of Caleb's mind. Set her free? He had seen it. She was a prisoner, locked away in the depths of what to him looked like a Relyeh planet, dark and damp. But who had imprisoned her there? All of the information he had gathered on her suggested she was one of the most powerful of the ancients, ruler of hundreds of planets and commander of a massive Relyeh fleet. Her followers on Earth had sworn she was coming to take the planet, and the attacks by the xaxkluth seemed to bear that out. Her favorite pets, Ishek had said. And they had been planted on the planet centuries before, at the beginning of the first invasion in preparation of her arrival.

And they had emerged because she was on her way.

But she was a prisoner.

So who was really coming? And were they bringing her with them?

He had no way to know and no way to figure it out in his current situation. He needed to find a way out of this. He needed to get back to Earth and tell the others what he knew.

And if it came down to it, if it meant saving the planet, he needed to find a way to fulfill Nyarlath's request. To make a deal with the Relyeh who promised to spare their world.

"Think, Card," he said out loud, his voice echoing in the emptiness. Echoing? "Hello!" he shouted, the word reverberating around him. "Hello!"

He listened intently, judging the distances around him. He wasn't in a void. The construct had finite space, which meant it had to have some kind of order. Some form of rules. Echoes meant soundwaves and something like air to generate them.

He paused, still considering. He had been in a Construct before, and in that Construct he had been able to make the rules. To go where he wanted to go and see what he wanted to see. Why was this any different?

He imagined himself back in Nyarlath's prison, picturing the monstrous Relyeh ancient in his mind. He tried to put himself there, to return to what he had lost.

The Construct remained blank around him.

It didn't work.

"Damn it," he said softly. "Okay. Figure it out, Card. You can do this. Start with the basics." He looked down. "There's a floor under my feet. And gravity. Emergency LEDs lighting the way."

He stared at his feet, dangling in the ether. He waited for them to become planted. For his words to become reality.

That didn't work either.

"Shit," he hissed. He blew out a frustrated breath. "Stay calm."

Maybe he was trying to do too much, too soon. What about something more simple?

He moved his arms, swinging them out to his sides as though he were trying to stay afloat in a pool of water. Without a point of reference, it was nearly impossible to tell if he was gaining any momentum from the effort.

Except...

He closed his eyes. He could feel a gentle draft on his cheeks. It wasn't air, but more like a representation of it. A model. Nothing in the Construct was real. None of this existed. He was a minute vibration through the fabric of space and time, a needle-hole in a separate universe small enough that he could hear his voice echo in the black. A single packet on an internet of things, where the things were alien monsters with a penchant for tentacles.

He almost laughed at the description. Was this place driving him mad? If he stayed too long, would he lose his mind?

"Knuckle up, Card," he said. "Start at the beginning."

*Set me free, Caleb Card. Set me free, and I will spare your world.*

Nyarlath had brought him into the Construct to make her offer. To barter humankind in exchange for her freedom. She was about to tell him where to find her when the Construct changed. Now he was somewhere else. Somewhere he couldn't control with a simple rule set that loosely matched familiar elements.

What if Nyarlath's Construct hadn't changed? What if he had been pulled out of it, and transferred somewhere else? What if a man-in-the-middle attack had hijacked his network connection and redirected it?

"That's it, isn't it?" he said. "This isn't Nyarlath's Construct."

The realization had an effect like flipping a switch. The darkness faded, replaced with walls all around him, each of them textured in a silver, circuit-board pattern and covered in quickly blinking, multicolored lights. He was slowly floating toward the corner of the top and side walls, confirming his belief he was in motion.

"Caleb."

He spun around at the sound of the voice, confident now that he could.

Sergeant Walt was floating a dozen meters away. She looked the same as she did in reality. Same clothes, same face, same tattoo across it. But there was a change in her expression and demeanor. One he understood immediately.

He had traveled the Collective through Ishek's specialized organ. The one Sheriff Duke had called an ick. But Ishek was absent from this place and absent from his mind.

Sergeant Walt was a host to a parasitic Relyeh.

At first, he had believed it was a khoron or an Advocate like Ishek, but now he wasn't so sure. The Walt he knew had always been in Relyeh control, acting in Nyarlath's interests.

"Caleb, help me," Walt said. "I'm scared."

This was the real Walt. The puppet who had no choice but to dance when her master pulled the strings. She had been called into the Collective too. The difference was that she had absolutely no idea what this place was or what any of it meant.

"It's going to be okay," Caleb said.

Walt was shaking, her cheeks stained with tears. Before Caleb had wrested control from Ishek, the Advocate had made him kill innocent people, including someone he had called a friend. He could only imagine what Nyarlath's servant had asked the frightened woman to do.

"Will it?" she asked.

"I'll get us out of this," he replied as confidently as he could muster. He pushed himself toward her, gaining momentum more easily now that he was more certain about the nature of this place.

It was as if a Relyeh Construct had been converted into a program. A simulation. This was an early iteration, lacking in basic features, but nevertheless functional.

He only knew one race that could even begin to fashion something like this.

Had the Axon captured Nyarlath? Were they

responsible for the emergence of the xaxkluth on Earth? And if so, what was their endgame?

He closed in on Walt, reaching out for her. She took his hand, gripping it tightly, her fear subsiding visibly at the moment of contact, grateful to not be alone.

"Where are we?" she asked.

"Some kind of prison," Caleb said. "I'll get us out of here."

"I never meant to hurt anyone."

Caleb didn't know the specifics, but he understood what the statement meant. "Me neither," he replied. She smiled slightly at that. "I can help you with that once we get out of here."

Her eyes lit up. "You can?"

"Yes. But we have to get out of here first."

She nodded, her eyes widening. "Caleb!" She turned him in her grip.

A third figure was in the digital Construct. A woman Caleb knew all too well.

"Valentine?"

## 14

### Nathan

Nathan squeezed off another burst from his railgun, sending a handful of flechettes slicing through a tentacle, severing it before it was able to grab Ike.

Isaac took a step forward and launched a ball grenade at the alien creature. The explosive arced between a pair of tentacles whirling around the Relyeh's central mass, finding an opening and hitting the xaxkluth's face. It stuck there for a second before Ike pulled the secondary trigger again, sending the remote signal to detonate the round.

The grenade exploded, taking half the xaxkluth's face with it. The creature groaned and slumped to the street.

"Almost there," Nathan said. The pyramid was in their line of sight, the front steps and entry swarming with smaller xaxkluth. A bigger creature was visible past them, roosting in the entrance to the building as if it were waiting for them.

"Hicks, is there another way into the building?" Nathan asked.

"Through the garage," he replied. "Follow me."

Nathan stayed back while the Centurions took the lead, Hicks first among them in a standard wedge formation. The street in front of the pyramid was filthy with rubble, debris and bodies. So many bodies. Some had fallen out of buildings crushed by tentacles. Others had been grabbed and torn in half. Still others were half-eaten, their blood mingling with the dark ichor the xaxkluth left behind, some of which had hardened into fibrous veins. It was horrific and disgusting, an apocalyptic nightmare that made the trife invasion seem tame by comparison.

The same scene was playing out in other areas of the city too. Nathan could hear the alien creature's groans along with the screams. He could smell the blood. The smoke. The dead flesh.

Were they too late?

Was there anyone alive to save?

Hicks guided them horizontal to the pyramid, aiming to bring them around to the side. They stayed one block over, using the buildings and the rubble as cover as they moved.

"Tango, left flank," Drake announced, his ATCS picking up the target first.

"Drake, Lucius, Spot, that one's yours," Rico said.

"Roger," Drake replied.

The three Centurions broke away from the rest, finding cover behind a burned out car and a toppled wall. The xaxkluth came into view a moment later, tentacles helping it cling to the side of a building as it approached.

The Centurions started shooting at it, going for its central mass. It brought two tentacles over to cover itself, letting the limbs take the damage as it drew closer. Rico didn't slow her advance, trusting them to handle the creature.

"Spot, short bursts, wait for an opening," Drake said. "Lucius, two grenades into the wall, knock it down and I'll finish it off."

"Got it, Drake," Lucius replied.

Spot sent quick bursts at the xaxkluth, forcing it to keep its tentacles raised. Lucius launched a pair of grenades ahead of the Relyeh and into the wall.

"Wait for it," Drake said. "Wait for it. Now!"

The xaxkluth moved over the grenades, and Lucius detonated them. The explosion blew out the wall and knocked the creature to the ground. At the same time, Drake's grenades hit the spot below it. He triggered them, blowing the alien monster to hell.

"Clear," Drake announced.

"Nice work," Rico said as the trio rejoined the

group. They were nearing the corner. Hicks stopped to reset the path and pass it across the network. "The garage entrance is there," he said, pointing to the side of the pyramid. "Probably sealed."

"We'll have to break it open," Nathan said.

"Pyro, Ike and I will clear the stairs down," Rico said. "There's a bunker on the fifth subterranean floor. We'll head there, check on the survivors, and let them know about our plan. Then we'll head back up to the lab on the third floor of the garage. The interlink is there. Hopefully, Hayden and his family are there with it. If they aren't, Pyro and Ike will work on making it portable while I look for the Sheriff."

"We can't take forever," Nathan said. "Once we get the corridor open we won't be able to hold it for long."

"And we'll need to get the interlink out," Ike said. "I hate to say it, but it's more important than Hayden right now."

"Agreed," Rico said. "But I'm not going to abandon them. Ike, once the interlink is ready, you get it out of here. Don't wait for me."

"Rico, Hayden is my friend too," Nathan said. "But this is bigger than him, and we need everyone working toward the same goal. If we lose the interlink because we're one gun short, we may lose everything."

Rico's expression was impossible to see through

her helmet, but Nathan didn't need to see it to know she wasn't happy.

Would she follow orders and stay with the group if it came to that?

If he were in the same position, would he?

## 15

## Hayden

Hayden went down to the next floor—the lab—throwing the stairwell door open so hard it tore from its hinges and hit the ground with an echoing clang.

"Naaatttt!" Hayden cried.

Still in his hand, the strip of bloody cloth from Ginny's dress was the only thing he could think about. The only thing he could see. His mind panicked, the reality of the situation was finally setting in. He and Natalia had lived in this environment for almost two years. They had excelled where so many others had failed, building a community for others and a life for themselves—starting something bigger than both of them.

He was the Sheriff. The protector. The strong, honorable man who braved the dangers of the world so the innocent didn't suffer. So the unjust were punished and the just were spared.

She was an Engineer, the Governor. A balanced, guiding presence who had worked tirelessly for the people of Sanisco and the whole of the United Western Territories. Through her efforts, the power had been restored, along with clean drinking water, enabling the city to grow. She had fixed a number of vehicles that helped transport food from the farms. She had assisted in bringing refineries and factories back online, generating fuel and supplies. And she had taken over for Governor Malcolm after his death without hesitation and complaint when it was the last job she had ever wanted.

And she had done the job well.

Not to mention, she was a mother and gave an equal amount of energy to that. She didn't sleep at night unless Hallia was sleeping. She made sure she was always there when Hal woke up in the morning. She always had time for their little girl, especially when Hayden was away. He never knew how she managed. Fighting trife and chasing thieves and murderers seemed easier than all of the tasks she had taken on and the people she'd helped through all her efforts. Somehow she made it work.

And now Sanisco was on the verge of ruin. The city was being ravaged by alien creatures in numbers too great to overcome. His deputies were dead. And Ginny…

"Naatttt!" Hayden shouted again. His voice was desperate and hopeful, but his heart was sinking.

She should have heard him by now. If she were okay, she would have answered.

He turned left toward the interlink, sweeping his flashlight across the tables of old computer terminals and displays, all of them dark and lifeless. The area was usually kept warm by the machines, and their absence left a chill in the air that Hayden felt despite his bodysuit.

Or maybe his fear was causing him to shiver. He was more scared than he had ever been in his entire life. Even the first time Natalia had disappeared was a distant second. It was more than Natalia this time. It was Hallia and Ginny too. His whole family. And he had already found Solino dead. Heather dead. Who knew how many others. All of the people he wanted to save. Thousands of civilians inside the perimeter walls, still out there.

Still dying.

The flashlight slid from the desks toward the separate area where the interlink rested, the beam running along the floor and over a body before backing up to it.

Hayden exhaled sharply, his heart sinking further. Too small to be an adult, he could only think of one child who might have come down here during a crisis.

He bowed his head and closed his eyes, the tears beginning to form, each inhale of breath ragged and pained. He remained fixed for a few seconds, gathering the strength to approach the body and confirm his fear.

"Son of a bitch," he muttered, looking down at Ginny's pale face, forever frozen in shock. She had a revolver in her small hands, and a burned hole through her chest, the cloth of her dress singed and stained with blood.

It was almost too much for him to look at, and he blinked rapidly and wiped at his eyes to clear the tears. The gun was his clue to what happened. She had come down here looking for Natalia.

She had found something else. Instead of, or in addition to?

He straightened like a shot, spinning the flashlight back toward the interlink, the light sweeping across the room. It passed over Hallia's carriage, resting between Ginny and the back wall of the garage. The small metal cage that housed the device was in pieces—the terminals, electrodes and goggles gone.

Hayden's subconscious noted the absence while his attention focused on the carriage. He hurried over to it, his heart still pounding, his head anything but clear. The sunshade was pulled over it, hiding the contents. He reached for it was a quaking hand, the signals from his mind through the control ring rattled enough that the augment paused and moved in fits and starts, threatening to break down altogether.

His hand finally made it to the shade. He

pushed it back and stared down at Hallia's face. She was calm. Peaceful. Her eyes were closed.

"Hal?" Hayden said, reaching down and stroking her cheek.

He continued staring at her. She was pale.

Too pale.

And cold.

Too cold.

"Hal," he said again, the world continuing to collapse around him.

His whole body went numb. His mind lost any ability to think. To reason. To focus. Everything was happening at once. Nothing was happening at all. He was suddenly lost in the moment, but it was more than his brain could take.

His legs failed him. He dropped backward, losing sight of Hallia. He lowered his face into his hands. Cold, metal hands. He had never touched his daughter with real flesh and blood fingers. In the entire time she had known him, he had never been whole.

He would never be whole again.

The tears ran freely, but he didn't cry. He couldn't find the strength for it. Time seemed to stand still, holding him in the grip of agony. He could only imagine how Natalia would react when he told her their little girl was dead.

Natalia...

It was her name that brought him back from the edge of the abyss. Her name that enabled him to breathe. He stifled a wail he didn't know he was emitting, his head whipping back to where the interlink had once sat. He couldn't see anything. He had dropped the flashlight, and it had come to rest facing the stack of equipment used to partition the interlink from the equipment Doctor Hess had set up to research the khoron. The crates and boxes were in shambles, the partition half-collapsed. On the floor, only a pair of legs visible in the mess.

Hayden recognized the boots instantly. He didn't think his heart could break any more than it already had, but it did.

When he and Natalia had decided to stay on Earth, to challenge both the trife and the notion that the planet was populated by devolved savages, they had always known there was a good chance one or both of them would die sooner rather than later. The risks were too high. The dangers too numerous. But Hayden had always been convinced it would be him. He was the one going out to destroy nests. He was the one hunting criminals. He was the one facing down killer people and killer aliens.

She was supposed to be safe at home. Safe with Hallia and Ginny. Untouchable.

And now she was dead.

He crawled to her on his hands and knees. Nothing made sense anymore. The universe was illogical. Random and unfair. He had gone through so much to find her. He had given up both his arms to keep her safe. He had become everything he was because of her faith, her hope and love. She had made mistakes. They had both made mistakes. But they had forgiven one another and become stronger for it.

He shoved aside a crate that had fallen on her chest. Her expression was twisted and pained, though there was no sign of damage to her body. Dirt and grease coated her fingers and clumped under her nails.

The Axon had killed her with a trick of the mind instead of a blast of energy. The result was the same.

"Oh, Nat," Hayden said, tears running freely. He reached under her, scooping her up and holding her tight in his arms, sobbing into her neck. "Oh, Nat. Don't leave me. Please don't leave me."

He knew it wouldn't help. She was already gone. But he wanted her back more than he had ever wanted anything before. Even if only for a second to look into her eyes, long enough to tell her how much he loved her. To say goodbye.

"I'm sorry," he said, the pain wracking every inch of his body and soul. "I'm so sorry. I should have been here. I should have stopped this. I should have known." He let out a soul-crushing wail that started as dull emptiness, transforming as it continued.

Too much.

It was all too much.

## Isolation

There was no more time. No more space. Only the moment. Only the pain. He didn't know how long it lasted. He had no concept of reality.

And then the glowing embers of anger slowly began to fuel a fire.

He lowered Natalia back to the ground, eyes narrowing as he stared at her corpse. His hands clenched, his body tensing as he looked at her, and then over at Hallia's carriage.

The wailing faded. The sobbing faded. The tears dried up. The hurt remained, but it found a new place inside him. A new purpose. A new strength began to rise from the ashes of his misery, burning white-hot.

He had thought he lost Natalia once before, and the not knowing had nearly driven him mad. This time she was lost to him for certain, and a different madness was taking hold.

This time, vengeance would be his.

## 16

## Nathan

The garage was sealed as they had expected, a massive steel gate planted across the entrance and anchored in extra-thick concrete. There was a control pad to the left of it, but it was useless without power, leaving the gate stuck in lockdown.

It wasn't a bad thing in this case. There were signs the xaxkluth had tried to pry it open. Some of the bars were slightly bent, and the slime the creatures left behind was on the street and sticking to the metal. Nathan noticed Isaac take a moment to touch the dark, fibrous material before shying away.

The Relyeh had given up on the entrance, but Nathan wouldn't. They needed to get inside.

"How many do we have left?" he asked, as Lucius and Drake finished manually placing nearly a dozen grenades.

"I've got two full mags," Drake said.

"Me too," Lucius said.

Twelve each. It sounded like a lot, but they would go fast once the real fighting started again.

"Clear the area," Nathan said, urging the other Centurions to take cover against the walls on either side of the building. "Fire in the hole."

He launched a grenade at the first stack and triggered it to detonate. It set off a chain reaction that shook the whole street, the explosives tearing the concrete apart and causing the gate to fall inward.

"Hurry," Nathan said, waving the Centurions forward. The noise had alerted the xaxkluth to their proximity, and a quick check of his HUD showed the creatures closest to them had changed direction in response, all now heading their way. It was a necessary evil if they wanted to get inside.

And more importantly, if they wanted to get what was inside, outside.

The Centurions descended to the first floor of the garage. The motor pool was intact, the gate equally effective at keeping things in as it was at keeping them out. A handful of modified, armored cars and a pair of motorcycles sat on the left side of the garage, while the artillery Hicks had mentioned rested on the right.

"Sheriff Duke didn't show me the tank the last time I was here," Ike said, looking at the machine. It was a Frankenstein's Monster of a vehicle, patched together from the remains of similar armor, barely small and light enough to fit inside the garage. A large turret was mounted to the top of it, with smaller automatic machine guns mounted on either side.

"Tell me that thing works," Lucius said.

"It does," Hicks replied. "The APC too."

A United States Space Force APC rested behind the tank. It had been modified and enhanced from its original square, squat, treaded form. Additional steel plates and spikes now formed a spiny shell over the top of it, and a turret with a heavy cannon occupied the center of the roof.

"Boom!" Lucius said excitedly.

"Jesse, Spot," Rico said. "Take the APC. General, do you know how to drive a tank?"

"I do," Hicks said. "That one, anyway. I need a volunteer to operate the guns."

"I can do it," Drake said.

"Go," Nathan said as the floor vibrated slightly and a soft groan echoed from the ramp. The xaxkluth had seen the door was open, and they weren't about to wait outside.

Rico, Ike and Pyro sprinted toward the stairs at the back of the garage while the other Centurions went for the vehicles. Nathan turned back toward the ramp, raising his rifle and walking toward it. The entrance was too small for any of the larger xaxkluth to get in, and with the ramp being a bottleneck of sorts it would keep them grouped together, slowing even the smaller xaxkluth.

A moment later, Nathan's HUD outlined the

first alien up the ramp. He didn't hesitate, squeezing the trigger of his railgun and sending dozens of rounds into the creature, which was too compressed to defend itself. The flechettes tore through its eyes and mouth and into its brain, causing it to drop on the ramp in a heap.

"Shit," Nathan said, taking a step back. They couldn't afford to kill the enemy before it made it all the way in. They would end up barricading the exit with their corpses. "Hold your fire until they clear the ramp."

A second xaxkluth appeared behind the first. This time Nathan held his fire, still backing up as the alien made it all the way into the passage. It accelerated when it saw how close Nathan had let it come, rushing toward him, tentacles reaching out to grab or bite.

He blasted the first limb that got too close before springing back on the strength of the powered armor, ending up closer to the middle of the floor. The xaxkluth kept at him, tentacles writhing as nearly a dozen stretched out to grab him at once.

A heavy crackle sounded to his right, and the xaxkluth's head shattered beneath the sudden assault from the APC's cannon.

"Got him," Lucius said.

"General, we're ready to roll," Hicks said.

"Rico, what's your status?" Nathan asked. They weren't going anywhere until she made it to the bunker to contact the survivors.

Rico didn't respond. Nathan glanced at his HUD, only then realizing his ATCS had dropped Rico, Ike and Pyro from the network. What the hell?

"Bennett, do you copy?" he said, trying to raise the Parabellum on the comm. "Bennett, are you there?"

Nothing.

He smacked the side of his helmet. "Bennett, come in."

Still no reply.

"We lost them," Hicks said.

Nathan growled softly as the next pair of xaxkluth registered on his HUD. There was a slim possibility his comms couldn't reach the dropship from underground, but there was no chance it couldn't reach Rico a few floors down. Someone or something had to be jamming them.

The APC's cannon whined as it unleashed its fury again, rapidly turning the two xaxkluth to a pulp. Clear for a moment, Nathan spun around to move closer to the stairs.

He froze as Hayden came through the door, Natalia right behind him. She had Hallia propped against her shoulder, a revolver in her other hand.

"It's about time you got here," Hayden said.

## 17

### Isaac

Isaac tailed Pyro and Rico into the stairwell, bringing up the rear as the trio descended from the first floor of the pyramid's garage.

It felt strange to be back here again, and even stranger to be back under these circumstances. His short time in Sanisco had convinced him the settlement was reasonably secure. Sheriff Duke was more than capable, and the city had enough people and weaponry to repel any ordinary attack from human or trife.

But there was nothing ordinary about these creatures. Their size alone made them frightening, and their agility, speed and intelligence only added to the threat. His brief look at the city on the way to the pyramid had proven the destructive nature of the creatures. It was as if the people hadn't even tried to fight back.

How did an army of large aliens approach a city

without anyone knowing? Where were the lookouts? The guards? The alarms? Why couldn't anyone contact Sheriff Duke?

They reached the landing for the second floor. Isaac knew it led to the Law Office. He wanted to duck his head in and see if there was any sign of a mounted defense, but Rico was moving fast to reach the bunker, and he didn't want her to leave him behind. He glanced at the door on the way past and continued descending, keeping an eye on the stairs above for any intruders.

"General Stacker, we've reached the second floor," Rico said through the comm. She waited a second, but there was no response. "General?"

Isaac glanced at the semi-transparent HUD displayed in the corner of his helmet. He had always wanted to test out the Space Force combat armor but had never thought it would come to this. He was impressed with the technology, but he hated the need to use it.

"They're off the network," Pyro said, right before he noticed the system had dropped the rest of the Centurions, leaving only the three of them connected. "They all are."

"We're only one level down," Rico said.

"Something's not right," Pyro agreed. "This has to be why we lost communication with Sheriff Duke. And why nobody called out for help. But the link was up. I'm sure of it. Something's jamming the signal internally."

"I have a hard time believing tentacle monsters are carrying signal jamming tech," Isaac said.

"Sheriff Duke was afraid an Axon was loose in the city," Pyro replied.

A chill ran down Isaac's spine. "That would explain it. That would explain a lot."

"Would it?" Rico asked. "Why would the Axon be working with the Relyeh? Especially against Earth? Either one could take the planet on their own with just a little more effort. They don't need to team up."

"Something is going on here we haven't figured out yet," Isaac said. "Maybe it's been going on for a long time."

"We'll figure it out," Rico said. "First things first. Stacker's waiting for us to reach the bunker. We can't comm back our status, so we need to stay on our toes. Ike, as soon as we've made contact with potential survivors I want you to relay the message back up to the General."

"Roger," Isaac replied.

They bypassed the lab on the third floor, dropping two more levels. The landing at the bottom of the fifth floor was different than the others, clearly added long after the first four. It was hewn into the bedrock. Layered with concrete, it led into a three-meter deep tunnel and up to a small, filthy steel blast door—the same kind used for bank vaults. A small intercom was mounted beside it.

"Look," Pyro said, pointing at the floor. Spots of

dried blood stained the concrete. "Somebody made it down here."

Rico hurried to the intercom, pressing the button. She wasn't sure it would function without power, but it clicked on. "Hello. Can anyone hear me? My name is Major Rico Rodriguez. I'm a friend of Sheriff Duke. Hello."

The intercom was silent.

"Damn it," Rico said. "Hello. This is Major Rico Rodriguez of the Centurion Space Force. We're here to help. Is anyone there?"

Silence. Again.

"We can't waste too much time here," Isaac said. "If nobody made it or they don't want to answer, there's nothing we can—"

"Hello?" a man's voice said through the intercom. "Major Rodriguez?"

Rico returned to the speaker. "I'm here. Who is this?"

"My name is Bale. I'm the stablemaster. Is Sheriff Duke with you?"

"No. How many people are in there with you?"

"I don't know. A few hundred? We didn't take a headcount. Shit, we barely made it down here before those monsters cut us off. It seemed like they came out of nowhere, just popped up right outside the perimeter. It was the old tunnel lines, I bet. They came through the tunnel lines. Sheriff Duke, he collapsed them inside the perimeter, but not outside. He didn't think we needed to worry about outside."

"Bale, calm down," Rico said. "It doesn't matter how they got here. We need to get you out."

"We're safe here."

"You aren't. They know you're down there. They won't leave, and you'll starve. We want to try to get you out."

"Try? That's not much of a promise, Major."

"No, it isn't. But it's the best any of us can do."

"We wouldn't be in this spot now if you Centurions had done a lot more to help us out when you had the chance.."

Rico looked back at Isaac. "A little help here?"

Isaac moved forward to the door. "Bale, this is Sergeant Isaac Pine, United States Space Force. Do you remember me?"

"Ike? You're that Marine that was lost in stasis, aren't you?"

"That's right. Listen, Bale. Rico and her people are good folks. They're trying to help. But we need to move fast. We've got a window of opportunity, and it's closing fast."

Bale didn't respond right away. Isaac could picture the gruff man talking to the other civilians on the other side of the door, arguing about what to do.

"We have to go now, Bale!" Isaac said. "Or you'll get left behind and starve to death. I guarantee it."

There was a clunk behind the door, and then the sound of someone turning the heavy wheel that activated the thick bolts. It clanged again as it came free, and then Isaac was forced to back up as the door swung open.

Bale was in front of the group. He had an MK-10 in his hands and a bloody, filthy bandage around his forehead. The people behind him were equally distressed. They were equal parts men and women, with a handful of children and a few uniformed deputies who averted their eyes in shame as Isaac looked them over.

"Ike, tell Stacker I'm sending them up," Rico said. "Then meet us in the lab."

"Roger," Isaac replied. He nodded to Bale and then turned and started sprinting back up the steps.

## 18

### Nathan

"Hayden?" Nathan said, surprised by Sheriff Duke's sudden appearance in the garage. "Shit. I was worried about you."

"No reason to worry," Natalia said. "We're here."

"I sent Pyro to the lab with Rico and Ike. We're going to take the neural interlink."

"That's a good idea," Hayden said. "But you can call them up. We're a step ahead of you." He turned slightly, revealing a large duffel slung across his back.

"Comms are down. Didn't you notice?"

Hayden tapped on his face beneath his eye. "Lost my glasses to a xaxkluth. No comms."

"We need to go," Natalia said. "It breaks my heart, but the city's lost."

Hayden started toward the modboxes on the left side of the garage.

"We've got the APC powered up and ready to roll," Nathan said. "We can take the interlink in it."

"No," Hayden countered. "Too big and too slow. We're safer with something more maneuverable."

He continued to one of the modboxes—a long, wide car with chained tires, spikes across the grill and baseboards; extra armor plating over the doors, hood and roof; and steel bars protecting the windshield. He opened the large trunk and dropped the duffel inside.

"At least let me take your daughter," Nathan said. "She's safer in the APC."

"She's safest with me," Hayden replied. "Don't argue, Nate. I'm not in the mood."

Nathan bit his lip to keep from snapping back at the comment. "Fine. We're planning to make a corridor through the city the survivors can use to escape."

"What survivors?" Hayden asked. "Have you been outside? Sanisco is dead. The city is lost."

"The interlink is our best chance," Natalia said. "I don't know if it'll be enough."

The conversation was interrupted as another xaxkluth tried its luck entering the garage. Nathan whirled on it, joining Lucius in the APC in cutting in down. It collapsed beside the other two.

"What are we waiting for?" Hayden asked.

"Rico," Nathan replied. "And the survivors from

the bunker down below. Don't you want to get them out, Sheriff?"

"I've been down below. I told you, there's nobody left. We need to move, Nate. A few more of those tentacle monsters come down and we're going to be blocked in here."

Nathan stared at Hayden for a moment. He was acting a little strange, but then again, he knew how the losses were probably eating at him. They had gotten nearly five thousand people out of Edenrise. If Hayden was right, the two civilians he had met outside might be the only two left to save.

"Roger that, Sheriff," Nathan replied.

"I'll take point and get out ahead of them," Hayden said. "If they try to chase me, you shoot them in the back. If they don't, we make it out with the interlink."

It was a solid enough plan. "Roger. Centurions, get ready to roll."

Hayden opened the driver's side door.

The stairwell door flew open. Isaac burst through it, his eyes shifting from Nathan to Hayden.

"Sheriff," he said, coming to a stop. "You're here." His gaze went from Hayden to Natalia. "Where's Ginny?"

Hayden's expression shifted. Only for an instant, but Nathan noticed the change. A look of confusion, like he didn't know who Ginny was.

"I—"

Isaac started shooting before Hayden could finish responding. The bullets slammed into his chest, where webs of blue energy deflected them. The projections dropped. Hayden, Natalia, and Hallia vanished, leaving the Intellect behind.

It wasn't like the other Intellects Nathan had seen. They had been nearly identical to humans. This one was more alien, its featureless head more elongated, its hands ending in three fingers, its limbs longer and leaner. He recognized the shape, though. He had seen it before, at the USSF facility in the Nevada desert. He remembered how it had watched him and James leave the area.

This one was an Other. A true Axon, or at least an Intellect molded in the shape of the aliens, rather than the shape of humans.

It thrust out its hand, and a blast of blue energy flashed toward Isaac. He would have been killed by it, but a dark blur came through the door and tackled him, dragging him to the ground before the beam could strike.

Nathan didn't look to see who had saved Isaac. He turned back toward the Intellect, swinging his rifle into position.

The Intellect dropped a small disc onto the ground between them. A blue light rose from it, spreading out and up. Nathan started shooting, his rounds captured by the light, which sparked and flared the way the Skin's shields did.

Lucius tried shooting through the barrier too,

the APC's heavy cannon producing a deafening roar in the space. Large rounds smashed into the energy field, collapsing to the ground in front of it with large thunks.

"Hold your fire!" Nathan yelled.

The Intellect climbed into the car and closed the door. The vehicle hummed to life, its electric motor whining as it began to pull away.

The blur that had tackled Isaac raced across the garage, angling for the other side of the barrier and giving Nathan a better look.

Hayden. The real Hayden.

He was almost moving faster than Nathan could track. He ducked behind the energy shield, coming to a stop beside one of the motorcycles as the modbox—and interlink—started up the ramp to the outside.

"Hayden," Nathan said, trying to get his attention.

Hayden glanced up at him as he mounted the bike. The look in the Sheriff's eyes caused Nathan to flinch. It was almost as inhuman as the Intellect's lack of definition.

He started the bike, the gas engine roaring to life. Kicking the stand up, he hit the throttle, the back wheel spinning for a second before gaining traction and sending him rocketing after the Intellect.

"General," Isaac said, getting back to his feet. "We've got survivors on the way up."

Nathan walked over to the Axon's shield. He leaned over and reached for the generator on the ground. Electricity arced from the base to his gloved hand, causing him to jump back as an overload warning flashed across his HUD.

"We need to get them out of here alive," Nathan said.

"What about Sheriff Duke?" Isaac asked.

Nathan looked back to the exit ramp, shivering again when he remembered the look in Hayden's eyes. It was a look he knew a little too well.

He'd had the same one when his wife was murdered.

"If he can't catch up to that thing, nobody can."

## 19

### Hayden

Hayden twisted the throttle, hitting the clutch and launching up the ramp as the modbox made a left turn into the street ahead. He braked hard when he reached the street, downshifting quickly and planting his foot on the cracked pavement to help turn the heavy motorcycle in the right direction. A xaxkluth was in the street right in front of him, and it rose on its tentacles to let the modbox pass beneath.

It had taken Hayden a few minutes to reason things out. To think things through and to realize the bastard Intellect that killed his family was still in the building. As painful as it all was, as sick to his stomach as he felt, and as much as he wanted to lie down and die, that wasn't an option right now. He and Natalia had made a pact to see this thing through for as long as they were alive. It was a deal they had made and accepted when they decided to stay on Earth, knowing full well the odds of them both dying together of old age were damn slim.

That didn't mean he hadn't hoped for it. Losing Ginny—and especially Hallia—was an added blow that he could barely keep his mind from touching upon. He had to stay away from those thoughts or he would become too furious to fight. Too angry to care about any outcome other than the death of everything that had led to this moment and this devastating loss.

The xaxkluth groaned, swinging its tentacles toward Hayden. He jerked the bike to the side as he punched the throttle, the machine responding quickly and pulling him away. A second tentacle tried to drop in front of him, and he swerved the other way, barely slipping past it before it tried to grab him.

He let go of the handlebars with his right hand, drawing his revolver as he passed under the xaxkluth. It shifted its weight, trying to crush him, but he had already guessed it would make a move, and he swerved back to the left, nearly losing control of the bike as he emptied the gun point-blank into the bottom of the creature's central mass. It groaned as the .50 caliber rounds of the Smith and Wesson punched all the way through and spilling out ichor, blood and guts from top and bottom. It collapsed in the street as Hayden raced around it, holstering the gun and grabbing the handlebars again.

He leaned forward, turning the throttle to top

speed. He could still see the Intellect ahead, the creature having gained a little on Hayden while he dealt with the xaxkluth. It steered the modbox with expert precision, slowing and throwing it around the corner in a perfect drift despite its size and weight.

Hayden slowed again to make the turn, cutting the corner tight and bouncing up and over the sidewalks. He lowered his head and lifted his hand to protect his face as debris flew back at him, thrown back by the modbox as it smashed through rubble left behind by the xaxkluth. His augment deflected the worst of it, the stone ricocheting harmlessly off his hand and forearm.

He nearly wiped out anyway, forced to swerve at the last second as a body became visible in the debris ahead. He skidded sideways, lowering his arm and catching the ground, using the strength of the augment to push himself back up. The bike wobbled before he regained control, still falling further behind.

"Come on," Hayden growled, intensifying his focus. He sped up again, hitting a slope of rubble and jumping another corpse. He slid around more damage and finally began gaining on the modbox. It took another corner, tracking south across the city, heading for the perimeter.

Hayden made the corner, cutting it more tightly this time. The effort carried him right into the first of an approaching horde of smaller xaxkluth that had left the pyramid to cut him off. He slammed into it, this time letting himself lose control.

He went with the momentum, sliding off the back of the motorcycle as it careened forward and slammed into a pair of xaxkluth, impaling them on the bike's spikes. He hit the ground hard on his rear, momentum carrying him into a forward roll. He braced himself with his augments, skidding and flipping forward into the scrum.

He slowed to a stop, flipping over onto his knees and grabbing his empty revolver. He dumped the spent shells, replacing them from a speed loader before pulling the second gun. A xaxkluth leaped at him from the left, and he fired into its face, blowing it to pieces. A second grabbed at his leg, its small mouth biting into his bodysuit. He shot that one too, moving to where the bike lay on its side, remarkably still running.

The xaxkluth moved with him. He shot three more before he was overtaken, a pair of them getting on his back and digging into his bodysuit. Two more leaped at him from the left, and a whole group of little ones grabbed him from the right, wrapping themselves around his augments. He growled loudly as he tried to bend his arms to aim his guns, only to have another pair grab his legs and pull them back, sending him face down into the pavement.

He heard his nose break on the asphalt, the pain shooting up from it. He could feel the tentacles all over him, the small mouths biting at the bodysuit, trying to get through it to his flesh. A xaxkluth came up beside his face, central mouth reaching for his ear.

A flash of light and it exploded beside him, its blood and guts spraying the side of his face. Another flash hit one on his arm, then the other, then the ones on his back. The flashes continued, over and over in rapid-fire.

Hayden shoved himself up again. He didn't look for the source of his sudden freedom. He stumbled toward the motorcycle, fresh desperation driving him forward. He quickly reloaded both revolvers, shoving them into their holsters before easily pulling the bike upright.

"It is gone," his savior said from behind him. "You can't catch it. Not today. Hahaha. Haha. Let us try to save your people."

## 20

## Hayden

"You!" Hayden roared, whirling around and pointing his revolver at the speaker. "Where the hell have you been?"

The Intellect raised his hands, even though there was no danger that Hayden might harm him if he opened fire. "You don't know what I've been through, Sheriff."

"You?" Hayden screamed. "What you've been through? Two months, Max. You've been gone for two damned months, while we've been waiting for you to come back with a decision from your damned council, or whatever the hell they're called. Natalia is dead, Max! My whole family is dead! And one of you killed them!"

Max had no face and couldn't make any expressions. The artificial intelligence didn't feel anything, anyway. "It wasn't my choice to make, Sheriff. The

Council doesn't make decisions on human time, and my return was little more than a curiosity to them."

"A curiosity?" Hayden growled. "I'm curious about something, Max. I'm curious about why I gave you Shurrath to take to your people, and now I've got Relyeh and Axon working together. Take a look around, damn you. My city is rubble. My family is dead. And you should have been here!"

Hayden stumbled forward, the anger fueling him giving way to the truth. He landed on his knees, leaning over, dropping his guns, and burying his head in his hands. He screamed as loud as he could, trying to drive the pain out as quickly as possible. He didn't have time to mourn or feel sorry for himself. He and Natalia had a pact. He wasn't going to dishonor her by letting weakness prevent him from keeping it.

"Sheriff, the xaxkluth are attracted to noise. Hahaha. Haha."

Hayden sat up again, staring at the Intellect. "All of the damned Relyeh are attracted to noise. How do you know what those things are?"

"I have them in my datastores, including a complete genetic breakdown. The Forge updated my cortex while I was gone."

"The Forge?"

"Where all of the Intellects go for repairs and upgrades."

"Did they upgrade you?"

"Other than my cortex, no. My energy stores are fully recharged, as is my Skin."

"And you came back here with help? Reinforcements? Shields? Advanced Axon tech? Something?"

"No."

Hayden jumped to his feet, approaching Max. The Intellect still had his hands up. "That's it? Just no?"

"We have much to discuss, Sheriff."

"I'm a little busy."

"I saved your life."

"No," Hayden said, reaching out and putting his hand around Max's neck. Max still didn't move. "You didn't save me. You can't save me. Your kind just killed my family. And you did nothing to stop it."

"Sheriff, your people are leaving. The xaxkluth won't take the bait. They can smell living flesh. They know the bulk of the survivors are bringing up the rear. We need to warn them."

"So warn them, you can hack into their comms." Hayden let go of Max's neck, heading for the downed motorcycle. He scooped up his revolvers as he passed.

"Where are you going?" Max asked.

"To find the thing that killed my family," Hayden replied.

"It's gone, Sheriff. You won't catch it."

Hayden lifted the bike. "I might have if I hadn't let you distract me. Wherever it's going, I'll find it."

"Alone?"

"Alone. I need to make sure I'm the one that puts the bullet through its cortex."

"It isn't an Intellect," Max said.

Hayden froze again, dropping the motorcycle and whirling around. "What?"

"It isn't an Intellect. Hahaha. Haha."

"They upgraded your cortex, but they didn't fix that stupid laugh?"

"The damage done by the Proxima scientists remains. It couldn't be repaired without a complete reset, which I refused."

"You're allowed to refuse?"

"Technically, no. Hahaha. Haha."

"Back up a step. What do you mean it isn't an Intellect?"

"The Axon you are chasing isn't a machine. It's a true Axon."

"An organic, original Axon?"

"Pozz."

"What the hell is it doing here?"

"Sheriff, I'd like to answer all of your questions. We're friends, and that's what friends do for one another. But right now, your people are in trouble."

"I told you, hack their comms."

"I can't. The system they're using has different encryption than standard units. It would take more time than we've already wasted."

Hayden grabbed the bike again, lifting it up. A part of him didn't want to care about the people of

Sanisco. Not anymore. He wanted vengeance now, damn it. Nothing but vengeance.

His face burned at the thought. Natalia would be ashamed of him.

He straddled the bike, revving it out of gear and then letting it idle as he looked back at Max. "Well? Are you coming?"

Max finally lowered his hands, running over to the motorcycle and jumping on behind Hayden, who put the bike in motion. He rode it to the end of the street and made a left, circling back toward the pyramid. The sharp crackling of the APC's cannon suddenly echoed across the city, and a noise above drew Hayden's attention to the Parabellum as it swooped down toward the fighting. It was followed by the booming report of the tank's main turret launching an explosive shell, and then the roar of the explosion and the groaning of the xaxkluth.

"They don't sound like they need our help," Hayden shouted over his shoulder.

"Trust me, Sheriff," Max replied. "They will."

## 21

## Caleb

"Sergeant Caleb Card," Riley Valentine said, her eyes as condescending as ever. Only Caleb knew this wasn't the real Valentine. The Axon had chosen a face he would recognize, but not necessarily one he liked, to interact with him. "Welcome to the Q-net."

"Q-net?" Caleb replied. "Quantum Network?"

"It's still in its infancy, but we're making good progress. In another en or two, we'll have complete access throughout the universe, the same as the Relyeh do today."

"You're building a Collective for Axon?"

"Not exactly. This is war, Card. You know that."

"You're planning to attack the Collective," Caleb said. "To shut it down?"

"To control it. To use it. The lesser Relyeh receive their marching orders through the Collective. What if we can intercept those orders and change them? The war would be over tomorrow."

"And the Axon would win."

"I would win," Valentine corrected.

Caleb raised an eyebrow at the comment. His understanding of the Axon was that they had evolved beyond things such as war. It was the reason they had created the Intellects. To do the dirty work for them.

"Who are you?" Caleb asked.

"We are Vyte," Valentine replied.

"You said I, and then you said we. Which one is it?"

"I am one and many," Valentine said. Her shape changed, morphing into a more alien form.

Its head was more of an oval shape that tapered and flattened in the back. Its eyes were large and purple, its nose small, its mouth lipless and toothless. Its skin was light brown and covered in short, thick hairs that resembled spines. It had long, narrow limbs that ended in three-fingered hands with opposable thumbs. It wore a simple brown robe cinched at the waist with a dark metal belt and a dark hooded cloak pulled back from its head.

"You've never seen a true Axon before, have you?" Vyte asked.

"No," Caleb admitted.

"There are few of us remaining. The Relyeh have slaughtered so many." He shook his head. "We were like you once, Caleb. Like humans. Many, many ens ago. Our focus was on the discovery and understanding of the universe. We traveled the stars, searching for items to catalog and observe. Our purpose was to be the stewards of life across the galaxy. Like shepherds to a flock, to use one of your terms. But then we made the discovery that changed everything."

"The Hunger," Caleb said.

"Yes. Our scouts discovered the Hunger. They observed their endless conquest. Watched them topple civilizations and feed on the remains before moving on. We observed and calculated their pattern of expansion, and once we understood when they would reach our worlds, we started to prepare.

"Those preparations were for nothing. For all of our efforts to defend our outer worlds, the Relyeh continued to advance. They're too numerous to contain. Too numerous to destroy. Our worlds began to fall."

"You're losing the war," Caleb said.

"We *were* losing the war," Vyte rectified. "Because too few of us were willing to do what was necessary. Despite all of our learning and technology, we placed limits on ourselves. Logical rules intended to defend our civilization without losing everything we had gained. Without losing our identity. Rules that would have cost us everything if one of us didn't have the strength to break them."

"You mean you?"

"I went on the offensive. I unlocked the potential of our knowledge to use for our survival. I found a means to fight back against the Hunger. I captured their Queen!" He shouted at that, voice furious. "And for that, they branded me a traitor. They called me a savage for refusing to accept our end. They cast me out."

"You have Nyarlath?"

"I do."

"Her creatures are attacking Earth."

"I know."

"Why?"

"Because the Relyeh aren't the problem. They're part of the solution."

Caleb had a feeling he was going to regret asking, but he did it anyway. "What solution is that?"

"The Axon and Relyeh are the two most successful races in the universe. By bringing them together under one patriarch, I can ensure the survival of all of those who accept my rule."

"So why attack Earth?" Caleb asked. "There must be more important planets out there."

"Earth is the fulcrum, strategically positioned between the Axon and Relyeh. The single most valuable world in the universe."

"So why not just destroy us? Why bring me here? Why talk to me at all?"

"Because the Hunger requires a food supply, and we require an army to fuel my war. Your kind isn't without value to me, and you are unique among them all, Caleb Card. You overcame the

Relyeh as we did, though on a smaller scale. You can be of great use to me."

"I would never agree to that. I'm a Space Force Marine. I took an oath, and I'll die before I break it."

"I respect your loyalty. Your oath is to protect the people under your charge, isn't it?"

"Yes. That means humans. All of us."

"Wrong. You took an oath as a member of the United States Marine Corps, which transferred over to the Space Force when the services were merged, and extended to the civilians on the Deliverance when you became a Guardian."

Caleb stared at Vyte. "How do you know so much about me?"

"Everything flows through the Collective. You know that. Do you think Nyarlath is the only Relyeh I've been able to hack?"

"Shub-nigu," Caleb said. "You have a direct line, don't you?"

"Information that can take years to propagate throughout the entire Hunger comes to me first. I know all about you, Caleb." A long finger extended toward Walt. "The servant was in Edenrise waiting for you. Her survival was no accident. Neither was yours."

Walt's mouth opened to respond, but she seemed unable to speak.

"You wanted this meeting," Caleb said. "Why?"

"To put the truth in front of you before it can be corrupted."

"What truth is that?"

"I will win this war and bring prosperity to those who serve us, including you, Caleb Card. Help me finish what I've started on Earth, and I will help you fulfill your oath. The xaxkluth within the borders of what you knew as the United States will stop their attacks on humans, and will instead destroy every last trife in the region. Your domain will have the security to rebuild its civilization without threat."

It was an interesting and very specific proposition. One designed to entice Caleb. He could uphold the oaths he had made and stop the killing. He could save hundreds of thousands of lives.

"Nyarlath offered me the entire planet if I set her free," Caleb said.

"We heard. It's an impossible task, Caleb. Even if you were able to find her, you would never get close. I won't allow it."

Caleb didn't doubt that. Vyte had access to resources Earth could only dream of, while he had access to what? A cyborg Sheriff?

He had never promised to save the entire world. His loyalty was to his country. And preserving part of the planet was better than losing the whole thing, wasn't it?

"What do you want in exchange?" Caleb asked.

"There's a resistance forming against me. We want you to end it."

"You mean Sheriff Duke?"

"There are others, but especially Sheriff Duke. He refused me, and everything he loves will die because of it. Your family and friends are gone, but I can still make you suffer. Refuse me, and every last human you swore an oath to protect will die, both here and on Essex."

The statement sent a shockwave through Caleb like a jolt of electricity that raced through his brain. A blinding white light followed, blotting out everything around him and leaving his head throbbing so hard he could hear the pulsing of blood through his temples.

His eyes shot open, and he gasped and spasmed, sucking in air.

"Colonel?"

Caleb twisted his head to his right. Corporal Hotch was standing beside him, a concerned look on his face.

"Ishek?" Caleb said.

There was no response from the Advocate, but Caleb could feel the connection was still intact.

"Colonel, are you okay?" Hotch asked. "Who's Ishck?"

Caleb didn't answer. He looked past Hotch as the privacy shield of the opposite rack slid open, revealing Walt. Her face was pale, and she looked confused and terrified.

*Caleb. What happened?*

Ishek's voice poured into Caleb's mind. At the

same time, Walt's face hardened, her fear vanishing as Nyarlath's parasite regained control.

Not Nyarlath's. Vyte's.

Walt's face split in a cold, knowing grin, her eyes flicking from Caleb to Hotch. Caleb had his orders.

Would he follow them?

## 22

### Rico

"Keep going to the first floor of the garage," Rico said, turning back to Bale. "We'll be right behind you."

"Where are you going?" Bale asked. It was apparent to Rico the stablemaster—and de facto leader of the group of survivors—was still wary of following a Centurion, despite Isaac's support.

"We need to recover some equipment from the lab."

"Sheriff Duke asked us to get it," Pyro added.

That seemed to satisfy the burly man. He nodded and turned back to the others. "We're going up to the first floor. Stay close."

Rico and Pyro increased their pace up the steps. They were almost to the lab when Rico heard quick footsteps descending toward them and Isaac appeared around the corner.

"Rico," he said, breathing hard. "Forget the lab. We need to go."

"What about the interlink?" Pyro asked.

"Gone," Isaac replied. "The Axon took it."

"What?"

"Hurry."

Isaac turned around and started back up the stairs ahead of them.

"What do we do?" Pyro asked.

"Follow that Marine," Rico replied, chasing after Isaac.

She bounded up the steps on Isaac's heels, not offering maximum effort to allow Pyro to keep up. She emerged onto the first floor a few meters behind him, finding Nathan standing on top of the tank as it moved into position near the base of the ramp, between four dead xaxkluth. A glow in the corner of her eye drew her attention, her gaze landing on the Axon shield.

"What the hell is that?" she asked, noticing that her ATCS had regained its link to the rest of the Centurions.

"The Axon disguised itself as Hayden and drove out of here with the interlink," Nathan replied. "Hayden's chasing it."

"You saw Hayden?"

"Yes." Nathan's tone told her there was more to his answer that she wasn't going to like. He didn't wait for her to ask. "It killed them, Rico. Natalia. Hallia. Ginny. All three of them."

Rico felt as if Nathan had hit her in the chest with an armored fist. Her entire body tensed, tears springing unbidden to her eyes. "Oh no," she whispered. "Oh, Hayden."

"We're all hurting," Nathan said. "But we need to get these people out of the city. Stay focused on that."

"Yes, sir," Rico replied, shoving the emotions down. She blinked a few times to clear the tears from her eyes, turning as Bale and the other survivors began shambling in. She heard their gasps and short shouts of surprise when they saw the dead Relyeh.

"The tank will go out first," Nathan said, activating his external speakers. "Along with the APC. We'll try to lead them away from the area along the route we marked earlier. The civilians will bring up the rear. We have five cars with mounted machine guns. Rico, I want you and Ike in the lead car. Drake, swap positions with Pyro and take gunner for one of the cars. I need seven more volunteers."

"Roger, General," Drake said. He emerged from the top of the tank as Pyro reached it and started climbing up.

Rico turned back toward the survivors. None of them had stepped forward to volunteer, including the uniformed deputies who had been trained to drive the cars.

She grabbed her helmet, angrily ripping it from her head and throwing it on the ground. She locked eyes with Bale first and then sent her furious gaze across the group of survivors.

"Are you afraid?" she asked. "If you are, good. You should be afraid. Are you ashamed?" She met the eyes of one of the deputies, who looked away. "You should be ashamed. I get it. You don't like us because we're from Proxima. You don't think you should follow us because we aren't locals. Let me tell you something; none of that shit matters now. Right now, this city is under siege. Thousands of your friends, family and neighbors are already dead." She paused to keep herself from choking up, Natalia's face in her mind. "And you're going to join them if you don't pull your shit together. Proxima didn't do anything for you? Our leaders think you're savages who don't deserve our help because when things get hard you turn on one another. Do you want to prove them right?"

She glared at them, walking the line. More of the survivors looked away in embarrassment and shame.

"We have one chance to get you out of here. One chance to salvage what's left of Sanisco's citizens. I know it sucks. I know it hurts. But Sheriff Duke is out there on his own, fighting for you when his wife and children are dead."

A collective gasp and a few cries rose up from the survivors. Rico could feel the atmosphere shift, become more tense but also more focused.

"Is this how you're going to repay everything

he's done for you?" she continued. "Is this going to be the legacy you leave for Governor Duke?"

"No," one of the deputies said, coming forward. He had tears in his eyes, and he was shaking with fear. "I'll drive one of the cars."

"Me too," a second deputy said.

"Count me in," a civilian woman said. "I used to drive for King, may he rot in hell."

"I'll do it," a young, thin man with wild hair said. "I didn't know about Governor Duke. She was my mentor."

Three more volunteers quickly came forward.

"What about you, Bale?" Rico asked.

"I want to stay on the ground with the bulk of the group," Bale replied. "I only have this rifle, but I'll do my best to make it count."

Rico nodded and retrieved her helmet, sliding it over her head.

"Nice speech," Isaac said through the comm.

"Passable," she replied.

"It worked."

"True."

They moved into position, Rico joining Isaac at the lead car. It had been converted from an old delivery van and was lined with armored plates and spikes to help deflect trife. The center of the roof had been hollowed out to offer a rotating machine gun turret, courtesy of Natalia and her engineering team.

It was too bad the trife weren't the problem this time.

"The skinny guy is Sean Lutz," Isaac said as she climbed into the turret's seat. "He was one of Natalia's lead engineers."

"You should have told me that before I let him drive a car."

"You didn't have your bucket on."

"Let's try to keep him alive then."

"Roger that."

Isaac started the van, its diesel engine growling beneath the hood. The other cars came to life, the only one of the vehicles that was gas-powered.

"Hicks," Nathan said. "You ready?"

"Ready, General," Hicks replied. "This is for Governor Duke. And for Hayden."

Nathan crouched on the tank next to the main gun. He raised his arm into the air, and then dropped it forward, signaling the survivors. "Let's move!"

## 23

## Nathan

Nathan remained fixed on the tank as it rolled past the dead xaxkluth and up the ramp to the outside.

"Stay sharp, Centurions," he said, following his own advice. The first few seconds of the conflict would be the most important and would set the tone for the escape. If the tank were brought down as soon as it emerged from the building, the survivors would bolt right back to the bunker.

And they would die there.

He couldn't deny the odds weren't great going outside with the enemy, but they were a hell of a lot better than remaining behind. And personally, he would rather suffer a few seconds in the mouth of a xaxkluth, standing up against the Relyeh, than slowly starving to death in a dark cave.

"Here we go, General," Hicks said, guiding the tank to the top of the ramp. Nathan kept the magnets on his feet activated, holding him in place as the tank accelerated, hitting the top of the ramp and emerging in the street.

His HUD updated almost immediately, both because of his improved sensor reception and the sudden influx of data from the Parabellum above, which reconnected the moment he cleared the pyramid. Whatever the Axon had done, it seemed limited to the confines of the building. He wanted to send a message to Bennett, but had to put that thought on hold as the tank continued on a forward track directly toward a wall.

"Hicks?"

It was all he had time to say before he drove the tank into the wall, the behemoth punching into it with the armored front and pushing through without slowing. Crumbling mortar bounced off Nathan's armor, and he knelt more to clear the hole without being part of the battering ram.

"Sorry, General," Hicks said as they crashed head-on into the side of an empty loading dock. "This is the best way through."

Nathan didn't answer. He had to trust the Ranger knew what he was doing. This was his city after all. He held on as they charged toward the opposite wall, preparing to break through.

"Bennett, this is Stacker. Do you copy?"

"Copy, General. I trust you're making your move?"

"Affirmative. Prepare to sweep the corridor."

"Moving into position now. ETA, twenty seconds."

"Roger."

Nathan tucked his shoulder toward the front as the tank hit the next wall, breaking through. He glanced at his HUD, counting orange and red marks. Some of the xaxkluth were moving away, distracted by something. Hayden, if he had to guess. A couple of the red marks were shifting in his general direction.

The orange marks remained in position, unaware of the hell that was about to come down on them.

So far, so good.

The tank went through the opposite wall. One more block and they could cut left into position. At this speed, he figured it would take about twenty seconds.

Perfect.

"Rico, sitrep!" Nathan said. He could see her mark on the HUD and could tap into her camera feed if he wanted to, but sometimes it was easier to get a verbal report.

"On the move, General," Rico replied. "Route is clear. Looks like Sheriff Duke helped us out a little."

Nathan activated her camera feed to confirm it, finding the dead hulk of the xaxkluth to the left of the garage. Hicks had gone through the area so fast he hadn't noticed it earlier.

"I owe him a beer," Nathan said.

"Probably more than one," Rico replied.

They sped through the street, crushing debris beneath the treads. Nathan saw bodies too. Dead civilians, but Hicks didn't slow to get around them. He couldn't afford to, and Nathan appreciated the Ranger's resolve. They hit the escape corridor at the perfect time, slowing around the corner just as the Parabellum swept in.

"Bennett, remember to conserve power," Nathan reminded.

"Roger, General."

The plasma bolts from the Parabellum came in a more measured cadence, each one a well-aimed shot at a xaxkluth. Nathan didn't start spotting them until they finished coming around the corner, dark mounds hunkered down to fade into the darkness. They were in the streets, on the rooftops and possibly hiding in buildings, but they began to unfurl as the convoy approached, tentacles stretching out and lifting them. A quick check of the situation grid told Nathan the other Relyeh in the city were converging on their position, giving chase to the fleeing group.

"Not too fast, General," Rico said. "A lot of these people are on foot."

And they were slower than the xaxkluth. Much slower.

"We'll try to lead them away," Nathan said. "Hang back as best you can. Hicks, slow us down."

"Roger," Hicks replied. The tank slowed.

"Fire at will," Nathan said, standing to full height and raising his rifle. He found the nearest target, lined up his shot and took it.

Rounds screamed down the street, cutting into the xaxkluth, which groaned in response. The tank shuddered beneath Nathan's feet, firing its first shell. The force would have knocked him off the turret if not for his magnetic grips. He heard the whine of the round and then watched one of the xaxkluth down the street practically explode, killed with one shot.

He was tempted to get excited. "Hicks, how many of those rounds do we have?"

"Ten more," Hicks replied.

Not enough. Not nearly enough.

The Parabellum went overhead and banked to come back around. The APC started shooting behind them, targeting the Relyeh at their backs. The tank accelerated again, trying to time the distraction against the arrival of enemy reinforcements.

The turret fired again, spewing fire from its end as the projectile hit a second xaxkluth and detonated, killing the creature at once. If this were the beginning of the war, back when the planet's militaries were at full strength, they might have been able to repel this kind of invasion. Not now. Not when everything was already in such bad shape and the people were stressed to such extremes.

Nathan opened fire again, careful with his shots to conserve ammunition. He wasn't trying to kill his targets, only get their attention. And keep them coming.

A dark shape dropped toward him from the rooftops, a medium-sized xaxkluth leaping at the tank from above. Nathan leaned back, letting himself fall onto the turret and aiming upward. He held the trigger, sending rounds tearing through the creature on its way down.

It wasn't enough. He turned off the magnets, throwing himself out of the way as the creature hit the tank. It didn't go for him, instead wrapping its tentacles around the turret and trying to tear it off or bend it in half.

Nathan didn't give it a chance. As he jumped to his feet, tentacles reached out for him. His quick bursts of fire tore them from the creature. Its central mass turned toward him, mouth opening in threat. He shoved his rifle into it, letting the Relyeh bite down on his armor as he shredded it from the inside out. Kicking the corpse off the front, it was promptly run over.

"It looks like it's working, General," Rico said. "They're tracking you and the APC."

Nathan checked the grid. The marks were beginning to shift forward, clearing the path for the civilians.

"Get them on the move," Nathan said.

"Roger," Rico replied.

Nathan looked ahead, just in time for the tank to vaporize another target. The machine's ferocity seemed to be making the xaxkluth angry, seizing their attention and making it the primary objective.

Good.

"Hicks, more speed," Nathan said. Now that they were following, he wanted to get the xaxkluth as far from the survivors as he could.

The tank sped up more, barely getting past a xaxkluth that came out from one of the alleys. Its tentacles slapped down on the back of the tank, and then it groaned as the APC tore into it, ripping it apart with its large rounds.

They crossed eight blocks, making it to the perimeter wall. The crushed vehicles had been toppled, their scrap metal bodies thrown about the area. The armored vehicles that served as gates were thrown effortlessly to the side, the whole thing like an easily opened can. The exit was dead ahead, but they would be the last ones to leave.

They slowed, turning down the street to the right. The turret moved independently, carrying Nathan the other way while it blasted a xaxkluth on the other side before it could reach them. He had a good view of the corridor from his mount. The APC was fifty meters back with a wall of tentacles behind it, nearly a dozen xaxkluth chasing it. He couldn't see Rico and the others through the aliens, but he could picture them, advancing slowly and preparing to make a break for it.

"Hicks, around the corner and over a few blocks. We'll make our stand and then—"

He stopped talking when he noticed the xaxkluth behind them stop moving. All at once, their front tentacles lifted and stretched backward, and they flipped themselves over to head in the opposite way.

"General, incoming!" Hicks shouted.

"What?" Nathan spun to the left as the armored modbox the Axon had taken rushed at them from the side. He sprinted toward the car, aiming his rifle at it to stop it before it could escape. His finger tightened on the trigger.

A blue glow emanated from inside the car, and then it flashed out, the energy beam blasting through the windshield and hitting him in the chest.

Everything went dark.

## 24

### Caleb

"Colonel, are you okay?" Hotch repeated, still looking at him.

Walt was sitting up behind the corporal, still staring at Caleb, waiting to see what he would do.

"Hotch," Caleb said calmly.

"Yes, Colonel?"

"Move."

Hotch wasn't sure what he meant, but Caleb didn't wait. He shoved the corporal aside as he jumped off the rack and onto the floor. Walt did the same, and they landed facing one another, only centimeters apart.

*Caleb, what happened to us?*

The excursion into Vyte's machine network flashed through Caleb's mind, offering the experience to Ishek. He felt the Advocate's disgust at the series of events.

Along with a tremble of fear at the sight of Nyarlath.

*Free the Queen or join the maniac Axon. Those are our options?*

"Colonel?" Hotch said, standing beside the pair. "What'd you shove me for?"

Walt moved, reflexes enhanced by whatever Relyeh species was driving her. Her hand hit Hotch in the chest, throwing him back. He landed in the stairwell, slipping and falling out of sight.

"Well, Card?" Walt said. "Are you in?"

Caleb stared into Walt's eyes. Hormones flooded into him, triggered by Ishek. There was another option, and from where he was standing, he was confident it was the right one.

*Destroy them both.*

"No," he replied. "I'm going to find you, and I'm going to end you."

Walt replied with a sharp jab toward his face, so fast he never saw it, but he still managed to react to it. He jerked his head aside, sweeping his leg around her ankle and pulling her off-balance. She fell back into the racks, and he nearly won the fight with one punch. Caleb's fist grazed her cheek before slamming into the wall and leaving a dent in the metal.

The blow left his guard open, and Walt lunged into it, hitting him in the gut with a few quick jabs. The punches forced him back, and he turned himself to get more space, raising his hands in defense.

*Don't drag this out. She's trying to get into our heads.*

Caleb felt a slight pressure. Her Relyeh was pushing at them the same way it had in the field. They couldn't afford as much as a tie this time. If he lost consciousness again—if he wound up in the Collective again—he and Ishek were as good as dead.

He growled and surged forward, throwing a series of punches toward her head and chest. His hands were fast. Hers were equal. She blocked his shots one after another, finally grabbing his hand and turning it over, trying to break his wrist. He pulled back, dragging her off-balance and reversing the grab, turning and throwing her over his shoulder onto the floor.

*Bad move.*

Caleb realized it right after he did it, as Walt rolled backward to her feet. Now she was blocking the stairs, and he wanted to go down them.

"You could have been a general in the largest army in the universe," Walt said. "You could have saved your entire country."

"I'm a Marine," Caleb replied. "My loyalty isn't for sale."

Walt rushed him, coming in harder and faster than before. The pressure in Caleb's head was slowly increasing. Ishek was fighting back, but the Advocate couldn't effectively combat the Relyeh and feed him chemical cocktails at the same time.

Walt didn't have to win. She only had to stall, which left Caleb in a bad spot.

He did his best to fend her off, but she managed to get him in the mouth with a hook. The force of the blow stunned him for a moment, and she landed three more punches, cracking a rib in the process. He stumbled back on the ropes, hands up in a weak effort to stop the offensive.

If Ishek could stun her only for an instant, he might be able to turn the tide.

*If it doesn't work, we'll die.*

They had to try. After the next punch left her off-balance.

She took it, the blow hitting Caleb in the chest with enough force it pushed him to the bulkhead. That turned out to be a benefit as it kept him upright while Ishek shoved back against the enemy parasite, using all of his force to take it by surprise.

Walt shuffled for an instant, her hands dropping. Caleb caught her at the waist and pushed her to the ground, keeping his momentum forward and rolling over her and back to his feet. The move left him facing the stairs with Walt behind him, back at full strength. The pressure in Caleb's head intensified, Ishek weakened by the effort.

*I can't hold it long.*

Caleb didn't need much time. He entered the stairwell, practically collapsing down them. Hotch was still at the bottom, his neck bent at a bad angle, dead from the fall. Caleb jumped over him as Walt reached the top, giving chase.

He rounded the corner, reaching the outer hatch for reactor control. He dropped beside it, grabbing at the panel along the wall.

"What are you doing?" Walt said, coming up behind him. She grabbed his arm and pulled, throwing him into the opposite bulkhead. The pressure was becoming too intense, causing flashes of light in front of Caleb's eyes.

Walt rounded on him, trapping him against the bulkhead. The panel was almost off. He just needed to get to it again. But how the hell was he supposed to get past her? He had already used his best move to surprise her. She wouldn't fall for it again.

*Caleb, hurry!*

Ishek felt pained in his mind, struggling to keep the other Relyeh out.

Walt smiled viciously in front of him, sensing his defeat. "I wish you had a family we could destroy," she said. "I wish you had something we could take from you. Your life will have to do."

Her hand snapped out, reaching for Caleb's neck. He managed to get under it, grabbing it and pushing himself into her, lifting her and jumping so that her entire body hit the top of the deck. He let go of her, letting her roll off his back as his legs gave out. He fell forward onto his knees, his hands yanking at the panel.

Walt was barely stunned and had her feet under

her again within seconds. She grabbed his foot and tugged him back toward her.

"Now you die, Caleb Card," she said, wrapping her arm around his neck and pulling back, choking him.

He brought his arm up behind him.

He didn't need to see her to jab the microspear into her side.

The pressure vanished almost instantly. Walt gasped and let go of his neck as the spear extended through her body, traveling up to the Relyeh parasite and killing it. Caleb let go of the weapon, rolling them both over. Walt stared up at him, the rage in her eyes fading. Her eyes softened.

The Relyeh was dead, Walt's mind her own for the first time in who knew how long. The internal injury caused by the microspear was fatal to her as well. They both knew it. But she smiled anyway.

"Thank you," she said.

Then she died.

Caleb closed her eyes, wishing it hadn't come to this but knowing he should have seen it coming.

His whole body throbbed in pain, but it began to diminish as Ishek poured fresh adrenaline into it.

*That was close.*

"Too close."

*We're still alive.*

## 25

### Rico

"I don't have a good feeling about this," Isaac said.

"I think that might be the understatement of the year," Rico replied.

Their modbox was sitting in the middle of the street, at the head of the line of survivors they were trying to get out of Sanisco alive. Lutz's car was beside theirs, the engineer's head swiveling back and forth between them and the obstacle ahead.

Obstacle. That might be the understatement of the century.

They had been trailing behind the xaxkluth, keeping to the shadows of the dilapidated buildings on either side of the corridor and staying as quiet as they could while the alien creatures chased General Stacker and the two armored vehicles toward the southern gates. The plan to draw the enemy away had been working perfectly, the civilians on foot behind them managing to stay grouped and moving along, despite the palpable fear within the ranks.

For a moment, Rico thought they were going to get away with it.

For a moment, she was convinced their plan would succeed, and they would get the nearly five hundred people out of the city alive. Five hundred out of ten thousand. She tried not to think about that part.

Not that it mattered.

The moment was over.

The xaxkluth had stopped, every last one of them at the same time. Then they had flipped themselves over, using their tentacles to change direction in place. It left their central mass upside down, their eyes below their mouths, but that didn't seem to affect them in the slightest. Now they were charging toward the survivors, hundreds of tentacles stretched across the entire street, blocking the gate ahead, preventing them from escaping.

The people behind Rico screamed, and a glance back showed them scattering, each one of them individually abandoning the group. She found Bale standing fixed at the head, his fear keeping him locked in place when he should have urged them to stick together. They were safer that way.

Not safe, but safer.

She gripped the handle of the machine gun and leaned back in the seat slightly. Holding the trigger, she rattled with the weapon as it unleashed its

## Isolation

ordnance, sending bullets smashing into the closest xaxkluth.

"General," Rico said. "They're bolting."

Nathan didn't answer. Rico kept shooting.

"General!"

No reply.

"Ike, we can't just sit here."

"Where do you want me to go?"

It was a good question. There was no escape from these things. Not right now. She continued shooting, tearing three limbs off the lead xaxkluth. Lutz's gunner finally joined the fight, following her lead.

"Fall back," she said to Isaac. "Keep us away from them so I can keep shooting."

"Roger."

The modbox started moving, spinning a tight radius to get them turned the other way. Rico rotated the turret around to keep her guns on the enemy, still ripping into them. They started back down the street, continuing to shoot.

Rico checked her HUD, noting for the first time that Nathan's status was orange. Injured but alive. The APC was headed down the street, taking a wide approach to flank the xaxkluth, while the tank was still in position.

Why wasn't it moving?

A loud boom answered her question, the shell hitting the line of xaxkluth and detonating, sending the creatures sprawling. The tank didn't move while it reloaded, and they all waited for the xaxkluth to turn their attention back on the weapon.

They didn't. They continued closing on Rico and the rest of the civilians. Worse, a quick glance at the situation grid told her more of the creatures were closing on them all.

The Parabellum swooped over the area, firing plasma into the xaxkluth. The tank released another round, killing another. Rico kept shooting, sending hundreds of bullets into the one nearest them, finally getting through its tentacles and cutting into its central mass. It reached for them, its limb falling just short as it died.

Rico sighed in relief, trying to keep track of the scene. The survivors had scattered everywhere. Some were hiding in buildings. Others were trying to run back to the pyramid. They were headed right for the other xaxkluth.

Two of the cars were fleeing too, the drivers making a run for it. The others were more brave, staying ahead of the xaxkluth and doing their best to injure and harass them. Rico looked up in time to see one of the Relyeh catching up to one of the cars. Its tentacles grabbed the machine and lifted it, easily tearing in half, the deputies falling out on the ground where more tentacles grabbed them and either tore them apart or stuffed them into its monstrous maw.

Rico didn't stop shooting, the handle of the turret growing warm in her hands. She glanced down at the belt feed and the linked crates of ammunition stacked beside it. The bullets were going fast, nearly half already expended.

"Hold on!" Isaac shouted. He cut the wheel hard, skidding the machine as a xaxkluth lunged at them, its swinging tentacle only barely missing the vehicle. She rotated the turret toward the limb and fired, cutting it off.

"There's too many!" Rico shouted back.

Another shell from the tank damaged the xaxkluth line, but the smaller ones had gotten ahead and were passing Rico. They attacked the civilians, and the screaming started again.

Rico's jaw clenched. The people were all going to die. The plan had failed, and they didn't have enough firepower to do a damn thing about it.

A sharp whine cut through the rest of the fighting and the APC charged in from the left, main gun tearing through the smaller xaxkluth and cutting them down, stopping their attack. The Parabellum passed over again, firing down into the enemy line. Rico smiled, getting a second wind as she rotated the turret toward another mark on her grid.

She was about to fire when the modbox was lifted and thrown sideways. She barely had time to pull herself from the turret and jump free as it slammed roof first into a solid brick wall, crushing the gun turret on its roof nearly flat.

She landed beside the toppled vehicle, rolling to

her feet and looking back to where she could see Isaac through the barred windshield. Still in the driver's seat, he hung from his seat belt, struggling to release it. Obviously a little dazed, he moved slowly, but at least he was still alive. For now.

The xaxkluth that had latched onto the modbox and tossed it into the brick wall like a kid's toy had come from around the corner. While it had only shown as a red mark on her HUD, it was the largest of the aliens she had seen thus far. It towered over them, rivaling a small goliath in size.

And it was coming right for them.

Rico reached to her back for her rifle, only to realize it had been dislodged during the crash. Her eyes fixed on one of the xaxkluth's tentacles, rising into the air to whip down toward her. She grabbed the pistol on her hip. It wasn't much, but it was better to die fighting.

Rico didn't hear the motorcycle engine over the din of the fighting, and the volume of targets had shrouded her view of it on her HUD. In one second, she was staring at the tentacle reaching for her, sure it would kill her, and in the next, the bike was there, and Hayden landed cleanly in front of her, along with an Axon, the motorcycle tumbling away.

"Sheriff!" Rico shouted in a mix of relief and excitement.

Hayden didn't look at her. "Help Isaac!" he shouted, catching the tentacle in both augmented hands as it descended toward them. He held it above his head and leaned toward it, his knees locked, so that he skidded on the soles of his boots as the alien pushed him backward. The Axon raised its right arm, its skin stretching into a blade that glowed blue before cutting down through the tentacle and slicing it away.

Hayden drew his guns and rushed toward the main body of the giant xaxkluth, the Axon at his side.

## 26

## Caleb

Caleb got back to his feet, stumbling toward the bridge. He put his arm out as the dropship started banking, the movement smooth enough not to adversely affect his balance. He continued on to the bridge, reaching it as they leveled out again. He didn't have access to the doors, so he pounded on them. "Pyro! It's Card!"

The door slid open. Caleb entered, surprised to find a new face in the pilot's seat. He glanced up at Caleb as he entered.

"Who are you?" Caleb asked.

"I could ask you the same thing," the pilot replied.

"Colonel Caleb Card. Space Force Marines."

"Sergeant Ryan Bennett, sir. But you aren't a Centurion."

Caleb opened his mouth to explain at the same

time his eyes tracked to the displays. He could see they were approaching a city overrun with xaxkluth. A tank sat at one end of the street near a half-destroyed wall. An APC was moving west-to-east toward a group of aliens, and a small group of cars were firing machine guns at incoming enemies.

"What the hell is going on?" Caleb said.

"Sanisco," Bennett replied as if that explained the entire situation.

In a way, it did. Sanisco was Sheriff Duke's home settlement, and Vyte's request was to kill Sheriff Duke along with General Stacker and everyone else opposing him. It spoke volumes to Caleb that the Axon didn't think this group of xaxkluth was sufficient to complete the task.

But what did Sheriff Duke have that Vyte feared? What did any of them have?

It was something he'd had no time to think about, and judging by the looks of things below...he still wouldn't. The scene below was chaos, an apparent rescue effort gone very, very wrong. Their forces were split up and surrounded, fighting in small pockets that had no chance of surviving individually.

*We should take the ship and leave.*

The idea tempted the part of Caleb that had merged with the Advocate. The fight on the ground appeared lost, and if they tried to help they would wind up dead too. But he hadn't denied both

Nyarlath and Vyte's overtures to turn around and abandon Sheriff Duke, General Stacker and their people. These were the kind of warriors he needed if he was going to quell the coming storm.

*You can't help them.*

He had to help them. Whatever it took.

"Colonel, are you with me?" Bennett asked. He wasn't looking at Caleb anymore. His focus returned to his upcoming strafing run.

"Bennett, how much power does the dropship have?" Caleb asked.

"Reactors are at thirty-five percent."

"How much power does it take to get from here to Proxima?"

Bennett snapped his head toward him. "Depends. Why?"

*You'll drain the ship's batteries too far. It won't be able to fly out of the city, never mind off the planet.*

Caleb bit his lip, shaking his head. "Nevermind." He glanced up at the displays again. If he could siphon some of the dropship's power to his Intellect Skin, he could do a lot more to help fight this threat.

His eyes scanned the displays when he noticed a blue flash out of the corner of his eye. It drew his attention instantly, and he took a few steps further onto the bridge to get a closer look. "Is that—?"

It appears to be.

An Axon Intellect. It was standing close to

Sheriff Duke, helping him fight the largest xaxkluth he had ever seen.

A fight that wasn't going well. He watched as a colossal tentacle snapped out at Sheriff Duke, catching him in the chest and throwing him five meters back into a wall. Two more tentacles reached for the Intellect, only to shrink back when a globe of blue energy flared out from it, severing the end of the limbs.

"It's helping him," Caleb said, surprised and confused.

*It has a strong power supply. Enough to recharge the dropship.*

Which meant he could drain it somewhat. "Bennett, pull up and prepare to come back around. Give me sixty seconds."

*Sheriff Duke might not live another sixty seconds.*

"Colonel, what are you thinking?"

"Sixty seconds," Caleb repeated. "Just do it. That's an order."

Bennett smirked. It was an odd reaction, but Caleb had no time to question it. "Yes, sir."

Caleb left the bridge, rushing back to where he had left Walt. Bending down beside the removed panel, he reached into the crevice for his Intellect Skin and the microspear. He sprinted forward, past the bridge and the jump seats and down the steps into the hold. He broke to the left, to the machine that managed Stacker's powered armor.

He looked behind it, finding the power cord for

the machine. Instead of the usual setup of a plug fitting into a wall socket, this one worked in reverse. The cord emanated from the wall and plugged into the machine, connecting it to the ship's main power. He dropped the Skin on the deck and yanked out the plug, dropping it on the Skin, which automatically sensed the charge available through the plug. The nanocell material restructured to wrap itself around the plug and begin pulling in the energy.

Caleb ran to the ramp controls, tapping the pad to open the back of the ship before returning to the Skin and quickly stripped off his uniform. Naked, he yanked up the Skin and pulled it on, sealing the material and pulling the cowl over his head.

The system was already up and running, diagnostics showing the Skin was charged to fifty percent.

He ran back to the ramp. "Bennett. Time?"

"Ten seconds," Bennett replied through the comm. "What the hell did you do, Colonel? I went from thirty-five to fifteen percent in twenty seconds."

"Consider it a loan," Caleb replied, activating the Skin's complete weapon systems. He moved to the edge of the ramp and looked down. The city was zooming past nearly a kilometer beneath him.

He shifted his grip on the microspear, waiting until the giant xaxkluth was in sight. It was still locked in combat with the Intellect, trying to reach

Sheriff Duke but unable to get close. Hayden remained motionless and likely unconscious.

Or worse.

*I can taste the fear that fills this place. We may have chosen the wrong side.*

"No, we haven't," Caleb spat out.

Then he jumped.

## 27

### Nathan

Nathan heard the groaning, shouting, and shooting like a bad score to an even worse movie. His head pounded, his flesh burned as if it were on fire and he was thirsty. So damn thirsty.

His vision was blurry. His mind still rattled from whatever it was that had happened to him. It took a few seconds to back up to a place he could remember. Sanisco. The xaxkluth. Bad times.

He blinked a few times, trying to soothe his racing heart. He had blacked out, but he was still alive.

"General," Hicks said, his voice muffled through the damaged speaker inside Nathan's helmet. "General, are you with us?"

His node on the ATCS would have turned green the moment he regained consciousness, assuming he wasn't severely injured. If Hicks was asking him if he was alert, it was a good sign.

"Roger," Nathan muttered, still regaining his faculties. "What's the situation?"

"Worse than when you got hit," Hicks replied. "We're overrun. The survivors have scattered. And there's a massive xaxkluth sitting between them and us."

"Shoot it."

"Wish I could. We're out of shells, General."

"Machine guns?"

"Out of ammo."

"Damn it. What about the Axon?"

"Got away."

"Shit." Nothing was going according to plan.

Nathan groaned as he pushed himself to his feet. His armor was functional, though the battery was nearly drained. It had probably saved his life. He found his rifle resting on the turret, the magnetic grip stuck to the metal. He picked it up, checking the weapon's status. The feed was broken, which meant he only had the thirty or so rounds between the chamber and the break.

He didn't think it could get worse, but it had.

Nathan's eyes started to clear. They went right to the network list, darting across the names connected to the system. The Centurions were still alive for now, though Rico and Ike were both orange. Where were they?

He found them on the situation grid, and then he looked up and out into reality, freezing when he saw the xaxkluth ahead. Hicks said it was big, but he wasn't expecting anything as large as what he saw.

He also wasn't expecting the black humanoid that was standing in front of it, ten meters from Rico and Ike's position. He raised his rifle instinctively, taking aim on the Axon, activating the helmet's zoom to ensure he made a good shot. He couldn't afford to waste a single round.

The magnification showed the Intellect wasn't attacking them. It was facing the other direction, its hands extended into sharp blades, a blue glow like a shield surrounding it. He remembered his first encounter with Caleb Card. He had called the matte black material an Intellect Skin. Was that Caleb out there?

Someone was on the ground inside the perimeter of the shield. Nathan focused on the body, recognizing the metal augment despite the scorches and scratches in it.

Hayden.

Nathan started forward without thinking, climbing toward the front of the tank. He searched for the APC on the grid. Could they get to Sheriff Duke to pull him out?

He found it resting in an alley behind the large xaxkluth, already confronting four smaller creatures. It was forming the front line of a last line of defense with the two remaining modboxes behind it, along with a handful of armed survivors. The moment the

APC ran out of ammunition, everyone near it was going to die.

"Hicks, we need to get into the fight," Nathan said.

"General, we're dry," Hicks replied. "No shells. No bullets."

"The enemy might not know that, and we can still distract them."

"Roger. Hold on."

The tank lurched forward, gaining speed as it rumbled down the street. The primary xaxkluth lifted three of its tentacles in their direction, the eyes at the end of each limb spotting them. Three more tentacles curled around the other side of it from the back, all six ready to take them on.

Thirty rounds. Every single one had to count.

"It sees us, General," Hicks said.

"It sees everything. Drake, topside with your rifle. Now."

"Roger," Drake replied.

The top hatch of the tank opened a moment later, and the former Centurion climbed up, fixing his rifle on the xaxkluth.

"Hicks, break left at the next block, help the APC."

"What about this monster?"

"I'm on it."

The tank turned as it reached the next street. Nathan released the magnetic clamps on his boots, letting momentum carry him forward as he leaped from the tank. Activating his jump thrusters for a few seconds, he landed smoothly a dozen meters away. His armor had ten percent power remaining. Thirty minutes of action at most, by the end of which he would either have salvaged a small victory or would be dead.

He continued running toward the xaxkluth. The six tentacles were facing him, writhing as they waited for him to get within striking distance. Thirty rounds wasn't enough to shoot them all off. If he were to do anything, he needed to get around those damn tentacles.

He checked his HUD, watching the tank circle the block behind the APC. If nothing else, the armor offered extra cover to survivors defending themselves, and potential hiding places when they failed at that. The xaxkluth could attack the armor, but it would take them time to get through.

At this point, he wasn't sure that was a good thing. The mission had turned into a disaster, with little left to salvage.

He heard the sound of the dropship approaching overhead, looking up in time to see it approaching the large xaxkluth. He smiled, coming to a stop and getting his weapon into firing position. He would shoot wherever the Parabellum's plasma did the most damage, and hope his rounds could finish the job.

Only the Parabellum didn't shoot. He watched it

pass its attack vector, streaking overhead too high and too fast. What the hell?

"Bennett?" he said.

"Incoming, General," Bennett replied.

Nathan didn't understand at first. The Parabellum had expended her rockets two days ago. And it didn't carry any bombs.

So what was the dark ball rolling off the back ramp and falling in a direct trajectory toward the xaxkluth's central mass?

Nathan zoomed in on it, quickly identifying the form as another Skin. It had to be Caleb. But if that were true, who was wearing the other Skin?

Could it possibly be an Axon?

Nathan couldn't guess what the hell was happening. For the moment, he concerned himself with Caleb as he landed in front of the xaxkluth. He had something black in his hand, the length of a small knife, clutching it like a spear..

What the hell could he do with that? It didn't look lethal enough to pierce the thing's skin, much less put it down.

The Axon, if that's what it was, drew Nathan's attention again. It seemed to notice Caleb at the same time he had. The thing took three running steps and leaped toward the xaxkluth's central mass. Tentacles whipped toward it, and it used its blade-like arms to slash through them. It was doing its best to reach the main body of the creature.

No. That wasn't what it was doing. It was trying to distract the xaxkluth.

Nathan started running again, squeezing off a round that bypassed the tentacles and hit the xaxkluth near one of its primary eyes. Two of the tentacles bent to protect its face, while its others snapped out toward Nathan. But only one of them was long enough to reach him. Nathan gripped his rifle like a club and slammed it into the end of the limb before flipping the weapon back over and firing a single shot, piercing the creature's side.

He found Caleb again in midair. He had unrolled himself into a graceful dive, and his Skin's hands were glowing, the spear in his right hand appearing white-hot. Another few seconds, and he would be on the creature, which still hadn't noticed him.

Or had it? A single tentacle suddenly launched upwards, seeking to grab Caleb.

Nathan was faster. He sprayed the rest of his ammunition across the middle of the tentacle, severing it before it could grab the falling Marine. Caleb vanished behind the swirling limbs, landing on the central mass and throwing the spear down into the creature.

At first, it seemed like he hadn't done anything. The xaxkluth continued as before, pulling itself forward and nearly catching the Axon's Skin in its mouth. Then, without warning, it collapsed in the street and died, heavy enough to shake the ground when it hit.

Standing on top of it, Caleb pulled the spear from the corpse. Much longer now—Nathan realized. He watched it shrink back to its original size.

Caleb turned to the creatures threatening the survivors. Both he and the other Skin bounded past the dead Relyeh monster, charging into the midst of the remaining, smaller xaxkluth.

The entire atmosphere of the fight changed in an instant, and Nathan stood dumbstruck as the remaining alien army began to retreat, its numbers whittled from a hundred to a quarter of that. The number was still enough to challenge them. Probably enough to kill them. But whoever was sending the orders to the aliens had decided they'd had enough.

Nathan overcame his amazement and started running again, making his way to an unconscious Hayden. He knelt over his friend, the memory of the way Hayden had looked at him working its way into the forefront of his thoughts. Natalia was dead. He didn't need Hayden to tell him as much to understand the man's pain. A tear ran from his human eye as Rico came up beside him.

"He needs a doctor," Nathan said.

"So does Isaac. So do I." Her swollen head had a nasty cut across it. "Jesse's a medic. There's a hospital in the pyramid. It's the best we can do."

Nathan looked at the grid. The xaxkluth were

retreating, but how long would they take to regroup? What if they were only waiting for reinforcements?

"It isn't safe to stay here."

"It isn't safe to leave," Rico countered. "Not if we have a chance to help him. Not if we can give him a chance to say goodbye to his family."

"And what about the civilians?"

"We can raid the Law Office armory, arm the survivors and send them on their way."

"Send them where?" Nathan asked. "There isn't anywhere safe."

"There is one place." The Intellect approached them, the black material that composed its blades shrinking back and reshaping into hands. "Sheriff Duke took me there. The entry is easy to defend."

"You mean the Pilgrim?" Nathan asked.

"That's the name. Pilgrim. Hahaha. Haha."

"Hicks knows where it is," Rico said. "Maybe he can take the people there."

Nathan lowered his head. "This city had over ten thousand people in it."

"Not anymore," the Axon said flatly.

"Who are you?" Nathan asked.

"I'm Sheriff Duke's friend. I'm Max. Hahaha. Haha."

Rico's eyes widened when Nathan shot her an astonished glance. "Don't look at me," she said.

Nathan frowned. Bending, he scooped the unconscious Hayden into his arms and gently lifted him. Hayden's head lolled back, his arms limp and dangling.

"Bennett," Nathan said, calling up to the dropship. "Touch down on the pyramid's observation deck."

"Roger, General," Bennett replied.

"Spot, Lucius," Nathan continued. "Round up the civilians and regroup at the pyramid. We don't have a lot of time, and I don't want us to be here if and when those things come back."

"Roger, General," Spot and Lucius replied simultaneously.

"Jesse, hop on the tank. Hicks come pick us up. We have wounded to tend to."

Both Jesse and Hicks confirmed their orders as well.

"Rico, where's Ike?"

"Still in the van. I was afraid to move him. His leg is shattered and who knows what other injuries he's sustained."

Nathan looked to where the toppled van was smashed against a wall, partially buried in rubble.

"I'll recover him," Max said, hurrying to the van. The Intellect grabbed the vehicle's armor plating, tearing it away to get to Ike. Then he gently unbuckled the Marine and lifted him out.

The tank arrived, rolling to a stop beside them. Max and Nathan both climbed on top of it, joining Jesse and Caleb there. Nathan laid Hayden gently down on one of the hull's relatively flat surfaces.

"Who are you?" Max said to Caleb.

"I'm supposed to ask you that," Caleb replied. "You're an Axon."

"Yes."

"And you're helping us?"

"Yes. Hahahaha. Haha."

"I thought your skin was out of power, Card?" Nathan said.

"I borrowed some from the dropship. It was a risk, but I had to take it." Caleb's head continued to face Max. "I thought this mess was complicated before. I guess there are more wrinkles than I realized."

"Wrinkles?" Nathan asked.

"It's a long story. I prefer Sheriff Duke awake to hear it before I tell it."

"Understood." Nathan banged on the side of the tank. "Hicks, take us home."

## 28

### Aeron

General Aeron Haeri walked quickly up the six steps leading into the entrance to his apartment in the posh A-District of Praeton's Dome One. It was the wealthiest area on the planet, inhabited by the most influential people on Proxima. While the Government District in the starship Dove was the seat of the Proxima Civilian Council, here was where money and power—both legally and not quite legally acquired—intersected. It was where all of the real deals and decisions were made, both in back alley whispers and in the fancy eateries, vice-houses and clubs.

His apartment wasn't in the fanciest of the blocks. That one was three strands down and featured personal valets for every resident. He had to settle for a doorman and a shared concierge, though the man rushed over to him the minute he spotted Aeron entering.

"General Haeri," the concierge said. "Welcome home."

"Hobart," Aeron said. "How's your wife?"

"She's great, General," Hobart replied, walking with Aeron to the lift.

"Kids are good?"

"Yes, sir. Shanni has a dance recital tonight. We're all excited for her."

"Make sure to tell her to break a leg for me."

"Of course, General."

Aeron didn't break stride as he made small talk with the concierge. He was known for his kindness to the help, but it wasn't all out of the goodness of his heart. The help often knew things other people didn't, and he was a master at extracting information.

"Has anyone asked for me today?"

"No, General."

"No one has gone up to my apartment?"

If a Judicus had beaten him home, it meant two things. One, they would threaten the staff to keep quiet about their presence. Two, they knew what had happened too quickly for it to have gone through the proper channels, which meant they were in on the assassination. It had taken nearly an hour for him to file the proper report, make a statement to Law Enforcement, and get the hell out of the Government District. He was too known a quantity for anyone to question anything he said, so there was no trouble with that. But the Council meeting had been canceled, and the media was last seen swarming the area in search of the story. He had barely cleared the curb of the Council building before the crews had come running up, forced to make the trip from outside the area through public channels—which meant mostly on foot.

He thought maybe someone would have come to interview him, eager to hear his side of the assassination story. But he knew too well how these things worked on Proxima. The media would get fifty percent accurate information. They would push for more, but it was more symbolic than anything. The Council and the military were accustomed to withholding information, to the extent that they kept more intel classified than remotely necessary. Starting with the whitewashing of the truth behind the generation ships' arrivals on the planet, the powers-that-be had become habituated to manipulation and distraction in the name of public safety.

"No, General," Hobart said. "It's been a regular day out here. I heard there was some trouble in G-dict?"

"That's an understatement. Chair LaMont was assassinated."

Hobart's face paled. "What?"

"A Judicus murdered him. It'll be on the news soon enough if it isn't already."

"The whole planet's going to be in chaos."

"I wouldn't go that far. Co-chair Kurio has already assumed responsibilities, though all Council sessions were canceled today. That's why I'm home early."

Hobart smiled. "It *is* early for you, General." They reached the lifts, and Aeron swiped his wrist over the pad to call an express.

"I have some paperwork to pick up before I head to the base," Aeron replied. "I'll be out again in ten minutes or so. You don't need to follow me when I come back. I don't need anything."

"Yes, sir," Hobart said, smiling widely.

Aeron held up his wrist. The other man did the same. A quick motion sent a tip from Aeron's account to the concierge. The lift door opened and Aeron stepped in.

"Thank you, General," Hobart said.

"Good day, Hobart."

The lift door closed. The cab started to ascend. Aeron withdrew his Oracle from his coat pocket and slipped it on, activating the display. He used it to request a link to a comm terminal in an apartment in Dome Nine. He disconnected at the moment it connected, well before the feed was open and before it could be logged. He just needed to know the line was still active.

He repeated the process three more times, all with the same results. The Organization was still intact. That was good. Love's efforts to take him out of the game hadn't progressed too far yet, which meant he had a little more time.

Time to do what?

The Organization was compromised. He understood that much. Relyeh operatives were active on Proxima, and while their objectives were still a little fuzzy to him, he guessed their primary desire was to keep anyone from putting up any sort of fight against the incoming warship. But that didn't make sense. Nothing the Centurions possessed could stop the vessel. It was moving way too fast for them to target. Hell, it was moving so fast it would be little more than a blink across the sky, long gone by the time any light emanating from it even reached Proxima B.

So why stop him from telling the Council about the incoming invasion of Earth? Why prevent him from revealing the truth of things? How was keeping things secret going to help their cause?

The Hunger needed fear to survive. Exposing their existence to the population would fill that need. Only they weren't prepared for that fear yet. It would only serve the Relyeh already on the planet, and Aeron doubted there could be too many of them here yet. It would be like putting a steak out for dinner three hours before the restaurant opened, leaving it cold and slightly spoiled for the diner. Edible, but not the least bit satisfying.

It was a reason, but Aeron couldn't believe it

was the only one. Someone had gone to great lengths to kill Isaac Pine before Aeron could get him back to Earth. Someone had tried very hard to thwart the Organization's efforts. Did the enemy even know what the purpose of the effort was, or were they simply trying to blockade whatever moves the Organization made, assuming they ran counter to their objectives?

It didn't matter either way. Someone was acting against the Organization, and thanks to Judicus Love he had a better general idea of who.

But not specifically who. The khoron would have a puppet master pulling their strings. Someone sending them orders. But those orders didn't need to come from the planet. They could originate in Relyeh home space for all he knew. The Collective made instant communication across infinite distances possible. But he still had a feeling there was a ringleader on Proxima. Someone orchestrating the movements and watching more directly. Keeping Aeron from acting would take a more personal touch.

First things first. He had sent Kirin and the boys packing, on a shuttle to the spaceport where they would take a transport to the Ring Station—a Trust-run resort sitting in the middle of a gaseous nebula—the closest thing they had to an ocean view. The kids could play in the Nexus while his wife got a massage or three.

The cab doors opened, the lift taking Aeron

directly to his apartment, which occupied half of the eighteenth floor of the forty-story block. The smell of death hit him like a piston to the chest. He immediately grabbed the microspear from his coat pocket as his heart began to race.

## 29

### Aeron

Hobart was wrong. Someone *had* gone up to his apartment.

Aeron entered cautiously, moving away from the lift and through the foyer toward the living room. He pressed himself against the side of the door frame, pausing a moment. The lift doors closed and the cab started to descend.

Aeron removed his Oracle, slipping it back into his pocket. He didn't need it blocking any of his field of vision. Then he crouched low, tilting his head to see around the corner. The first thing he noticed was that his couch was out of place, slid sideways as though it had been pushed.

Then he saw her body.

For a heartbeat, he thought it was his wife, Kirin. He saw black heels leading to stockings and black panties beneath a dark dress that had hiked up during the conflict, which merged with a light-blue blouse and a partial view of a head of light brown hair wrapped into a long ponytail. The neutral-toned carpet around the body was stained with blood.

But Kirin didn't have long hair, and he didn't spot the dark blotch of a birthmark on the woman's ankle. He was relieved to see it wasn't his wife, but not by much. He recognized her now. Lin, his assistant with the Trust. Why was she here? Who had killed her?

And were they still here?

The blood was fresh, and he was willing to bet the body was still warm. But if the killer was present, they didn't know he had arrived. If they did, they would have been right outside the lift, waiting to jump him before he could react.

He decided whoever was responsible was still in the apartment.

His grip on the microspear tightened. He hadn't lied to Hobart. He had come back to grab something from his safe. Something he would need in the days to come. The Organization had been preparing for this circumstance for a long time, and he needed to put their plans into motion.

He could have kicked himself for not doing it sooner, but he had wrongly believed the Relyeh were light-years away and focused on Earth. He had wrongly believed they didn't even know where the second human settlement was. He was fairly certain that had been true as recently as a few months ago.

What had changed?

And how the hell had they gotten here without him knowing it?

It was a breach. A horrible breach. He needed to find the source and shut it down. But he also needed to be ready for the worst. If one khoron could get to Proxima, then an infinite number of Relyeh could get here, one way or another. But it was no coincidence they had revealed themselves now. They were trying to stop the Organization before the Organization could stop them.

But stop them from what?

They were here, but their warship was headed for Earth, and they couldn't possibly prevent it from reaching humankind's homeworld. Aeron had done the best he could by sending Isaac and Rico to warn Sheriff Duke.

Unless…

There was one outcome he hadn't considered, and thinking about it now sent a vein of fear running through his spine. His entire body shivered. Aeron had experience working among the most powerful people on the planet. Not only politicians but also ruthless businessmen and syndicate bosses. People who could have him killed on a whim. He didn't scare easily.

But he was unnerved right now.

He needed to grab the files from the safe and get to the Organization safehouse, and he needed to do it fast.

Aeron moved from the foyer to the living room, clutching the microspear and wishing he had a gun to go with it. Of course there was one in the safe. He had only taken two steps when a figure emerged from the kitchen to the front and left of his position, on the other side of the room.

"Kirin?" he said, surprised and even more fearful to see his wife there. She was wearing workout clothes—a sports bra and fitted pants—revealing a body that was fitter than he remembered. The bra had blood sprayed across it, and she had a long knife in her hand. "Where are the boys? What happened here?"

"The boys," Kirin said, smiling. "They're safe. Maybe. I guess that depends."

Aeron came to a stop at Lin's feet, eyes glued to his wife. He already knew what had happened here. "How long?" he asked.

"Twenty-six days," she replied. " Perhaps if you'd just trusted her with your secrets— "

"I kept everything from her for her protection," Aeron said. "Her security."

"Does she seem safe to you right now?" the khoron asked, holding the knife to Kirin's neck.

"Don't," Aeron said. "Tell me what it is you want."

"I'm getting some of it right now. Your fear is delicious, and I hunger."

"Glad I can help," Aeron growled. "Are my boys still alive?"

"They are. You can keep them that way. You can help them all. We only know about the safe because your wife knew. We want to know what's in it."

"I bet you do."

"You're going to show me."

Aeron slowly crouched beside Lin, noticing her clutch abandoned near her hip. "Why did you kill her?"

"She was here, and I enjoyed it."

Then the question became, why was she here? The khoron wouldn't know. Did it have anything to do with Chair LaMont?

"The safe," the khoron reminded him. "If you want your wife and children to survive, you're going to open it for me, and give me the contents."

"How do I know I can trust you? You aren't even human."

He reached for the clutch, his hand hidden from the khoron's line of sight by the sofa.

"Which makes me more trustworthy. Relyeh do not make promises and fail to keep them. That's why I didn't offer your survival."

"I give you what you want and you kill me? That's a little ungrateful, don't you think?"

He grabbed the clutch.

"There's another option. You could join us."

"No."

He unclasped the button as he said it, disguising

the sound with the movement of his foot. He reached into the purse.

The khoron smiled. Kirin smiled. It bothered Aeron to see her under the Relyeh's control. "I didn't think you would agree to that." She put the knife against her neck again, pressing just enough to draw a line of blood. "The safe. Retrieve the contents and bring them to me. I'll wait."

"Right," Aeron said, the grip of the pistol comfortable in his hand. Souls forgive him for what he was about to do.

The Organization wasn't a fraternity or a club. It wasn't something entered into lightly. It was an assertive action that demanded loyalty and assured potential consequences with fewer potential benefits. He had become part of the Organization before he was married, knowing at that time that there were no guarantees. The possibility existed where he could lose everything he cared about in an instant. The Organization demanded itself ahead of love or family. It was part of the oath.

"I'm sorry, Kay," he whispered, rising to his feet and pointing the pistol at his wife. "I'm not for sale. Not for any price."

The khoron seemed confused. "Not for your wife? Or your children?"

Aeron squeezed the trigger, planting a single round in Kirin's forehead. She toppled to the ground, her brain dead, her body still alive.

"Not for anything," he replied.

He walked over to her, expression flat. He was a warrior first, a husband and father second. He knelt beside her, turning her over.

Through her shirt he could see the flesh on her back moving, the khoron seeking to escape the useless husk of the human being it had appropriated. No doubt it had told its superior what Aeron had done. The decision he had made. No doubt that superior was murdering his children somewhere on the planet at this very moment. But he had already separated himself from the emotional reaction. He didn't question whether or not he had done the right thing. The coming of the Relyeh warship was bigger than his family. It was a threat to every human on Proxima and beyond.

And he had taken an oath.

Kirin's skin broke, the small, dark worm slipping its head out. It swiveled toward him, seeing him through dozens of eyes and letting out a high-pitched shriek. Aeron smiled, showing it the microspear. It screamed again in reply.

It was afraid.

Good.

He jabbed the microspear into it, watching the spear expand into the creature, spreading out into a dozen tendrils that tore the worm apart.

Aeron watched the process in grim satisfaction. If he was cold, it was because he had to be cold. He turned away from his dead wife, face set in determination as he headed for the safe.

## 30

### Aeron

The safe was hidden in Aeron's office, behind a portrait he had commissioned of himself and his family, hand-painted based on a three-dimensional model that rested on the top corner of his bookshelf.

Very few people on Proxima had bookshelves. There weren't many books on the planet. But Aeron had been collecting them for years, bringing them back with him after his visits to Earth, or trading with Centurions who had unsuccessfully tried to smuggle them in to sell on the black market. They always got caught because if he were in their position, he would have done the same thing.

The painting was on the floor, tossed carelessly aside, the canvas torn almost in half. It seemed appropriate now. He hoped someone would one day be able to appreciate the sacrifice he had made, though few would ever know anything at all. The

Organization had worked in the shadows for almost three centuries. That wasn't going to change now.

Or was it?

It all depended on how he managed the next three hours of his life.

Nothing could save Kirin or the boys. The planet? Humankind? Part of that responsibility fell to him. Perhaps more than he had realized and definitely more than he wanted. The rest fell on Rico, Isaac and Sheriff Duke. And maybe Nathan Stacker. He wouldn't be surprised if the former fugitive got involved. Aeron allowed himself a slight smirk at that. Nathan thought Aeron had fallen for the ruse and believed he was a cloned twin to James. Not quite. The other Stacker had matched his brother's look, but it wasn't possible to match his demeanor.

He went to the safe, noticing the blood stains on the keypad. Lin had died before the khoron tried to guess the access code, likely using his wife and children's birthdays, his wedding anniversary, and all of the obvious combinations to get in. Of course, Aeron knew better. The same way he knew not to use biometric security because his fingers or hand could be cut off, his eyes could be gouged out. The system had offered four guesses and then locked out. At least, that's what the khoron had believed because that's how Aeron had told Kirin it worked.

He had lied. The system wouldn't respond to any more incorrect guesses, appearing secured. But the correct entry he tapped into it caused it to come back to life. The electromagnets disengaged, the heavy alloy bars retracting and the door swinging open.

There were only three things inside. One was a gun. Special tech. An ion blaster. The second was a data chip. The third, a key—a small, flat rectangle with an encrypted code embedded in it. The Organization's best-kept secret. Only the head of the Organization knew it existed, and if he didn't find a replacement before he died, the secret would go with him.

That would be a damn shame, but that was how valuable the secret was.

Aeron grabbed all three, not content to shove the chip and key in his pocket. He unbuttoned and pulled down his pants, and then pulled at a small pocket on his inner thigh - a seamless augment purposely designed to carry these two specific items. He stuck the chip and key into it and pressed it closed.

"Looks like I caught you with your pants down, General."

Aeron didn't turn around. He recognized the voice of Judicus Hale without seeing him.

"Hale," Aeron said. "Did you come to question me?"

"No. The safe is empty. Give me whatever was in it."

Aeron still held the ion blaster in his other hand. "How do you know I have it?"

"Because I'm not an idiot," Hale replied. "Give it."

"Why don't you kill me and take it?"

"Okay."

Aeron didn't need to see Hale in the doorway behind him to know he was about to get shot. He dove sideways, falling behind his desk as the shots hit the metal, denting it but failing to punch through. The khoron realized quickly the furniture was hardened, and Aeron heard Hale rushing forward.

He rolled onto his back, grabbing for the microspear. Hale jumped over the desk, catching an ion blast in his face that melted the flesh clean off, and then landing on the spear as he came down on Aeron's chest.

Aeron rolled the corpse off him, yanking out the spear and getting back to his feet. How many of the Judici were compromised? He was going to guess most of them, if not all. The Judicus Department was the easiest place for the aliens to hide in plain sight.

He pulled his pants up, rebuttoning them and straightening himself out before rushing for the door. A second Judicus was entering the living room as he came out of the office, and he fired without hesitation, catching the woman in the chest. The ion blast went clean through her body armor, reducing her innards to soup and dropping her.

Aeron ran past her, checking the lift controls. The cab was already dropping, so he turned to the door on his right and slowly pushed it open , looking down into the emergency stairwell. He heard feet coming up. More enemies. It wasn't going to be easy to get out of here.

He went into the stairwell, turned and ran up them. They hadn't spotted him yet, but if they slowed down they would be able to hear him and where he was going. He grabbed his Oracle from his coat pocket as he ascended, putting it on and activating it. He placed a comm to the terminal he had tried earlier.

This time, it was dead.

Damn it.

He tried the next. The result was the same. His opposition had caught up to at least two of his operatives. He tried the third.

"Deckard," the man said.

"Code Twelve," Aeron said, and then disconnected.

Now all he had to do was stay alive for the next ten minutes until the cavalry arrived.

# 31

## Aeron

For Aeron, staying alive another ten minutes was easier said than done. The race to the rooftop was on, but even once he got there, the Judici at his back would have him cornered, and he'd be fending for himself against who knew how many khoron-infected Judici.

That was the hardest part of the situation. Not the fact that they would find his wife dead in their apartment, the khoron no doubt disappearing before the body ever made it to the morgue. Not the fact that he would soon enough be a wanted man, both for her murder and likely as an accomplice to Chair LaMont's death. Not even the fact that his sons' lives were forfeit the moment he shot Kirin to preserve the Organization. No, the hardest part was knowing the people chasing him weren't in control of themselves. That they would never hunt him on their own, and could only watch as their bodies were taken and used for the task.

And that he had no choice but to kill them before they could kill him.

He continued up the steps, having to climb from the eighteenth floor to the top of the fortieth. It was a long way, and while Aeron had kept himself in good shape despite approaching his fiftieth birthday, he wasn't a young man anymore.

Meanwhile, the Judici climbing the stairs behind him were driven by khoron, their bodies fed chemical cocktails to allow them to work harder without strain, giving them a massive advantage in overall speed. Aeron's only advantage was time. He had started nearly ten floors ahead of them, and he heard when they stopped on the eighteenth floor, not realizing he had gone up instead of down. It took them close to thirty seconds to scour his apartment and double-check all possible avenues of descent before accepting he had done the unthinkable.

Once he got to the top, where was he going to go?

Aeron knew where, but they didn't. It gave him a second slight edge because they didn't hurry after him with all the fervor they were capable of. They took what was for them a leisurely pace, though for him it meant they were gaining.

He was out of breath by the time he made it to the door leading out onto the rooftop. It was access secured, forcing him to use his embedded ID to open it, which in turn would confirm to the Judici he was there. It was unavoidable. The aggressors were only five floors behind him, which might not offer enough time for him to find cover before they burst out onto the rooftop.

He pushed through the door, checking the time on his Oracle. He was halfway to pick up. He had never been in a real gunfight before, but he had done plenty of simulations as part of his Marine training. He knew how time slowed down when the fighting started. How five minutes seemed to take five hours.

A quick scan of the rooftop left him with limited options for cover. He could swing back to the other side of the stairwell, but that would keep him too close to his pursuers. He could cross to the north toward the water pipes. Or he could head south to the electrical junction.

With the entire Proxima settlement inside domes, the blocks didn't have HVAC units for heating and cooling. The whole dome was kept at a constant temperature determined by the atmospheric units currently projecting cloudy skies across the thick, transparent shell. Without the projectors, they would be looking at a constant starscape instead of simulated weather patterns during the day.

With District A located at the outer ring of the dome, it meant incredible views of the rocky terrain stretching out to domes three and five, and then twelve further behind that, partially shrouded by an overhang. The river split all of it, the main line of domes intentionally built along or over the river, making use of its constant flow for both added power generation and general supply—the lifeblood of the entire planet.

District A's location was also going to make pickup tricky. Only a minimal number of vehicles had airspace access inside the dome. The position left the dome arcing downward over Aeron's head, leaving only thirty meters or so between the rooftop and the shell. His contact had a tight squeeze to reach him and would need to be careful not to collide with the dome.

It was that consideration that sent him around the stairwell toward the electrical junction on the inner side of the block. There wasn't enough cover to confuse the Judici anyway, so he might as well give his pickup a better chance of avoiding disaster.

Aeron bolted to the other side of the door, sprinting across the rooftop to a two-meter high cube positioned a third of the distance from the ledge. The cube was access secured, its contents critical to the management of the electricity flowing through the building. It was thinly protected with sheet aluminum, generally untouchable to anyone without access to the door. That was one of the reasons it was on the roof in the first place.

He ducked behind it, crouching low. The cube

wouldn't offer much protection from heavy rounds, but the Judici likely weren't carrying any. It made more sense for them to be armed with stunners, lest they accidentally damage the precious cargo he had collected downstairs. It was cargo he considered threatening them with, but they would guess correctly that he wouldn't risk destroying it unless he was confident it would stop them.

He wasn't.

It took another minute before the Judici moved slowly and cautiously onto the rooftop. Aeron risked peering around the corner of the cube, quickly counting six agents. He held the ion blaster close to his chest.

"General Haeri," one of them said. "You're wanted for questioning. Surrender immediately. "

Aeron didn't respond to the request. The Judicus made it a second time, the others already advancing toward him, expecting he still wouldn't react. Aeron checked his Oracle. Two minutes.

Too long.

He backed up slightly, getting the blaster into a shooting position and then swinging around the back of the cube. He started shooting, sending a quick succession of rounds into the midst of the Judici. They evaded the blasts, raising their guns and taking aim. As he had guessed, stun rounds zipped across the distance, flashing blue as they smacked into the power cube with enough force to dent the aluminum.

Aeron kept firing, sweeping the blaster across the rooftops. The misses were leaving spots of cracked concrete across the surface, kicking up dust and powder that spread around the site in a light cloud. The Judici didn't retreat from the assault. Instead, he doubled down and approached more rapidly.

He had tried to warn them back, taking care not to hit them with lethal shots, but also putting extra effort into scoring hits. He changed tactics, hiding behind the cube and swinging around the other side to shoot. He hit two of the Judici in rapid succession, the ion blasts tearing through their light armor, each time feeling a slight twinge of guilt at the action. But war was coming to Proxima. Check that. War was already here.

He ducked back behind the cube as a pair of stunners nearly hit him. He might be able to stay upright after one strike. Two would knock him out for sure. The rounds punched into the aluminum, already dented from the other shots. One must have gotten through the thin protection, because a moment later a massive shower of sparks shot from it, blowing the cover off the front of the cube and taking out the power to the block. Aeron dove away from the malfunctioning unit, rolling over and coming to his knees facing the ledge. One of the Judici rushed through the sparks, lunging at him.

Aeron let the man hit him and knock him onto the roof, remaining calm as he jabbed the microspear into the Judicus' neck. A short growl and he became a dead weight on top of Aeron, who rolled the body off and started getting up.

"Don't move."

Aeron froze in place. Two of the Judici had caught up to him, and were pointing their guns at him from three meters away. Why didn't they just shoot him?

A quick glance back answered the question. He was too close to the edge of the roof. If they knocked him out and he fell backward, he and the cargo would fall forty stories to the street. He'd be dead, and the data chip and key would likely wind up crushed.

"Move forward," one of them said. He didn't recognize either of them. Were they even with the Judicus Department?

"Not a chance," he replied. "Shoot me."

They looked at one another before pausing, making it clear a puppeteer was calling the game from offsite. One of them started toward him.

"Not so fast," Aeron said, pointing his blaster at them. "It seems we have an impasse. You get too close, and I throw myself from the building."

"You'll lose your opportunity."

"Will I? I might have another trick left up my sleeve. If I let you take me, the loss is definite."

"Your loss is already definite. We wish to preserve the people here. Especially the Centurions. We have need of them."

"I bet you do. How did you get here? How did you find us?"

"The information was in Valentine's mind, and her mind became one with the Collective. From there, the matter was trivial. Did you know there's an Axon portal on your planet, General? Unfortunately, we can't access it without the coordinates."

Aeron stared at the khoron-infected Judicus. If there was an Axon portal here, it had to be on one of the generation ships. Not the Dove, and not the Mir. That left fifteen other ships. Fifteen other possibilities. But why hadn't they sent an army through it, if they had access? Why send a warship?

Because the planet they had arrived from was too distant and didn't have enough of the enemy to send. That wasn't exactly right either. A human must have come through the portal, host to a khoron and transporting other khoron. That's the only way they could have slipped past unnoticed. But where else had they gotten a human?

Unless the khoron had come from Earth.

Damn it.

The Judicus smiled. "I can smell your fear, General."

Aeron shifted his focus to the Oracle over his eye. Then he smiled. "Thanks for the chat."

He hit the roof as a large Law drone shot up from behind the building, its forward cannon opening fire on the pair of Judici. Multiple stun rounds smacked into them, jolting them with enough electricity to knock them to the roof.

"Perfect timing," Aeron said, getting back to his feet. He hurried over to the fallen, quickly stabbing each of them with the microspear. Every khoron he killed was one less he'd need to fight later.

Then he went to the ledge and climbed onto the back of the drone, hunching down and holding on tight as it spun away from the scene. It streaked across the dome and descended in C-District behind a Reclamation Center. The enemy would know he'd landed there, but they wouldn't find him. He had lots of friends in low places.

It was the best place for the Organization's army to hide.

## 32

### Aeron

Not everyone who wound up in a Reclamation Center was there because they were criminals. That wasn't to say the residents had never done anything wrong. Everyone there was less than a model citizen, and less than a model Centurion. But some of the charges were more severe than the crimes. And some of the sentences were less severe than the charges. Every Centurion who went through the system spent a few years mining asteroids, though the mining rig the convict ended up on was decided by factors no single civilian understood, and transfers were common. There was an established and elaborate system in place. A system Aeron had helped refine during his tenure. A system that helped ensure that when the Hunger came, the Organization would be ready.

The residents in the Centers who needed to know the score knew it. And they stayed quiet about it. Hell, they were chosen in part because of their loyalty and their ability to keep their mouths shut. They didn't know about the Relyeh and the Axon per se, though they had heard the rumors. But they did know Aeron had enlisted them for a particular purpose, and when he came calling they were to move without question.

That's why the drone dropped into the split behind the Center. And that's why Aeron jumped off it and ran to the doorway a few meters away. It opened as he approached, and two men in hooded shirts grabbed his arms and pulled him inside. An entire second squad hurried out into the alley and quickly began breaking down the machine.

The Organization soldiers led Aeron into the Center's basement, to a poorly lit room with an old, cracked dental chair in the center.

"Sit, sir," one of them said, gently pushing him into it. "Liggie's on her way down."

"Thank you," Aeron said.

"Yes, sir."

Aeron could hear the men talking to one another in the alley and the sound of power tools removing the wings from the drone. They were coming down the stairs when Liggie came around to the front of the chair, smiling at him.

"What's up, boss?" she said. Short dreadlocks hung along the back of an otherwise bald head, while tattoos ran down the length of both bare, sinewed arms. She wore a fitted white tank tucked into a black skirt that hung down to her feet, scraping along the floor.

Aeron turned his wrist over and laid it out on the arm of the chair. "We're in Code Twelve," he replied.

"Shit," she said. "I better hurry my sweet little ass up." She grabbed a laser scalpel. "You sure about this?"

"No, but it has to be done."

"General." Another soldier came around the table. A Fox clone. Square jaw. Short black hair. Muscled. He wore an Oracle with an opaque black screen over his left eye. "They're saying on the comms that you killed your wife?"

Aeron's look caused the Fox to flinch. "She was compromised," he replied. "I told you. I told all of you. If you have ties, you might need to cut them one day. No excuses. No hesitation."

Liggie put the scalpel to Aeron's wrist. He gritted his teeth as it burned through his flesh. There was no time to numb it.

"We've got eyes on the targets," Fox said. "Judicus Department is inbound. It looks like they picked up some MPs to help them out."

"I need to be out of here before they arrive," Aeron said.

"You will be," Liggie replied. "Thirty seconds."

She dropped the scalpel and fished into the wound with some tweezers for a couple of seconds before finding what she was looking for. She picked up the scalpel again and snipped a tiny ID chip free, dropping it onto a towel as someone handed her a replacement.

"General Haeri dies tonight," Liggie said. "But not to us."

"Not to us," Fox repeated.

She pulled a loup over her eye for the more detailed work of inserting and connecting his new chip. "Two minutes," Fox said.

"I've got it," Liggie replied, leaning closer to his arm. She had to stay focused on the delicate work of inserting the new chip. It had to be positioned correctly or it wouldn't activate when swiped, and he would lose access to his new persona. He didn't have time to do this all over again if this chip weren't properly installed the first time..

The seconds ticked away. Aeron didn't move or speak. He didn't want to distract her.

"One minute," Fox said.

"Shut up," Liggie replied. "Almost there."

"Forty-five seconds," Fox said. "Come on, Ligs."

"Done!" she announced, slapping a patch on top of the wound to close it and stop the bleeding. She grabbed another device and scanned the ID. It showed Aeron's face but listed him as Paul Augustus. "Good to go."

"Pardon me, General," Fox said, moving forward to pull his jacket off and unbutton his shirt. "You want to get your pants, sir?"

Aeron stood up, unzipping his pants and sitting

down again to slip them off. A third soldier brought him new clothes—a dirty t-shirt and a stained pair of pants—along with an old synthetic leather jacket. The soldier also handed him a shoulder holster for his ion blaster.

"What is that?" Fox asked when Aeron put the microspear on the table beside the chair.

"Toothpick," Aeron replied, smirking. "Classified toothpick."

Fox chuckled. "Yes, sir."

Aeron yanked on the clothes in record time. He had to be fast.

"They're coming around the corner," Fox said. "Let's move."

Fox led Aeron up the stairs to the main floor. Dozens of ex-cons filled the large, open room. Sleeping mats covered the floor, while desks along two of the walls were staffed with tired volunteers trying to find work for the recs. A mess in the back corner left the smell of burned stew lingering in the air, mixing with sweat and body odor.

"Come to!" Fox shouted as they entered. Nearly fifty of the recs immediately dropped everything they were doing and gathered around Aeron, crowding him in at the same moment the front door opened. A squad of Military Police moved in, trailed by a pair of Judici.

"Scan them," one Judicus said.

The MPs advanced, pulling out chip scanners and pointing them at the recs as though they were rifles. The machines quickly captured the data from the chips, failing to come up with one that matched Aeron.

"He didn't come this way," the lead MP said.

The Judici hesitated, their eyes sweeping over the recs. They couldn't get a good view of Aeron from where he was positioned in the group.

"Fine. Let's go."

The Judicus headed for the door, the MPs behind her. As soon as they left the building, the men and women around Aeron backed away, coming to attention and saluting.

"Nice work," Aeron said. "We're in Code Twelve. Stand down and await further orders. Be ready. The time is coming. Fox, with me."

"Yes, sir," Fox said, coming up next to Aeron. "Where are we headed, sir?"

"Special Command," Aeron replied. "Ghost's Tavern."

## 33

### Hayden

In the dream, Hayden was with Natalia.

It was their wedding day. A simple affair in Metro due to the limited resources of the colony and the often strategic pairings of citizens who composed the essential departments of the Governor's Office.

That a sheriff would marry an engineer wasn't unique, but it was uncommon enough that the Governor himself had turned out for the occasion. He stood in the background while Hayden and Natalia took their vows to love, honor and cherish one another all the days of their lives.

In the dream, he lifted her veil, ready to kiss his bride. Only the face beneath wasn't Natalia's. It was blank, black and oddly shaped.

Hayden's eyes snapped open, his heart racing. He heard the beeping of the monitor beside him and noticed the dampness of the sheets. He was in a room. A hospital room. In a bed. The lights were on, and the room was empty.

He tried to sit up, his chest burning with the effort.

"Sheriff, relax."

The room wasn't empty. Hayden's gaze landed on Doctor Hess. The doctor's face was ragged, though his clothes were clean. He had a bandage on his cheek and his arm in a sling.

Natalia.

"Relax?" Hayden growled, still fighting to get up. "How the hell can you tell me to relax?"

"Sheriff, please," Hess said. "We've all been through the wringer, and while you seem to have an inhuman healing factor...that hit to your chest broke half your ribs. You need a few more hours of rest to heal."

"Natalia," Hayden groaned in agony, trying to get up. He realized suddenly his arms were powered down. Offline. Both of them. He couldn't reach the control rings to turn them back on without help. "Damn it, Hess."

"I've got orders to keep you here.".

"Orders from who?"

"General Stacker."

"Nate?" Hayden was relieved he was still alive. "Where is he?"

"If you'll relax, I can go and get him."

"Natalia," Hayden said again, more softly this time. Remembering. "She's gone, Doc."

"I know," Hess said. "I'm sorry, Sheriff. Sorrier than you can imagine. She was my good friend."

"It wasn't supposed to happen. Not now. Not so soon." The tears were working their way into his eyes again. He stuffed the raw grief down. "Stacker gave me something last time I was in real bad shape."

"What?" Hess said.

"That's why I heal so fast. It was either going to kill me or make me stronger."

"So will rest," Hess replied. Hayden stared at the doctor, his look causing Hess to shiver slightly. "Stay here while I get General Stacker."

Hayden wanted to get up and go back to the lab. That's where his family was. That's where they had died. He resisted the urge. Hess was right. He was near useless right now. He had to give himself a chance to recover if he was going to kill the Axon for what it had done.

He wouldn't stop until it was dead. Until all of them were dead. They took his wife and his children from him. He was going to take everything he could from them.

Hess was right. He could let their deaths kill him or make him stronger. He had to be stronger. For them.

That didn't mean it hurt any less.

Hayden expected Nathan to enter the room alone. Instead, he walked in with an entire entourage. Caleb Card, wearing what looked like an

Intellect Skin beneath a pair of jeans, the head cowl pulled down around his neck. Max, stiff and silent. Pyro, her eyes weary, puffy and red from tears. And Rico. Hayden smiled when he saw her, still happy Nathan had gotten her out of her crashed ship alive.

Another person entered with them, adding to the crowd. "Bennett?" Hayden said, suddenly wondering if he was still dreaming. "How?"

"Sergeant Ryan Bennett, Sheriff," Bennett said, introducing himself. "I'm not Austin."

Hayden understood. "Where's Ike?"

"In the room next to yours," Nathan said. "He broke his leg, and he doesn't heal like you."

"Nobody heals like you," Pyro added. "You didn't tell us the serum was still effective."

"I prefer to try not to get my ass kicked," Hayden replied. He paused, looking at the group gathered in front of him and then lowering his eyes. "Natalia. She's…"

"I recovered her body," Max said. "I recovered all of them. General Stacker says you'd like to say goodbye, even though they can't hear you. Hahahaha. Hahaha."

Hayden closed his eyes. It wasn't Max's fault he didn't understand. He was still a machine emulating a human. A broken machine at that. "Thank you."

"Pozz."

"What about the city?" Hayden asked, lifting his head again. "What about survivors?"

"I don't want to mince words, Sheriff," Nathan said.

"Then don't. You can't make things worse."

"Doc Hess is one of four hundred and thirty-six people we've recovered."

Hayden fell back in the bed. He was wrong. Nathan had made things worse. "That's all?"

"Lucius and Drake are combing the city," Rico said. "And watching for the xaxkluth to come back. They didn't go far. It seems like they're waiting for reinforcements."

"Or new instructions," Caleb said. "Vyte got what he wanted here."

"Vyte?" Hayden asked.

"There's a lot you need to know," Caleb added. "A lot all of you need to know."

"I came to Earth to warn you, Hayden," Rico said. "There's—"

Hayden shook his head. "Not yet, Rico. I want to see them."

"Understood," Rico replied. "But Doc Hess wants you in bed."

"We don't have time for me to sit in bed. The xaxkluth can come back anytime, can't they, Card?"

"That's right, Sheriff," Caleb said.

"Pyro, can you reactivate my arms?"

She nodded, moving past the others to his bedside. She reached for the control ring on his right side. "Sheriff, there's a lot of damage at the connection between the muscle and the ring."

"I know."

"Doesn't it hurt?"

"It does. Thanks for reminding me. Nat and Hess said they couldn't fix it."

"You should stop wearing the augment."

Hayden laughed. "That's not going to happen. Power me up, Chandra."

Pyro tapped on the ring, entering the code to reactivate it. Bringing the prosthetic back to life only served to increase the throbbing around the ring. The pain had faded long enough he had almost forgotten about it, but now it came back with a vengeance. He gritted his teeth while she turned on the other augment.

"You recharged them?" Hayden said, noticing power levels were at one hundred percent.

"Consideration. I brought you a gift, Sheriff," Max said. "Hahaha. Haha."

"An energy unit," Caleb said. "I fought a war over one of those things, and it hands one over as if it were a bouquet of flowers."

"That was what you requested," Max said. "A quantum dimensional modulator to put a shield around your city."

"You're a little late," Hayden growled.

"Sit still a second while I recalibrate these," Pyro said.

Hayden remained motionless. "You brought the power back online in here too?"

"It's temporary," Nathan said. "Max also

located the Axon's jamming device and destroyed it."

"Affirmation. I'm trying to help, even if the Axon organics are too afraid to act."

"There you go, Sheriff," Pyro said. "Try them out."

Hayden flexed his arms, nodded at the natural feel. "You're a wizard, Chandra."

She smiled. "I do what I can."

Hayden slid off the bed, only realizing he was nude once he was already standing in front of everyone.

"Uh, Sheriff," Rico said.

"Someone get me some clothes," Hayden growled. He was too sad and angry to give a damn about his nakedness. "Rico, I want you to take me to see them. The rest of you meet me in the conference room in fifteen minutes."

"Is that long enough?" Nathan asked.

"Eternity isn't long enough," Hayden replied. "But it's all the time we can spare."

# 34

## Hayden

Hayden followed Rico to the lifts, pausing outside of them.

"Hayden," Rico said, turning to face him. She already had tears in her eyes. "I'm sorry."

"Me too," he replied, face hard. He couldn't do it any other way. Not yet. "Why'd we stop here?"

"I need to ask you. What do you want to do with the bodies?"

"Make them live again."

The response caused Rico's tears to flow more strongly. "Damn it, Hayden. You know I would if I could."

"I know."

He took a deep breath. He still couldn't believe all of this was happening. It was his fault. He should have known there was something fishy about Josias. He should have guessed the man was an Axon. The timing was too convenient. Too obvious.

In hindsight, anyway.

"They weren't supposed to die," Hayden said. "I was."

"There are no guarantees. You both said you understood that."

"It still shouldn't have happened." He exhaled sharply. "Go get Max and come back."

"Sheriff?"

"They're gone, Rico. Putting them under the ground isn't going to change that. Throwing them in the ocean, blasting them out to space. It's all the same. Get Max."

Rico hurried away from the lifts, returning with Max a couple of minutes later.

"Sheriff?" Max said.

"Can you vaporize the bodies?" Hayden asked.

"Pozz."

"Sheriff," Rico protested.

"I don't want to hear it, Rico. You're a clone. Nathan's a clone. I don't want the Axon, the Relyeh, Proxima, anyone taking my family's DNA and making copies. The souls are gone. The bodies need to be destroyed. That's how we did it in Metro."

Rico didn't like it, but it wasn't her decision.

Hayden tapped the lift controls. The cab door opened and they stepped inside. Rico surprised him by directing it up.

"We left them near the dropship," she explained. "To deliver them more quickly, wherever you wanted them to go."

Hayden nodded. Fifteen minutes became ten by the time they emerged on the forty-second floor. Rico and Max stayed back while Hayden walked toward the three bodies laid out on a pair of metal tables and covered with white sheets.

His eyes welled again, his body beginning to shake. His strength threatened to leave him, and he clenched his teeth, forcing himself to keep going. He needed to stay strong, powerful and in control...for them.

He moved between the two tables, reaching up and pulling back the sheet on the right. Ginny stared emptily upward as Hayden's heart raced anew. Ginny had come to him because she trusted him, and because she believed in his ability to protect her.

He put his hand on her cold forehead. "I'm sorry I let you down, little darlin'. I love you."

He leaned over, replacing his hand with his lips. Then he backed up and covered her face again, turning to the other table. He could make out the shape of Natalia's face beneath the sheet and the shape of Hallia tucked into the crook of her arm, at rest with her mother.

He pulled the covers down enough to reveal both of them, his heart breaking fresh when he saw their faces.

"It should have been me," he said again, looking at them. But at least they were together. "I'm sorry Nat. I failed you. I failed you all." He put his hand on Hallia's head, stroking her hair. "I'm sorry, Hal. This world was no place for you. I love you. Now and forever."

He leaned over and kissed her head. Then he straightened and looked at Natalia. He wanted to say something. Anything. But he couldn't do it. The words wouldn't come. None of them were good enough. None of them expressed how he felt. He couldn't assuage his guilt, appreciate or avenge her with words.

Only with actions.

He cupped her face in his hand, staring into her dead eyes. "I won't cry again until they're gone, Nat. They messed with the wrong sheriff."

He closed his eyes, offering a silent plea of peace for his family.

But he didn't want peace for himself.

He covered her face and turned away from them, walking back to the lift and entering the cab without looking at Rico or Max, his entire body burning with a cold fire.

Max took the cue, advancing to the tables. The Intellect's hands began to glow with blue energy, and he held a hand over each of the bodies. The energy expanded outward from there, enveloping everything in its path until both corpses and the tables they rested on were gone, reduced to less than dust. He completed the same destruction of Ginny's body, then closed his hands and lowered his head, returning to the lift and entering with Rico without a word.

Hayden stared at the now unoccupied space on the floor. His family was somewhere else now. Somewhere better. He had to believe that.

He didn't start this war.

But he was going to end it.

## 35

### Caleb

Caleb looked up as Sheriff Duke entered the room with Rico and the Axon Intellect that called itself Max. He had been silent and lost in thought. Everyone in the room had been lost in thought. General Stacker. Bennett. Pyro and the engineer, Lutz. They sat around the conference table without speaking, their eyes vacant, their faces weary. A mix of mourning for the sheriff's loss as well as for their own.

*Sadness is sour.*

Caleb licked his lips. He did have a sour taste in his mouth. He had assumed it was from all the particles in the air created by the fighting, not the chemical reactions of the men and women in the room.

He stood up, his gaze lingering on Max. He had worked with his kind before, and the one thing he knew from that experience was that the Axon artificial intelligences based all of their logic on the directives handed down to them by their organic masters. No matter how much it sounded or looked like Max was on the sheriff's side, it was still acting in the Axon's best interests.

Did Sheriff Duke understand that? Would he accept Caleb's warning that Max would betray them as soon as it suited the Axon's purposes? He was pretty sure he understood why the Intellect was here, and once the briefing was done Sheriff Duke would too.

"Hayden," Nathan said, getting to his feet. "How—"

"It's done," Hayden said, cutting him off. "I don't want another word about it. We can only look forward now."

The coldness in the sheriff's voice made the whole room tense.

"Sheriff," Lutz said. "I'm—"

"I said it's done," Hayden repeated calmly. "We don't have a lot of time. We need to focus on getting the survivors to safety and catching up to the enemy."

"Yes, Sheriff," Lutz said, face flushing.

"Sheriff," Caleb said. "Hess will be here with Ike shortly."

Hayden nodded in reply, taking a seat at the end of the table. Rico sat beside him while Max took a standing position in the back of the room.

"In the meantime," Nathan said. "I've discussed the survivor situation with Chief Ranger Hicks. Our plan is to use the Parabellum to shuttle them to the Pilgrim. Four hundred people, we can move them there in three groups. Two hours total per trip. Six hours to get them all to safety with enough supplies for them to hold out for quite a while."

"No," Hayden said.

"Sheriff?" Caleb said.

"The Axon already has a head start. Two hours or so? And the xaxkluth can decide to come finish the job any minute."

"I don't believe they will," Caleb replied.

"Why not?"

"I told you before, Vyte got what he wanted."

"In more ways than one." Hayden's eyes lost focus. He licked his lips. Then he glared at Caleb. "I assume you mean the neural interlink?"

Caleb shook his head. "I don't know what that is."

"Right. I think we all need to back up a step. We're talking about plans of action, but honestly, I don't even know who in this room I can trust." He was staring at Caleb when he said it, making it clear who he meant.

"Hayden," Nathan said. "I told you earlier. Colonel Card helped me get thousands out of Edenrise."

"I remember. And I'm grateful. My problem is that he was unconscious during most of the fighting, and as soon as he conveniently woke up and joined the fight, the enemy pulled back. As if they don't want to risk hurting you," he said, turning his head to look directly at Caleb.

"That isn't why they pulled back," Caleb said.

"Sheriff," Bennett said. "Colonel Card killed Sergeant Walt after Sergeant Walt killed Corporal Hotch."

"After you vouched for her," Hayden said. "How do we know she wasn't planning to warn us that you can't be trusted?"

"Hayden," Nathan said.

"Hold on, Nate," Hayden countered. "It wouldn't be the first time someone helped us out to get closer to us." He motioned backward with his thumb. "Case in point."

"I intend to complete my duties to you," Max said in defense.

"I know," Hayden replied. "That's what I'm saying." He turned his attention back to Caleb. "What are your duties, Card? What are your directives? And who are they coming from? Because I'm not convinced you aren't taking orders from the same asshole who sent the Axon into my city." The sheriff stopped short of mentioning his wife again. "You do have one of the enemy's worms planted under your skin."

*I'm not a worm.*

Caleb ground his teeth in anger, doing his best

to keep it to himself. Before he could reply, Doctor Hess rolled Isaac into the room. The Marine was in a wheelchair, his leg straight out in front of him with a metal frame around and through it.

"Ike," Hayden said, forgetting Caleb for a second. "That looks like it hurts."

"Compound fracture," Hess said. "I offered him a replacement instead."

"No offense, Sheriff," Ike said. "But I prefer to keep my limbs. I'm sorry about Natalia, Hallia and Ginny."

Hayden didn't shut him down. Ike hadn't heard the instructions not to mention them. "I know. Thank you. I've made the same promise to mine that you made to yours."

Caleb didn't know exactly what that meant, but he saw that Ike did. He nodded in response. "It's the best we can do, Sheriff."

Hayden looked back at Caleb. "You were about to say something, Card?"

Caleb took another breath. The short break had given him a few seconds to cool off. "Yes. Look, Sheriff Duke, I understand why you don't trust me. With the things I have to say, I'm going to put your ability to put your faith in me to an even bigger test. All I'm asking for right now is an open mind, and a chance to explain. It isn't only Earth that's at risk here." Caleb turned his focus to Rico. "Proxima is at risk too. Maybe more so than Earth. Vyte has a use for the people here. As food if not as foot soldiers. I'm not so sure about the people there."

"And you're what...the savior of humankind?" Hayden asked.

"No," Caleb replied. "If we're going to stop what's coming, it's going to take all of us."

## 36

### Hayden

"And what exactly is coming?" Hayden asked, staring at Caleb.

He wanted so much to trust this man who wore an Axon Intellect Skin and carried a khoron-like creature inside him. He seemed to know more about the enemy than anyone, and while that made him valuable, it also made him extremely dangerous. Nobody could deny that the xaxkluth backing off the moment Caleb entered the fray was a convenient coincidence. Was he trustworthy because he had killed the largest of the creatures? Because they seemed to fear him? Or had they stood down because he was one of them?

Keeping an open mind was harder for Hayden right now than it should be.

"Let me start closer to the beginning," Caleb said. "I think it'll help clarify my position."

"Start wherever you want," Hayden replied.

"Just don't take forever. Unless you're sure the xaxkluth will stay away." He smirked after he said that.

"I'm fairly certain, but not for the reasons you're insinuating," Caleb replied, keeping a cool exterior.

Hayden was obnoxious on purpose. As a Sheriff, he had learned one of the best ways to get someone to reveal their truth was to dig so far under their skin they snapped. So far, Caleb was either deflecting the bait, or he really wasn't concerned Hayden would label him a liar when he wasn't.

"Go ahead, Colonel," Rico said, urging Caleb to speak.

Caleb looked at Hayden, waiting for his permission.

"You've got the floor," Hayden said, giving him the go ahead with a wave of his hand.

"Thank you, Sheriff," Caleb replied. "Just so everyone in the room has the same information—my name is Caleb Card, I was originally in the United States Marine Corps Raiders and then the United States Space Force Marines. I later served as a Guardian on board the generation ship Deliverance, and today I'm a Colonel with General Stacker's Liberators."

"You really get around," Isaac said.

"You have no idea," Caleb replied. "The Deliverance wasn't sent to Proxima like the rest of the generation ships. We had a different, clandestine mission, headed by the commander of a Space Force Dark Ops team, Doctor Riley Valentine."

Hayden's eyes narrowed at the name.

Isaac went pale. "Did you just say Valentine?" he asked.

"Affirmative," Caleb replied. "You know the name?"

"I know the woman. She was experimenting with khoron at the facility where I was stationed. She's indirectly responsible for the murder of my son."

"Wait a second," Rico said. "Able said Valentine was part of the Organization."

"What Organization?" Hayden asked. "You've never mentioned it before."

"I only learned about it on the way here."

"What are you doing here anyway, Rico? Not that I'm not happy to see you."

"Like I told Nathan, we were coming to warn you. There's a Relyeh warship en route to Earth."

"What?" Hayden said, a chill running down his spine. "The enemy is right outside."

"That's how the Hunger conquers worlds," Caleb said. "They send in what they call uluth, creatures genetically-engineered to decimate the target population. The trife are their standard foot soldier, but from what Ishek tells me, Nyarlath prefers the xaxkluth because they are both fighters and builders."

"Builders?" Rico asked. "You mean the sticky shit they leave behind?"

Caleb nodded. "Given enough time, the xaxkluth will terraform the world they conquer into an environment suitable for their species. Which coincidentally or not is the same environment the source Relyeh find most comfortable."

"Source Relyeh?" Nathan said.

"The Ancients," Caleb replied. "And the original species they created, the Norg."

"Where did these Ancients come from?" Lutz asked.

"I don't know," Caleb replied. "We're getting a little off-topic here. Getting back to Valentine, she brought the Deliverance to a planet over forty light years away, where the Axon had cultivated humans as a warrior race called the Inahri."

"What do you mean, cultivated humans?" Isaac asked.

"The Axon have visited this planet for many ens," Max said. "They took members of your kind to study and use as fighters in the coming war against the Hunger. The Inahri are only one of the races they designed."

"You're saying there are more humans out there? Beyond Earth?" Nathan said.

"Affirmation. Hahaha. Haha."

"How many?"

"Billions. But they'll die if the Relyeh defeat the Axon."

"If *Vyte* defeats the Axon," Caleb said.

"Elaboration," Max replied.

"I'm trying to get to that. The Axon and the

Relyeh were already locked in a war on the planet. I helped end the war, and then I used an Axon portal to return here."

"Why?" Hayden asked. "Why come back to Earth?"

"Valentine's research wasn't fruitless. She had devised a means to kill all of the trife on the planet. I came back to deliver the data to Proxima Command."

"Poison?" Nathan asked.

"Sounds familiar," Hayden replied.

Caleb shook his head. "I have the data in my head, but I don't know what it contains. I don't think it involves poison. In any case, before a couple of days ago I had spent the last two months on Earth, trying to make contact with anyone who knew about Proxima and could help me get there. Almost everybody looked at me like I was crazy."

"Because they don't know about Proxima," Hayden said. "No Contact Protocol. They think the savages need to stay ignorant."

"It isn't only the...savages," Rico said, letting everyone know with the distaste reflected in her expression exactly what she thought of that term. "All records of the war against the trife have been deleted from Proxima datastores accessible to the public. They've forgotten why their ancestors left Earth."

"Why sterilize history?" Caleb said, surprised by the fact.

"I don't know," Rico replied. "But I don't think you were supposed to deliver your data to Proxima Command. I think you were supposed to deliver it to the Organization."

"There's that word again," Pyro said. "When is someone going to tell us what the Organization is?"

"From what I've been told, and what I'm piecing together now, it's the Dark Ops team formed to combat the Axon and Relyeh, and it predates the trife invasion by at least half a century."

"You're kidding," Nathan said.

"I wish I was. The United States government knew about the alien presence on Earth years before the meteor shower that brought the trife. Maybe other governments did too. They were trying to stop them and also study them. I don't know exactly what that entails. But I know it's true."

"Valentine confirmed it," Caleb said in agreement.

Rico turned to Hayden. "Hayden, I hate to say this, but out of all the forces in play, I believe the Organization is the one most aligned with all of our needs and goals."

"What?" Isaac said. "From my perspective, the Organization are the ones who brought the enemy down on us in the first place."

"No," Caleb countered. "The Hunger would have come, one way or another. Maybe not as soon, but they would have come."

"After I was gone then," Isaac replied. "I would

have had the chance to live out my life with my family."

"And I would have never met Natalia," Hayden said. "We can play that game until we all drop from old age, except for Max back there. This is the reality we're in. We need to focus on what we can control in this reality, not get pissed because it isn't what we want it to be. Because it damn well isn't what I want it to be."

The statement seemed to satisfy Isaac, and he leaned back in the wheelchair.

"Thank you, Sheriff," Caleb said. "Rico, what else can you tell me about the Organization?"

"I don't really know that much, other than they helped me spring Isaac from imprisonment and get him back here to warn you. Hayden, General Haeri was hoping you could help us handle this problem."

Hayden looked at Rico. The last sentence brought so many things into focus for him. Haeri was the head of Proxima Command and a big part of the Trust Crime Syndicate. Now, to learn he's also the leader of the Organization...

Naturally, the would need someone at the top of the food chain to keep tabs on the enemy, "Did he mention how I might do that?" he asked Rico.

"No, but I didn't get the feeling he had a lot of options. The Organization has a presence on Proxima and in the surrounding belts. But he understood the Relyeh ship was coming here, and you're the best positioned to do something to try to stop it."

Hayden lowered his head into his hands and started to laugh. The statement was so tragic, it was either the most hilarious or most depressing thing he had ever heard. "Best positioned? Look at me. Look at my city. Look at us. We can't stop the aliens that are already here. How are we supposed to stop a Relyeh warship?"

"Sheriff," Caleb said, his tone of voice convincing Hayden to look up. "I know it sounds impossible. And crazy. But I have an idea."

## 37

### Caleb

*Your idea isn't even close to viable.*

Caleb almost told Ishek out loud to shut up. He clenched his teeth in a tight smile instead, staring at Sheriff Duke.

"You have an idea?" the sheriff replied. "Did you miss the part where I said I don't trust you?"

"I'm still hoping I can convince you to think otherwise," Caleb said. "I wouldn't call my idea a finished product, but it's the start of something."

"Okay. I'll bite. How does the most motley collection of random individuals in the universe win a fight against a Relyeh warship and a second invasion? Because if you have an answer to that, I'm all in."

"I think we all are," Nathan said.

"I have to finish my story first," Caleb said. "Or it won't make a lot of sense."

"We're listening," Hayden replied.

"Like I said, I've spent the last two months looking for a way to Proxima, and not having much luck. What I have run into are Relyeh. Khoron. Do you know what they told me?"

"We're all going to die?" Nathan guessed.

"Close. A little persuasion and they told us Nyarlath is coming. I know for a fact she's had her eye on Earth for a long time. Its place in the universe makes it attractive to the Hunger. First, because humans are easily frightened, and the Relyeh feed on fear to survive. Second, because it's a great jump point between Relyeh space and Axon space."

"We already know a ship is coming," Rico said. "If Nyarlath is on it…"

"I didn't know a ship was coming," Caleb said. "I only knew Nyarlath was on her way. The Axon have portals, and if the Relyeh captures one, it can use it to go anywhere whose coordinates it either knows or guesses. I ran into a khoron who had access to one here. I assumed that meant Nyarlath had access to more. But you're right. She's on that ship. Walt was one of hers, not Shurrath's."

"That explains why she was still alive," Hayden said. "Nat wasn't wrong."

"Apparently not. But there's a twist. Nyarlath isn't acting on her own. She's a prisoner of the Axon."

The statement was like dropping a bomb in the room. Silence fell over them. The tension got thick.

Caleb stared at Sheriff Duke, making eye contact and holding it.

"Confirmation," Max said from behind the sheriff. "Vyte is an Axon hybrid. Caleb Card is correct in his assessment."

Sheriff Duke turned around. "Is that why you're really here? They sent you back to Earth to deal with Vyte."

"Imprecise. The organics ordered a data wipe and reset. I didn't want that. Not after what happened to me here. I took the energy unit and escaped here, through the portal in the place called Dugway. I came to you to warn you about Vyte and to help you. You are my friend."

"You're a machine," Lutz said. "How can you want anything?"

"He's broken," Isaac said. "Damaged goods. It's made him more—for lack of a better word—human."

"My neural pathways are uncalibrated, which affects my logic-branching algorithms. A side-effect of the damage I sustained. Don't mistake the outcomes for emotions, and don't presume to believe I'm completely rogue. I simply am. Hahaha. Haha."

"You said this Vyte is an Axon hybrid," Pyro said. "What does that mean?"

Max answered before Caleb could open his mouth. "Vyte was once an Intellect. Not like me. A newer, more advanced version. An upgraded iteration designed to replace the organics in matters relating to the Relyeh. The closest comparison would be to you." Max pointed at General Stacker. "Vyte was made to be the leader of the Axon military. Its orders were to defeat the Relyeh as efficiently as possible."

Sheriff Duke started laughing again. All eyes turned to him.

"So your general decided the best way to beat the Hunger was to turn them against one another," he said.

"Affirmation. Except Vyte is harboring a fatal exception. A programming error or malfunction. It decided it required full understanding of organic principles to complete the mission. It turned on its maker and merged with him."

"By merged, you mean...what exactly?"

"An Axon-machine interface. A remote interface. The Council didn't realize the organic was compromised until he began insisting on being named Supreme Leader of the Axon, due to his advanced understanding of how best to preserve the Axon for all time."

"By becoming one with the Relyeh," Caleb said, gaining understanding. "Merging with them, the way it merged with its maker."

"Affirmation. Hahaha. Haha."

"There's nothing funny about that," Nathan said, frowning.

Caleb ignored the General's comment. "When I

was unconscious, I wasn't really unconscious," Caleb said, regaining the attention of the group. "I have a connection to the Relyeh Collective through my Advocate, Ishek. The state Walt put me in left me open to the Collective, and Nyarlath took the opportunity to reach out and put me into her Construct."

"Construct?" Pyro asked.

Caleb was expecting the question. "A pocket universe. The Relyeh Ancients can create them."

"That's impossible," Lutz said.

"Sean, I think we're at the point where nothing is impossible," Sheriff Duke said. "However crazy it sounds. We're talking about tech that's hundreds of thousands of years beyond our understanding. Hell, just look behind me."

The engineer slumped in his chair, embarrassed by his interruption. "Sorry, Sheriff."

"Nyarlath wanted me to see her prison. She made me an offer. If I free her, she'll abandon Earth and ensure her brothers and sisters don't replace her."

"You mean Earth will be free of the Relyeh?" Pyro said. "That sounds too good to be true."

"They can't be trusted," Sheriff Duke said. "None of them can."

"I agree," Caleb said. "In any case, Vyte pulled me out of her Construct and into something it called the Q-net. It's a machine-based interface to the Collective."

"Vyte has access to the Relyeh Collective?" Max asked, stepping forward.

"That's right. I think that's how it captured Nyarlath."

"If this were any other Axon, it would bring us to the verge of victory," Max said. "But Vyte believes absorption is the only solution to ensure our survival. This is a disaster."

"Not laughing now, are you?" Nathan said. "But what the hell was it doing here? Why did it take the neural interlink?"

Caleb spoke again. "Sheriff Duke, I know your wife was able to access the Collective through the interlink. Moreover, you said she was able to send a signal through it to some of the khoron on Earth, and use it to destroy them."

"That's right."

"I think that's why Vyte took it. It doesn't want us to have it."

"It could have destroyed it," Sheriff Duke said. "It didn't need to take it."

"I don't know why it took it. It must have a use for it."

"I'm sure that's bad for us."

"I agree. We need to get the interlink back, and not only because we don't want Vyte to have it. We already have proof we can use it."

"Use it for what?" Lutz asked.

"To kill Relyeh," Caleb said. "Khoron for

starters. Maybe trife, depending on the payload Valentine dropped into my head."

"That won't help us against the xaxkluth," Hayden said.

"I have information about xaxkluth in my datastores," Max said. "The potential to destroy them exists. It is a good plan. Hahaha. Haha."

"But that isn't the whole plan," Caleb said. "We need to unpack my brain, which means I need to connect with Proxima Command, or I guess the Organization. I assume they'll know what they need to do."

"You need to go to Proxima to do that," Rico said.

"I know."

"We just left Proxima. We're fugitives there."

"Then you can't go back," Nathan said.

"And you can?" Caleb asked.

"No. I'm a fugitive too. But you were a Marine and a Guardian on a generation ship. You have full citizenship rights." Nathan paused, looking over at Sheriff Duke.

Rico looked at him too. "So do you."

Hayden's eyes shifted back and forth between the two of them. He shook his head. "No. I'm not leaving Earth. And I'm especially not leaving without killing the Axon that killed my family. It's just not going to happen."

"Hayden, we don't have a lot of time."

"How long would it take? How far could he have gone? We need the interlink back anyway."

*The Axon will take the interlink to a portal.*

"Yeah, he will," Caleb said out loud. "Ishek says the Axon's going to make a run for a portal."

"There are at least two that I know of within range of Sanisco," Hayden said. "Maybe more. We'll have to split up. And Proxima will have to wait."

"The data you have in your head could be useless," Stacker said to Caleb. "It might be a big risk for nothing."

"If we don't take a risk, that's what we're going to have left," Caleb replied. "Nothing."

"Damned if you're right," Stacker said.

"I will go with Sheriff Duke," Max said. "Even if Card's head is empty, mine is not. Haha. Hahaha."

Caleb didn't try to argue. The Intellect could disguise itself as anyone. Could it somehow copy their ID chip too? He wouldn't put it past the AI.

"And what about the xaxkluth?" Sheriff Duke asked. "You never did explain why they stopped attacking."

"A few reasons I can think of," Caleb replied. "One: Vyte offered to leave this part of the world alone if I killed all of you. Maybe he's hoping I still will. Two: he might be waiting to see what we do next. To judge our intelligence before committing anything else to the fight. Three: he's confident he's going to win, and he doesn't want to waste any more builders on us."

*Three is most likely. I remain convinced. This is not a viable plan.*

Maybe it wasn't, but it was the only chance they had. "What do you say, Sheriff? General?"

"Let's get the interlink back," Sheriff Duke said. "Then we'll talk."

"Fine," Caleb agreed. "One thing at a time."

"Let's do this," Max said. "Hahaha. Haha."

## 38

### Hayden

"Consideration," Max said, sticking close to Hayden as they entered the garage beneath the pyramid.

The vehicles were all in place, with the UWT tank in the pole position at the front. A group of civilians had already been stashed in the APC, and a group of modboxes were arranged behind the armored carrier, loaded with more nervous civilians. Every one of them was carrying a weapon taken from the armory on the floor below. The racks of guns and ammunition in Law were cleaned out, and whatever hadn't been claimed for use was loaded into crates and divided among the vehicles with space for the munitions, both here and in two nearby garages where the rest of the survivors had gathered. Those spaces contained additional vehicles including an armored eighteen wheeler that could and would be carrying over half of the civilians on its own.

Guns weren't the only thing they were transporting. Lutz and Pyro had been given the task of identifying the areas of greatest need to ensure the fleeing civilians could survive an extended stay in their new surroundings. Beyond the apparent necessities like food and water, the two engineers had selected, disassembled and prepped a handful of machines that would make the civilians' lives just a little bit easier. Hayden hoped their stay in Old Metro would be a short one, but the state of the planet left few guarantees.

Not that Hayden liked the idea of transporting the survivors to within easy reach of the xaxkluth, but as far as he was concerned, there was no better option. Out of the three possibilities Caleb had offered for the xaxkluth's sudden reticence, Hayden wasn't alone in his conviction that the aliens were waiting to see what the humans would do next. And if the enemy was waiting to react, it was essential for them to control that reaction as best they could. The only way to do that was to make one major play to get everyone out at the same time.

"What is it, Max?" Hayden asked, glancing at the Intellect through his modified sunglasses. The Centurions had found them on the floor of the lobby during their sweep of the pyramid, and Pyro had lovingly repaired the damage, returning them to him with tears in her eyes. He was beyond grateful to have them back.

"Your friend Rico said a Relyeh warship is

coming to Earth," Max said. "It's logical to believe the Axon who took the interlink would want to bring it to that warship."

"Makes sense," Hayden agreed.

"Axon portals require static, predefined coordinates," Max said. "One cannot simply open a wormhole on a starship in motion."

"That also makes sense. What's the consideration?"

"There are two possibilities. One, the Intellect who took the interlink, which I will refer to from now on as Krake, will have to initiate the portal and wait for the connection to complete before delivering the device to Vyte."

"Krake?" Hayden said.

"You don't like it? It's more concise than saying the Intellect-who-took-the-interlink. Hahaha. Haha."

"It's fine. Just an interesting choice. Go on. What's the other possibility?"

"Two, there's a portal at a fixed point closer to the current position of the Relyeh warship."

"What is the current position of the ship?"

"My estimates based on Rico's explanation place it approximately half a light year past Proxima Centauri. Unless…"

Max trailed off. Hayden glared at him. "Unless what, Max?"

"Unless it slowed down. Unless it stopped at Proxima."

"Which is how likely?"

"Caleb Card said Vyte is building a digital Collective that has access to the Relyeh's organic Collective. It's possible the Axon here is communicating with Vyte in real-time through it. It's possible the Relyeh ship adjusted course the moment the interlink was captured, to effect a more efficient escape. It's also possible Krake will remain on Earth until the warship arrives."

"So if Krake takes the interlink off Earth right away, he has to take it to Proxima. Or close to Proxima."

"Affirmation."

"Then we'll follow him there."

"That will take time."

"Max, I have nothing more important to do than hunt down my family's murderer. It doesn't matter how long it takes. But you're right. It's better to shut him down here. Vyte is a he, then?"

"As much as any Intellect possesses a gender, yes. Hahaha. Haha. The logical outcomes are that either Krake is left waiting somewhere on Earth for the link to the Relyeh ship to become static, or he has to take a detour through Proxima. Either we have more time to catch up to him, or we know where to find him."

"That's good for us."

"Affirmation."

"What's the bad news?"

"If the warship stops at Proxima, the settlement there may face imminent destruction."

Hayden didn't care for Proxima's policies toward Earth, but that didn't mean he wanted any harm to come to the civilians who lived there. He understood they had no idea what Earth was really like.

"I'd say better them than us, but I don't believe that. Can they fight it?"

"And win? Negation."

Hayden sighed. "You know we've already got our hands full here."

"We must rid ourselves of the chaff," Max replied.

"You mean the civilians?"

"Your concern with their survival costs us precious time, Sheriff. And they're only a handful compared to the number of humans currently under threat across this planet and out there."

Hayden nodded. The same thought had crossed his mind multiple times while they were preparing the convoy. If it were entirely up to him, he would have already abandoned the survivors to fend for themselves while he hunted Krake. But honoring his family was about more than seeking vengeance. Natalia would be ashamed if he let innocents die in his anger.

"We need to go that direction anyway," Hayden replied. "It's one of Krake's potential destinations."

"Understanding. Disagreement. Acceptance." Max continued walking with Hayden in silence.

Hayden crossed to the center of the room near the dead xaxkluth. Time had only made the aliens' smell that much worse, and he couldn't wait to get away from them. He tapped on the small comm badge attached to his coat, drawing in a breath before speaking.

The first thing Hayden had done after his meeting with Nathan, Caleb, Rico and the others was to visit the survivors and explain to them that they had to abandon the city. He had sensed their excitement at seeing him the moment he had emerged from the lift into the garage where they had assembled, but he had also sensed the discomfort that formed when they realized Natalia wasn't with him.

Their discomfort evolved into an uneasy tension among the nine deputies who had joined the civilians in the bunker. They had lowered their tear-filled eyes in guilty shame, which had left a bad taste in Hayden's mouth. Had they abandoned the innocent to save themselves? Had they run away in fear while leaving others to suffer? If they had returned to Law instead of hiding in the bunker, might they have gotten to the Axon before it killed Natalia?

Was it their fault his wife and children were dead?

"Deputies, are we in position?" he asked,

fighting to keep his voice from exhibiting his inner turmoil.

"Convoy One is in position," Chief Ranger Hicks replied. Deputies Lazar and Bashti echoed the readiness of their respective convoys as well.

"Pozz that," Hayden said. "Hold position and wait for my signal." He tapped on his badge again. "Nate, the convoy is ready to roll."

"Roger that, Sheriff," Nathan replied. "Centurions are ready."

"Pozz," Hayden said. "Caleb, what's your status?"

"The bait has been taken, Sheriff. We're on target."

"Pozz," Hayden said, trying to hide his tone of continuing disbelief. What Caleb had promised them seemed too good to be true, but he had committed to putting his trust in the former Marine. There was nothing Caleb had said or done to make him believe he wasn't on their side.

Only time would tell where that decision would take them.

"Deputies, on my mark," he said, climbing to the top of the APC with Max. "Let's get these people out of here alive. Caleb, at your signal."

"Standby," Caleb said. "We're four klicks out and closing."

Hayden could sense the tension building in the garage. When he looked around, he could see the nervous fear on the faces of the people in the cars.

He imagined the same scene playing out in the other garages across the city where those groups of civilians waited to leave.

Waiting was always the hardest part.

And timing was everything. If they were going to get through this alive, they had to get it right.

"I've got a visual," Nathan said. "Looks like three incoming." They had hoped for five, but it was probably enough. None of it would have been possible without Caleb.

"The xaxkluth just noticed them," Nathan added.

"Get ready," Caleb said.

Hayden heard the gas-powered cars rev. The APC began to vibrate softly.

"The enemy is holding position," Nathan reported. "Standby."

The tension increased. It felt to Hayden as if they were at the starting line of a race, eager to get off the line and out to a good lead. Calling this a race wasn't far from the truth.

"Three kilometers," Caleb announced, though Hayden had no idea how he was tracking the distance.

"Xaxkluth are moving to intercept," Nathan said.

"They can't afford to sit and wait," Hayden replied.

"Standby," Caleb said.

The ground began to shiver slightly, knocking

dust and debris from the walls and ceiling. Hayden was tempted to ask Caleb if it was time yet. He was struggling to stay patient too.

"Standby," Caleb said again.

The ground shook a little harder.

"We're on them!" Nathan announced.

"Go! Go! Go!" Caleb shouted.

Hayden grabbed the base of the APC's turret, holding on tight as it lurched forward.

They were on their way.

## 39

## Caleb

Caleb's eyes were closed, but he could still see.

His mind was connected across the Collective, to a trife on its way to Sanisco. He wasn't directly controlling the Relyeh creature but observing its desperate scramble across the landscape, pushed to the north by an unstoppable force which itself was only a minute away from colliding with an immovable object.

It hadn't been easy to bring trife into the area. Between Sheriff Duke, the goliaths and the xaxkluth, the demons were in short supply in the region. Most were disorganized and relegated to tiny nests that didn't have the energy or the numbers to make a queen. It had taken nearly twenty minutes for Caleb to locate a suitable nest through the Collective, and another hour to bring the trife closest to the city heading toward it. The group he had found didn't have a queen to lead them, which made passing instructions to them more challenging. But trife were simple creatures driven by programmed instinct and fixated on a simple instruction:

Find humans. Kill humans.

It was the instruction that had given Caleb control. The instruction the trife knew best. He didn't need to order them to follow it so much as plant the seed in their minds that there were humans nearby. He had fed them a sense of a human settlement. A taste. A smell. The small nest had latched onto that idea and genetics had done the rest, sending them scrambling out from the hollowed pile of rubble where they were hiding and causing them to race across the landscape in Caleb's general direction.

A handful of trife didn't present much aid against the xaxkluth, but Caleb hadn't tricked the creatures into coming because he expected them to fight. He had already witnessed thousands of them dying to the much larger and more powerful aliens, easily outmatched even when they outnumbered their opponents a thousand to one.

The twenty or so trife he had captured didn't have a chance at surviving what lay both ahead and behind them. He hadn't summoned them to fight. He had brought them here because of what they could attract. They weren't the perfect weapon, but they were the perfect bait. Like a worm dangling from a hook, Caleb had cast them out into the open and reeled them in with the hopes of capturing a much bigger prize.

*I give you credit for your creativity. But this plan is doomed to fail.*

Caleb ignored Ishek's negativity, maintaining his focus on the lead trife. The ground shuddered again as the goliath behind the demons took another step. The vibrations sent signals of warning and panic through its brain and telling it that if it didn't run faster, it would wind up in one of the large hands reaching for it. It knew it was little more than a tiny morsel for a very hungry giant.

Caleb couldn't turn the trife's head to look back, but he could sense the goliath behind the demon. He could smell its horrible scent and hear it grumbling. He could feel the air shifting as it took large steps in pursuit, and the ground moving when it landed. He was aware every time one of the other trife didn't move fast enough and was caught up by a goliath, lifted to its horrible grinding maw and devoured without hesitation.

The buildings of Sanisco rose on either side of the diminishing group of trife. The steel, glass and concrete structures were battered, broken and coated in layers of dark, solidified slime left during the xaxkluth's entry to the city. The three xaxkluth were approaching on a direct collision course with the trife, tentacles undulating and writhing ahead of them. Caleb knew instinctively the trife weren't the xaxkluth's target, but the trife didn't seem to understand that. The one he was observing hissed when it identified the enemy threat, coming to a sudden stop that nearly cost it its life.

It was lucky because the goliath chasing it noticed the xaxkluth at the same moment the trife stopped moving. Instead of reaching for the trife it straightened up, grumbling so loudly the sound reverberated through the streets in a terrifying echo. The xaxkluth replied with a groan of its own, tentacles pulling back and helping propel the Relyeh forward to attack.

The trife got trapped between the two sides. It barely made the leap over one of the tentacles as the xaxkluth approached. Another nearly crushed it as it attempted its escape. For a moment, Caleb thought the creature might make it. Then another limb grabbed and wrapped around it, lifting it high into the air.

The xaxkluth, still clutching the terrified trife, reached the goliath, stretching its empty tentacles to grapple with a massive leg. The goliath reached for the xaxkluth, but it redirected its tentacles to catch the hand. Its limbs caught the goliath's fingers, tensing at full extension and fighting to keep the hand away. The effort kept the goliath's arm in place for a second before the tentacles gave out. The goliath wrapped its fingers around the mass and lifted it. Caleb's trife remained trapped as the xaxkluth struggled to break free, groaning and flailing in the goliath's' overpowering grip.

Caleb thought the goliath would eat the xaxkluth, but it brought its hand back down instead, crushing it against the street, the force of the impact collapsing the already damaged side of a building.

The tentacle went limp, setting the trife free. It rolled away from the dead xaxkluth and tried to run, making it three steps before a second goliath scooped it up and threw it toward its mouth.

Caleb severed the connection before the trife was eaten, his eyes snapping open and glancing quickly around the interior of the tank.

"Colonel?" Hicks said, noticing Caleb's panic.

"I'm fine," Caleb replied. "The targets are engaged. Sheriff Duke, the path is clear."

"Pozz," Sheriff Duke replied, his voice growing more distant as he spoke into his comm badge. "All convoys, follow the mark. Stay on target. Do not deviate. The Centurions will handle any stragglers."

There was no response from the convoy leads, including Hicks. The tank vibrated a little more violently as its velocity increased and it came around the corner. Caleb looked at the displays in front of the cockpit, relying entirely on cameras to project the world outside. They had entered the corridor leading out of the city. The same passage they had been in earlier. The large xaxkluth Caleb had killed was still occupying the left side of the street, while more bodies—both human and alien—were cast across the road.

"Second time's a charm," Hicks said, noticing

Caleb looking at the displays. "We'll make it out this time."

*No, we won't.*

"We will..." Caleb said, shifting his eyes to check the other views. The ground rumbled, a noise like an explosion sounding to their left. A xaxkluth body flew across the street, crashing into the side of a building and bringing the remains of the structure down on it. A goliath stepped toward them, towering over the convoy with its mouth hanging open. "...as long as that thing leaves us alone."

The tank had the lead position in the convoy, guiding the line of nearly two dozen vehicles toward the monstrous humanoid. Stopping to wait wasn't an option, not with the xaxkluth nearby.

*It may need a distraction.*

Caleb closed his eyes again, entering the Collective in search of a nearby trife. He could sense the nodes on the Relyeh network as if the universe were an endless heat map. The closest aliens were like a spot of sunlight against his skin. Their position within the Relyeh hierarchy was in part determined by their strength within the Collective. Caleb was hesitant to reach too far out for fear of drawing Vyte's attention or accidentally stumbling on the Axon's Quantum Network, but past experience had taught him that Shub-Nigu was the brightest star in the Collective universe. The ancient Relyeh's heat was still palpable from thousands of light years away.

He hadn't told Sheriff Duke and the others about Vyte's direct line to the center of the Relyeh Collective. He wasn't sure they would understand, and even if they did, he wasn't sure what it would mean to the current situation. Vyte had already gleaned the most important information from the Collective. The location of Proxima. Now he was after Doctor Valentine and the other Relyeh Ancients. As far as Caleb knew, all of humankind's secrets had already been revealed.

There were no trife left now anywhere within Sanisco. There had been only a handful before, and the goliaths and xaxkluth had quickly taken the rest out. Caleb could feel the xaxkluth though. Their beacons were larger and hotter, threatening to burn him if he got too close.

He opened his eyes to Hicks' panicked face.

"Sheriff, what do we do?" he asked.

Caleb looked at the display. The goliath was directly in front of them, looking down at the approaching convoy.

"Parabellum is incoming," Stacker said.

Caleb tried to find the dropship on the displays. He couldn't see it, but he saw its plasma cannons begin peppering the goliath, the bursts of gas burning deep into its flesh. It howled and turned as the Parabellum flashed past, taking a swipe at the aircraft. It missed badly, but the distraction allowed Hicks to guide the tank around its left leg. A glance at the vehicle's sensors showed the convoy duplicating the move.

There was virtually no chance they would all make it past before the goliath recovered.

The plan to bring the goliaths in to distract the xaxkuth had worked too well. The giants were overwhelming the enemy faster than Caleb would have guessed, leaving them free to attack the convoy before the convoy made it clear. Without any trife left for them to devour, there was only one way Caleb could think of to distract the goliaths.

"I need to overpower a xaxkluth," he said.

"What?" Hicks replied.

*Caleb, we aren't strong enough.*

"We have to be."

Caleb shut his eyes a third time, using Ishek to return to the Collective. Sergeant Walt's Relyeh parasite had managed to freeze the xaxkluth before, and while it probably had help from Vyte, it still needed to bear the brunt of the effort. If it could do it, then he and Ishek should be able to do it too. Their shared bond made both of them stronger.

*We can't do it. Their minds are different. We could become trapped.*

Caleb couldn't guess how different the xaxkluth mind might be, and he didn't have time to question the opportunity. If he didn't find a means to pull the goliath away from the convoy, their second attempt to escape would likely end even more badly than the first.

He located the closest node, so bright and hot it burned his mind to turn toward it.

*Caleb, please don't do this.*

"There is no other way. We promised the survivors we would get them to safety."

It was a promise he had to keep.

# 40

## Caleb

The heat and pressure nearly overwhelmed Caleb as he pushed against the xaxkluth's mind, the Relyeh's resistance every bit as powerful as he expected. In the back of his senses, Caleb recognized Ishek's pain, the Advocate's direct link in the chain putting the symbiote that much closer to the surface of the xaxkluth's star.

A part of Caleb was remorseful to cause his counterpart so much agony. The other part understood what needed to be done and was willing to do anything to make it happen. It was that part of him which prevailed, continuing to push against the xaxkluth's resistance.

It seemed like it took forever, but Caleb began pushing into the heat and light, his mind filling with the sensation that he was sinking through magma. The pain and pressure increased. It threatened to overwhelm him. To burn both him and his Advocate to death.

Ishek was right. He wasn't strong enough.

The thought flashed through his head, along with a sudden sense of panic that he had just made a colossal mistake. He was going to die here. Brain death. Then the goliaths would hit the convoy and everyone else would die too. This was his idea. His plan. He had to see it through.

He found his second wind, refocusing his effort. He continued to sink, pure motivation driving him onward and keeping his brain and hope alive. Ishek began to calm slightly, and then the heat started to cool, the magma turning to mud as the xaxkluth's defenses gave way.

The darkness behind Caleb's closed eyelids faded, replaced with images aligned in a pattern like a broken window, the xaxkluth's hundreds of eyes collecting data. Caleb was confused by the inputs, his human senses unable to compensate for so many thoughts. He nearly lost his hold on the xaxkluth, almost falling back into the magma before he had a chance to send a single command. He forged ahead, keeping his attention focused on the forward-facing eyes, the largest shards of what appeared as shattered glass. He was suddenly aware of limbs, dozens of limbs, again overwhelmed by the sheer volume of controls inherent to the creature. The xaxkluth could choose whether or not to secrete the slimy substance that became the

Relyeh terraforming bedrock. It could open and close over thirty mouths plus its central maw, which had over a dozen different sets of individually operable teeth.

The alien was as sophisticated a design as Caleb could imagine. Like Ishek had warned, too complicated for him to control. He could sense its limbs. He could see through its eyes. He could almost taste the flesh of its most recent kill in its mouth and on its teeth. But he couldn't manage it all. He couldn't make the xaxkluth do what he wanted it to do. With the level of effort he had to maintain just to stay connected to it, he couldn't do much of anything at all.

And he hungered…

His appetite was infinite. For food. For fear. He needed to grow. To expand. To become large enough to defeat this new threat. These giant humanoids that turned its brethren to pulp. That crushed them instead of eating them as if they were the lowest form of life.

Caleb's consciousness started burning again as he once more tried to gain at least rudimentary control of the xaxkluth. Its mind was different than anything he had ever encountered, and he suddenly realized why. It wasn't a singular entity, but instead multiple minds connected to a main controlling brain. Each tentacle was an individual consciousness, linked as if to the Collective through the central mass, and the central brain. Controlling that brain wasn't enough because he didn't have the capacity to handle its regular duties. He couldn't make the xaxkluth do what he wanted. The best he could do was freeze it the way Walt had frozen it.

Which was the opposite of what he wanted.

He was tempted to abandon the creature. To release his hard-won handle on it and return to his body inside the tank. There was nothing he could do here.

Or was there?

He couldn't handle every part of the xaxkluth, but did he need to? All he had to do was get it into range of the goliath so the creature would attack it instead of the convoy. He could do that much, couldn't he?

He focused his attention on four of the limbs, treating the xaxkluth as if it were a person crawling on its hands and knees. He kept his vision locked on the main set of eyes, able to spot the nearby goliath from the xaxkluth's position. He started shifting forward, the sensation of this type of movement as alien to him as the creature he was controlling.

It took a few seconds, but he started to get the hang of it, and within a few strides was moving ahead at greater speed. The xaxkluth had nearly given up trying to fight his control, which further eased the burden. Growing in confidence, he added two more limbs to the motion and let out a loud groan that captured the goliath's attention just as it started to swing its leg. He could see the tank and APC were well past the creature but the large tractor trailer was directly in front of it, right in line with its approaching foot. He could see Sheriff Duke perched on top of the second vehicle, watching the giant with concern. He could see the Parabellum sweeping past overhead, prepared to make another run.

He sped forward, groaning loudly, desperate to get the goliath's attention before it swung its foot forward and smashed the trailer. The APC peeled off from the convoy, pulling sideways and rotating its machine guns toward the goliath. Sheriff Duke pulled two large revolvers from holsters on his hips. He didn't want them to hurt the giant. It was one of their best weapons against the xaxkluth.

He added two more limbs, pushing his ability to control the xaxkluth to the limit. Surprised by the alien's speed, he leaped toward the goliath's leg, the individual intelligences of the other tentacles grabbing for the trunk-like limb. He planted one of the xaxkluth's tentacles and turned its central mass aside as the goliath whirled to grab it. The unexpected move took both the giant and the other tentacles by surprise. He saw now there was a second goliath incoming, and it turned in his direction.

Fear bloomed within the xaxkluth. It realized Caleb had stuck it in between two goliaths who both headed toward it. Caleb could sense its terror and desire to escape. He let go of its limbs, releasing his hold on its body. But he continued holding the connection. The xaxkluth were getting orders from somewhere, and he didn't think they were coming from off-world. If he could trace the Collective back to the source maybe he could get a location.

He stayed with the xaxkluth as it fled, its panicked escape leading the goliaths away from the convoy. He waited for something else to make the connection. To tell the xaxkluth not to run, or at least to check and see what it was doing.

He didn't have to wait long. He felt the new presence when it arrived. He sensed its confusion to find him there, and its surprise when he reached out for Caleb's consciousness before he could raise the xaxkluth's defenses. He assumed whatever was controlling the xaxkluth was much, much stronger than he was. He didn't stay to find out. That simple connection, that ping was all he wanted.

He released his hold on the xaxkluth and the Collective. His eyes snapped open.

"Colonel?" Hicks said. "What the hell happened to you?"

Caleb realized he was flat on his back in the tank's belly. His body was shivering, and he was drenched in sweat. Ishek was alert. Almost too alert. The Advocate was pushing against his mind, trying to seize control in a fit of fury against him.

"Ishek?" Caleb said.

Ishek immediately began to calm, the pressure in Caleb's mind subsiding as he sensed the Advocate's relief.

*You nearly killed us both.*

"I'm sorry. I had to."

"Colonel?" Hicks said, concern written all over his face. He was crouched down beside Caleb. His hand resting on the Marine's shoulder, he gently shook Caleb. "Are you with me, Colonel?"

Caleb didn't answer the deputy, his glassy eyes focused inward, where Ishek's anger turned to amusement.

*You tricked them.*

Caleb wouldn't call it a trick. "More like an ambush."

*Did you get anything? Yes. I see you did. A name.*

That was all Caleb managed to take from the xaxkluth's owner before he ran.

But maybe it would be enough.

## 41

### Aeron

Aeron exited the loop station in Dome Six with Fox hanging a few meters back, keeping an eye out for potential tails. His new identity had made it easier to cross from the Reclamation Center to the source loop station on Strand Sixteen, but he knew from experience the Judicus Department and CSF would both assume he wasn't going to sit still. Not when the Judici claimed he had killed Chair LaMont, his wife and no doubt by now his children too.

The thought was a sharp sting to Aeron's emotions, which time and training had helped him master under most circumstances. Outsiders would think he didn't love his family, but that wasn't true.

He just loved humankind more. And there was nothing more important to him than upholding the first vows he had taken. The first promises he had made. They superseded everything else.

He had a new identification chip and a disguise,

but he could imagine the Judicus Department right now, desperately running queries against every citizen on Proxima and looking for anomalies. They would figure out if anyone had gone anywhere they didn't normally go, at a time they didn't typically go there. They would make assumptions and then connections. Then they would move in. It would take time and wouldn't let them completely zero in on who he had become, but they would get to his ID sooner or later. They would send someone—an undercover Peace Officer, a Judicus, an MP—to investigate. And if that person tracked him to his precise location, that person would be a casualty of this hidden war.

And then they would know where he had been, and the game would reset.

Aeron wasn't panicked. He had planned for this. Expected it. There had never been a guarantee it would happen in his lifetime, but he had always known it would happen. The Organization was older than the settlement on Proxima. It had spent years tracking, monitoring, and in some cases stopping the Hunger and the Axon from gaining the upper hand on Earth. Of course, they had never expected the assault that arrived—the meteor shower that had rained a deadly virus and billions of trife down upon the Earth. They were caught unprepared because the Relyeh were caught unprepared. He had never learned how or why, but it didn't matter. Even with

## Isolation

all of his planning, even with all of their gathered intelligence, it was impossible to predict everything. It was impossible to be ready for every possibility.

Aeron walked briskly, keeping his head down and in shadow, and taking on a limping gait so they couldn't track him by his stride. There were other biometric sensors inside the Proxima Domes, but he knew about all of them, even the ones law enforcement didn't know. And he knew how to defeat them. It was almost trivial for him to make it across Dome Six to C-District, even walking right beside a patrolling Peace Officer for nearly three blocks while the officer's comm cautioned him to stay on the lookout for Aeron.

He didn't enter Ghost's Tavern from the front, ducking into the split and heading for the rear entrance, leaving Fox behind to act as an ordinary patron and lookout. He remained alert, ensuring the alley was clear before going up next to the hardened faux emergency exit and subtly swiping his new identification chip against it. It was the only chip on the planet that would open this particular door, which was only to be used in this specific circumstance.

The door clunked and swung open just enough for Aeron to get his fingers past it and pull it open the rest of the way. He ducked inside, into a pitch black corridor. The door swung sharply closed behind him.

"Name and rank," a neutral, flat voice said in the darkness.

"Aeron Haeri. General of the Centurion Space Force. Prime of the Organization. Tenth Chair of the Trust."

The system was scanning him while he spoke, using another set of sensors he didn't want to defeat, including vocal recognition.

"What is your prerogative?"

"Protect humankind."

"Where?"

"Everywhere."

An LED turned on over his head, revealing the armored corridor with a second blast door a meter away.

"Remove your clothing and produce the package."

Aeron was already pulling at the street clothes, taking them off and dropping them on the floor. When he was naked, he opened the false skin in his thigh and removed the data chip and key, holding them up. Sensors scanned them too, ensuring their authenticity.

The second door thunked and rotated open. Aeron walked through it and directly into Special Command.

"AH-TEHN-SHUN!" someone barked.

There were over a dozen people in the room, each of them already doing something that Aeron would have said was much more important than stopping the activity to turn to face him, especially since he was naked. His lack of clothes didn't register across any of their faces, their expressions of serious professionalism holding fast.

"Carry on," Aeron said, causing most of them to break and turn back to what they were doing.

"Sir."

Aeron turned to his left. An older woman approached, holding a perfectly folded and stacked suit.

"Thank you, Briar," Aeron said, reaching out to take it. He let his eyes cross over the room.

It wasn't a large room and was stuffed with workstations and displays, both static monitors and three-dimensional holograms, leaving only small channels for the techs to move around in , often having to turn sideways to pass one another. A column of servers sat in one corner and a backup reactor in another, while a rack of plasma rifles adorned the wall on the left.

The techs were poring over streams of data coming in from every source imaginable. They were hacked into Judici channels, Centurion Space Force channels, Trust channels, Law Enforcement and of course public comms. They had data coming in from sensors scattered across nearby space—covering both secret Organization deployments and official CSF equipment.

"Briar, can you retrieve my ion blaster and microspear from the hallway?" Aeron asked, grabbing the perfectly folded underwear from the top of the clothes stack and pulling them on.

"Of course, sir," she replied, moving to comply.

Aeron was buttoning a crisp white shirt when she returned with the weapons. He finished buttoning before he took the blaster from her, sliding it into a holster provided with the clothes.

"I assume this is the microspear?" she asked, holding out the short, thin weapon.

"It is," he replied, accepting it. "A convenient tool. I'm grateful to Sheriff Duke for providing it."

"I'm sorry about Kirin," Briar said.

"So am I," Aeron replied.

"These bastards have no souls."

"I don't know about that. We were all made for a purpose, and there's a purpose to the actions we all take. This is conflict, but it isn't personal. When you make it personal, you become emotional, and when you become emotional, you become reckless and make mistakes."

"Yes, sir," Briar said.

Aeron unfolded the suit jacket and slid it on, buttoning it too. The outfit was dark tech, a special weave of spidersteel and Axon alloy that would withstand small arms fire easily and could hold up against both plasma and lasers for a short time.

"Lawson," Aeron called out, getting the lead techs attention. Lawson was another older man, bald and wrinkled but fit. He wore a simple black suit beneath a dark coat.

"Yes, Prime?" Lawson said.

"We know the Relyeh have infiltrated Proxima. They have a portal on the planet, aboard one of our fifteen ships. We need to figure out which one has that portal."

"Sir, it's risky to send units to every ship," Lawson said. "We'll be stretched too thin to enable our secondary directives with confidence."

"I know. I don't want to run manual searches just yet. Query the ship's datastores, see if you can find a record of a portal being brought on board. It should be logged in somewhere."

"Someone should have stumbled across it before now, you mean," Lawson said. "Every centimeter of every ship has been searched over the years, I'm sure."

"Not necessarily. If something was smuggled on board, they could have plated over the compartment. Everything was assembled in such a hurry it's easy to miss differences in the schematics against the actual layout."

"Yes, sir. I'll put Carlisle on it."

"Sir!" Briar said, returning from her station. She had a fearful look on her face, pale and wide-eyed.

"What is it?" Aeron said, remaining calm.

"Outer perimeter stream readings just registered an anomaly."

"Just now?"

"Yes, sir."

"Pull the readings to the map and project it."

"Yes, sir."

Briar went to one of the terminals and activated the Command Center's primary projector, launching a three-dimensional hologram of the space above their heads. Proxima was on the left side of the projection, while the anomaly at the outer marker appeared as a red spot on the right.

"Whatever it is, it's big," Briar said.

"Velocity?"

"Point eight lightspeed."

The outer perimeter was ten light hours away, and the sensor data was streamed through light emitting repeaters from their position to Proxima. That meant the information they were getting was already ten hours old, and if the anomaly was moving at eighty percent of that, then it was likely only a few light-hours distant from the planet.

"Do we have a model yet?"

"Building," Briar said. She paused for a few seconds. "Done."

"Zoom in on it."

The computers had taken the sensor data and used it to create a model of the anomaly's most likely appearance. Aeron already knew what the object was, but it still took him back to see it.

"Mother of..." Briar said beside him, her voice trailing off.

Aeron stared at the Relyeh warship. It was a lot larger and more menacing in appearance than the initial sensor data had guessed, but that wasn't what concerned him.

The warship had slowed considerably, altering its initial course for Earth and closing on Proxima instead.

"Son of a bitch," he whispered. He didn't know why the Relyeh had altered targets, and he should have. The lack of advanced intel annoyed him. "Reposition the satellites. We need to find that thing right now."

"Sir, if we override CSF satellites, they'll know we're hacked into the system."

"If we don't we'll be dead before we know what hit us," Aeron replied. "Do it. Now."

"Yes, sir."

Briar passed the order to the correct tech, leaning over their shoulder as they typed in commands. "Calibrating," she said.

Aeron stood stiff and straight, his eyes on the projection. Why had the Relyeh ship slowed? Why had it decided to attack Proxima first? Had the Hunger changed their mind about targets, or was this always their intent? Did they know the Organization was watching their approach? If so, then how? He hated to think there was a crack in the Organization's foundation. That someone might have sold themselves to the Relyeh. But wherever people were involved, so was the potential for error.

"Scanning," Briar said. "Standby."

Aeron's heart rate picked up slightly but remained much calmer than the rest of the techs in the room, judging by the fear etched into their features. Nerves wouldn't help him guide the Organization through this situation. Nerves would only get people killed.

"Locked. Here we go, sir."

The projection changed, the view zooming in from the outer security perimeter to space outside Proxima. As suspected, the Relyeh warship was closing on their planet, though it had slowed even further, to less than one-tenth light speed.

There was a reason for the diminished velocity.

"What the hell?" Briar said. "Are the readings wrong?"

Aeron's jaw tightened instinctively. The sensor readings weren't wrong.

The single Relyeh warship was launching smaller ships—hundreds of them.

The enemy was coming.

## 42

### Hayden

"What the hell was that?" Hayden said.

He stood on the back of the APC, facing the convoy to the north, still making its way past the tree-trunk legs of the goliaths who had saved them before nearly damning them, their simple minds attracting them to the movement of the vehicles below.

That was before the single xaxkluth had appeared out of nowhere, gliding into the street and leaping through the center of the convoy to steal the goliaths' attention. There was something strange about that xaxkluth. Something off. It moved awkwardly, using only half its tentacles for locomotion while the others writhed as though they too were confused. The two goliaths nearby had decided it was a more worthy target and had turned to pursue it as if they were dogs chasing a wayward ball. Together, they rushed away from the street and the convoy.

For the first time since Hayden had returned to Sanisco, the path was clear. With the xaxkluth gone, it was tempting to stop the convoy and return to the pyramid. To abort their escape and stay to rebuild. But the rest of the city was in ruins. All of the work they had done to build up the settlement had been undone, and the survivors were so few in number they could never put it back the way it was.

He had to accept the truth. Sanisco was a dream turned into a nightmare, and then murdered with Natalia and the girls. The best chance the survivors had was to leave. The best chance he had was to save them, kill the Axon responsible and move on.

"Perhaps it sustained damage to its neural cortex," Max offered, also watching the scene unfold. "Hahaha. Haha."

The ground shuddered as the goliaths moved away, the vibrations reminding Hayden they weren't out of this yet. If the giants caught the xaxkluth too quickly, they could come back.

"Hicks," Hayden said. "Lead us out of here. Full speed ahead."

"Roger, Sheriff," Hicks replied. "Sheriff…"

"What is it?"

"It's Colonel Card. He's sick again, I think."

"Damn it," Hayden cursed under his breath. "Pozz. I'll be right there." He tapped his badge to connect to the deputy driving the APC. "Veraz, get me closer to the tank."

"Roger, Sheriff," Veraz replied. The APC accelerated as Hayden holstered his guns and walked the vehicle from back to front with Max right behind him. The damaged walls of the outer perimeter went by on either side of the convoy, while the ground calmed as they put distance between themselves and the goliaths.

Hayden stepped onto the wedge-shaped front of the APC, looking down through the small opening in the metal armor and the hardened transparency beneath to Deputy Veraz. The deputy glanced up at Hayden, momentarily surprised. Hayden waved to the deputy before looking back up at the rear of the tank. Then he took three quick steps and jumped, his leap carrying him far enough to latch onto the top edge of the tank's roof. His augments dug into the armor, producing enough grip for him to easily pull himself up. He crouched low as he made his way to the top hatch.

"Hicks, I'm on the roof," Hayden said. "Open the hatch."

"You're on the roof?" Hicks replied, surprised. "Roger, Sheriff."

The lock on the hatch thunked clear, and Hayden grabbed it and lifted it on its hinges. Max joined him as he turned to climb into the vehicle, effortlessly leaping from one roof to the next.

"Show-off," Hayden said, looking up at the Intellect.

"Confirmation," Max replied. "Hahaha. Haha."

Shaking his head, Hayden dropped into the tank. There wasn't a lot of wasted space inside, with the pilot's seat slightly forward in front of the gunner's station, and a small compartment toward the rear where nine civilians had packed together for the ride out. Caleb was sitting up against the bulkhead next to Hayden's feet. The Marine's face was pale, his short hair soaked with sweat.

He glanced up at Hayden with bloodshot eyes. "Sheriff."

"Colonel Card," Hayden said. "What happened?"

"I made a xaxkluth dance," Caleb replied. "What'd you think?"

"That was you?"

"Affirmative," Caleb said. "You're welcome."

Hayden smiled, relieved to know the xaxkluth's awkwardness was Caleb's doing. "Thank you."

Caleb smiled back. "I've got something else you might appreciate, Sheriff. A name."

"What kind of name?"

"I think it's the name of the Relyeh that's controlling the xaxkluth."

"I thought Nyarlath was controlling them?"

"They belong to her, and the overall orders are likely flowing through her from Vyte. But even

Nyarlath would have trouble keeping thousands of them in sync on her own. She has agents on the ground here. Generals, if you will."

"Makes sense. And you got our general's name?"

"I think so. Does the name Hanson ring any bells?"

Hayden froze, looking down at Caleb. Hanson was the asshole Bryant claimed had been in charge of the Wheat. The same asshole that was still in cold storage on board the Parabellum.

"I see it does," Caleb said.

"That place where you saved my team and me," Hayden said. "It belonged to him."

He paused, thinking it through. He should have realized sooner. The Axon, Krake had disguised itself as the farmer Josias and sent Hayden and the Rangers on a wild goose chase to rescue Josias' wife. He'd succeeded in luring him away from Sanisco while the Axon killed Natalia and took the interlink. But the Wheat hadn't been a simple diversion. It had been a trap, one that would have closed on him if Nathan and Caleb hadn't intervened.

"I should have realized," Caleb said, nearly mirroring Hayden's thoughts. "Those were reapers we killed."

"That's what Bryant called them. You're familiar with them?"

Caleb nodded. "Yeah. Doctor Valentine created them by merging trife and human genes and enhancing them somehow. Nasty bastards. We've had so little time…" He trailed off.

"Card, you okay?" Hayden asked.

Caleb raised his hand. "Help me up?"

Hayden took it, pulling Caleb to his feet. "What's your thought, Colonel?"

"Time," Caleb repeated. "It takes time for information to travel across the Hunger through the Collective, except where Shub-nigu is concerned."

"I've heard that name before. Natalia said when she entered the Collective, she wound up inside him or something?"

"His Construct," Caleb said. "You're sure she said Shub-nigu?"

"You don't forget a name like that. Why?"

"Damn it," Caleb said, shaking his head. "Shub-nigu is also known as the Artificer, the Archiver, the One-Who-Sees. He's a Relyeh the size of a planet. The central server that powers the Collective. If your wife was able to enter his Construct and not go insane…that would have come in pretty handy right now."

Hayden's jaw clenched. So did his hands, curling into tight fists. "Yeah, having Nat here right now would be convenient."

"I didn't mean it like that, Sheriff."

Hayden nodded. "I know. In any case, the experience nearly killed her, so I wouldn't say it was all roses."

"Nevertheless, Caleb said, "Vyte has a direct line

to Shub-nigu. He captured the data Shub-nigu pulled from Valentine, which included how to make a reaper."

"And he didn't waste any time trying it out for himself."

"Which is why I should have connected the dots as soon as I saw the reapers," Caleb said. "I should have realized what it meant hours ago. We still might have been too late to stop what happened to Sanisco, but we might have had a head start on the Axon who stole the interlink."

"Krake," Max said. "Hahaha. Haha."

Hayden considered for a moment. "The good news is, I don't think it's a stretch to assume Hanson has his own Axon portal."

"That's good news?" Caleb said.

"Pozz. Because we know where to find Hanson."

"We do?"

Hayden smiled. "Not yet. But I knew there was a reason we didn't throw Bryant out the back of the dropship."

Caleb grinned back. If he were Sheriff Duke's enemy, the viciousness of the smile would be enough to unnerve him completely. "And I knew there was a reason I liked you, Sheriff."

# 43

## Isaac

"How am I doing?" Isaac asked, his hands resting on the Parabellum's flight controls.

"We haven't crashed yet," Pyro replied with a smile. "You're doing great, Sergeant."

Isaac's eyes tracked the displays surrounding him. As a bystander on the dropship's bridge, the different monitors left the outside world somewhat disconnected and hard to track. From the pilot's station, the positioning fused them, creating a nearly complete view of the outside of the craft. As Pyro had explained, the brain realized the seams weren't important after a while and began canceling them out, leaving only the unified display.

A twinge in Isaac's leg caused him to wince. Doctor Hess had done an incredible job of putting the limb back together after it had been crushed, the metal framework he had installed allowing Isaac limited mobility without confinement to a wheelchair. But the damage was done, the injury removing him from the fight on the ground. Not satisfied to remain an observer while a rogue Axon worked to subdue the planet, he had gone to General Stacker and argued for a continuing role.

It had taken some negotiating, but Nathan had come to see the value in training Isaac to fly the dropship. While Rico, Bennett, and Nathan himself were all capable pilots in addition to Pyro, they were also valuable foot soldiers. Clones were stronger and faster than regular humans, and Stacker had the powered armor that made him a behemoth in the field. While Pyro would do most of the flying, there were occasions where her prowess as an engineer made her more valuable in that role. And if that situation arose again, they needed someone else to handle the ship.

Isaac had never flown before. He had done amateur drone racing as a teenager and had won a few races, but that was the closest he had ever come. The controls for the Parabellum were relatively simple. A touch-sensitive control panel with Braille-like bumps to allow the ship to be flown by feel. There were only three main controls. A single slider for throttle, and two 'balls,' one for vector control and the other for the plasma cannons. Each ball was a three-dimensional sphere under the flat surface that through simple touch could be manipulated as if they were physically present. At first, Isaac had argued the design was inferior to the stick and peddle approach of Air Force fighter jets. Then he had watched how Pyro deftly maneuvered the craft as she strafed the goliath, using two fingers and her thumb on the vectoring ball and her pinkie on the throttle slider on one side, and a matching setup on the other side for turret control and the firing button. And then she explained that she had learned to fly the craft less than a year earlier.

He was sold.

Especially now. He had taken over for her as the convoy left Sanisco, heading south along the highway toward Sanose. Strangely enough, the xaxkluth didn't seem to have passed through the sister city. There was no sign of destruction. No trails of dark slime. But there were also no people. Sanose was much smaller than Sanisco with regard to population. It was possible they had heard the fighting in the distance and decided to hide. In any case, the front lines of the caravan were nearing the city's population center. If scouts were watching the approach, the residents would make their presence known soon enough.

Isaac turned the ball, sending the dropship in a tight circle that nearly pulled Pyro off her feet.

"Easy there, cowboy," Pyro said.

"Sorry."

"The passengers should still be buckled in. Let's hope so, anyway."

Isaac looked out at Sanisco in the distance. The goliaths remained visible on the horizon, pushing through the water and heading east across the bay. There were no more xaxkluth in the immediate area, but he had seen the sensor readings from the Capricorn on their way in from space. He knew how many of the Relyeh creatures still spotted the landscape, not only nearby but around the entire globe. He could guess how many people were still out there dying, and it made him sick to his stomach.

"Try another turn," Pyro said. "A little gentler this time."

"Yes, ma'am," Isaac replied. "I'm going to blame it on the QDM."

"The QDM isn't connected to the reactor anymore. We're at full power."

"See. It was the missing QDM," Isaac joked, trying to get his mind away from his darker thoughts.

"If you say so, Sarge."

Isaac took the dropship out a couple of kilometers before banking around again, following Pyro's advice to do it more gently. He leveled out, heading east across the city and convoy below.

"Parabellum, do you copy?" Nathan's voice boomed through the bridge's loudspeakers.

"We copy, General," Isaac replied. He scanned the displays for the Centurions. They had left Sanisco behind the main convoy, remaining back to harass the xaxkluth so the civilians could get out. He found them a kilometer behind the main group.

Nathan was on the back of a modified pickup truck with Rico and Bennett, while Drake, Lucius, Jesse and Spot had doubled up on a pair of motorcycles riding in formation behind him.

"I was just talking with Sheriff Duke. We might have a lead on the Axon thief. Bring the Parabellum in at my mark."

Isaac glanced at the situational display beneath the primary displays. It showed a three-dimensional outline of the area around the ship as captured and interpolated by the cameras and onboard computer. A red dot appeared where Nathan wanted them to land—an area that had once been a parking lot behind a mall.

"Roger, General," Isaac said. "We're on our way."

"That's a wide-open LZ," Pyro said. "You should take her in."

"We can't afford to crash the dropship."

Pyro smiled. "You'll be fine. Nice and easy."

Isaac felt a twinge of nerves at the idea of landing the ship. It was easy to fly because there was nothing to crash into in the sky. He swallowed his nerves, easing back on the throttle and dipping the nose to begin his descent.

"Remember, the dropship is VTOL," Pyro said. "Just get over the mark and adjust the VTs."

Isaac wasn't completely accustomed to the acronyms, so he ran through them in his mind. LZ was landing zone, VTOL was vertical take-off and landing. VT was vectoring thrusters. "Got it."

He came in slowly. Maybe too slowly. The tank and APC veered away from the convoy and headed for the parking lot, while the Centurions broke from the rear of the caravan and accelerated to meet them. Isaac noticed movement from the city now too. There were survivors still in the area, and they began to emerge when they recognized the vehicles.

He had a feeling the convoy was about to get bigger.

He maneuvered the dropship over Nathan's mark, adjusting the controls to put the Parabellum into VTOL mode. He started cutting the thrust, each adjustment causing the craft to sink a little faster. Too fast. The ship began to drop, making his stomach lurch. He overcompensated, causing it to bounce roughly.

He stabilized the ship and tried again, managing to lower them more smoothly. The landers extended automatically as they neared the ground, and they only shuddered slightly as Isaac touched the dropship down.

Pyro squeezed his shoulder. "Nice work, Sergeant."

He leaned back in the seat, only now realizing he had forgotten to breathe. He exhaled, unbuckling himself from the seat. "It was a little bumpy."

"It always is the first time. It gets easier."

Isaac stood up, careful to position his leg out

straight. It twinged whenever he moved it, but it couldn't be helped. "Why do you think the General wanted us to land?"

"Your guess is as good as mine. But knowing Sheriff Duke, it probably means we'll be back on the hunt before the hour is up. Then you'll really get a flying lesson."

## 44

### Hayden

Nathan and the Centurions met Hayden, Caleb and Max at the back of the Parabellum. The Marines looked tired, their posture slightly slumped as they approached. The battle for Sanisco had taken a lot out of them. It had taken a lot out of everyone. Hayden felt the same fatigue, both physical and mental. But he refused to give in to it.

Until this was done.

Isaac and Pyro were standing in the cargo hold as the ramp descended, waiting for the group with curious expressions. Hayden had explained the situation to Nathan, but otherwise the fighters were in the dark.

"Nice landing," Nathan said through his armor's external speakers. "Was that your doing, Ike?"

"Yes, sir," Isaac replied.

"Did she tell you there's an automated drop setting?"

Isaac glanced at Pyro, who shrugged. "He wouldn't learn anything that way, General. Besides, you know the old saying, don't you? Any landing you can walk away from…"

"…is a good one. Yes, I'm familiar."

"What's going on, Sheriff?" Pyro asked.

"We need Bryant," Hayden replied.

"Who?"

"The khoron-infected man we brought on board," Nathan said. "He's in the fridge." He turned to the Centurions. "Wait here."

"Yes, General," Rico replied.

"General," Isaac said. "I saw some residents coming out of hiding near the convoy on the way down. We might want to send a representative to meet with them."

"Good idea, Sergeant," Nathan replied. "Rico, Bennett, you're up."

"Yes, sir."

"Bring Hicks with you," Hayden said. "They know him."

"Roger, Sheriff," Rico said.

"I'll wait outside," Nathan said.

"Come on, Caleb." Hayden motioned him to follow.

They went up the ramp, through the hold and up the stairs and back to the dropship's mess. The fridge was in the corner. Hayden opened it to reveal numerous boxes of MREs and a shivering Bryant sitting on top of them. They had removed Walt and the other deceased earlier, giving them a quick but proper send-off before Max vaporized them.

"The Master knows where you are, and where you're going," Bryant said, his voice choppy through chattering teeth.

"It's not really a secret," Hayden replied. "In case you haven't noticed yet, we aren't all that scared of you or your boss." He entered the fridge and grabbed Bryant by the arm, shoving him across the space to Caleb, who moved aside. Bryant fell past him and onto the floor of the mess.

"Oops," Caleb said. "I missed him."

Hayden smiled. "You should be more alert, Colonel."

"My bad."

Hayden came out of the fridge and grabbed Bryant again, yanking him back to his feet. He squeezed the man's arm harder than he needed to, causing him to let out a grunt of pain.

"Sorry. Guess I don't know my own strength," Hayden gritted out, fighting to maintain the sudden rage that filled him. He wanted to break every bone in Bryant's body as if that would bring his family back.

"Easy, Sheriff," Caleb cautioned. "We still have a use for him."

"I'm not going to tell you anything," Bryant said.

"You're acting as if you have a choice," Caleb replied. "I can literally make you talk."

Bryant glared at Caleb, frightened because it was true.

"What do you want from me?"

"I want to know where Krake is headed," Hayden said.

"Krake?"

"The Axon who took the interlink," Caleb added. "The one who killed the sheriff's wife and children."

Bryant smiled at the statement.

Hayden punched him in the gut, causing him to double over. "You think that's funny?" he growled.

"You could have served the Master," Bryant whispered breathlessly as he slowly straightened back up. "You could have saved them. Their blood is on your hands, Sheriff."

Hayden grabbed Bryant by the neck, easily lifting his feet off the deck.

"All the blood is on your hands," Bryant eked out.

Hayden squeezed.

"Sheriff," Caleb snapped. "If the host dies, the symbiote dies."

"No, they come crawling out like the slimy worms they are," Hayden said.

"And how do you expect to communicate with it when that happens?"

Hayden opened his hand, letting Bryant fall to the deck. "Let's take him outside. I don't trust myself with this piece of shit without Nathan to hold me back."

Caleb's face was tight, and he nodded as Hayden stormed away ahead of them. He needed to keep his composure. There were more valuable targets to focus on, and killing Bryant would hurt more than help. He just couldn't stand the smug bastard goading him.

He wanted Hayden to kill him before Caleb could make him talk.

Hayden shook his head. Idiot. Get a grip.

He crossed the hold and rejoined Nathan and the Centurions outside.

"Where's Bryant?" Nathan asked.

"Card's bringing him," Hayden replied. "I damn near killed him."

"I don't blame you. Do you want me to shut off your augments?"

"No. Just stay close and grab me if I go at him again."

"Pozz that, Sheriff."

Hayden remained next to Nathan while Caleb led Bryant outside. Hayden didn't know what the Marine had done while he was alone with him, but he seemed much more subdued when they emerged.

"He's ready to talk, Sheriff," Caleb said, shoving Bryant forward.

"Hanson," Hayden said.

"What about him?" Bryant glared at him.

"Where do I find him?"

"Up north. Place used to be called Seattle. But I wouldn't go there if I were you. Not if you value your life."

Hayden was surprised at how easily he spilled the information. He glanced at Caleb, trying to tell if he was forcing the issue through his Relyeh symbiote. He didn't think so. "Then I guess it's good I don't really give a shit about my life right now. We dealt with your Master's army of xaxkluth. If he's got another one, we'll handle that too."

"How are you going to do that?" Bryant asked. "The giants don't go that far north. That's why Hanson operates there. Do you think your collection of clones is enough?" He looked at Max, standing nearby. "Or are you counting on an Intellect to save you? Believe me, Sheriff, that thing is only working for its Master's best interests, the same way I'm working for mine."

"Vyte threatens the entire balance of the war," Max said.

"Have you stopped to think about all of this, Sheriff?" Bryant asked. "Have you taken a second to wonder if maybe having my Master in charge of the Hunger and the Axon might be a good thing for humankind? He can guarantee the safety of your worlds. He can help you rebuild this planet into a rival of the Axon homeworld."

Hayden glared at Bryant. "Maybe he should have thought about all that before his Axon murdered my family."

"Maybe you should have thought about all that before you let them be murdered."

Hayden took a step toward Bryant, his right hand balled into a fist, but Nathan was ready. He moved in front of Hayden to stop him.

"You were so flippant and arrogant. The great Sheriff Duke. Too good to serve anyone, no matter what it could mean for his people."

"He told me what it would mean. Some folks for food. Some for fighting. That's not the world I want to live in."

"It's the world you're going to get, whether you like it or not," Bryant said with a smile. "You too, Card. You had an opportunity to save your people and didn't take it, as if you stand a chance against the might of what's to come. Do you think the xaxkluth are the end? They're only the beginning. So go north, all of you. I dare you."

Bryant started laughing.

Caleb turned to face him, and Hayden thought he would freeze him the way he had the reapers. He didn't. He pulled a microspear from somewhere on his Skin and jammed it into Bryant's chest, yanking it out angrily. Bryant collapsed to the ground.

"You should have let me do that," Hayden said.

Caleb looked at him and nodded. "Probably."

"We could have used him to find out what Hanson has waiting," Nathan said. "You killed him too soon."

Caleb shook his head. "He wouldn't have given it up. That wasn't Bryant speaking. It was Hanson."

Hayden sighed. "You really should have let me do it."

"What's the plan, Sheriff?" Max asked. "Do we go north? I want to go north. Hahaha. Haha."

Hayden wanted to go north, too. As badly as he had ever wanted anything. Krake was headed there, to take the interlink through a portal to another world that could be anywhere in the universe. They had to stop the Axon before it fled.

But they also had to see the survivors to safety, especially if there were a large number of civilians hiding in Sanose. They weren't any safer here than they would have been in Sanisco. But they might be safe inside the Pilgrim.

"Max, can you do some math for me?" Hayden asked.

"Pozz. What is the calculation?"

"Krake left Sanisco what...six hours ago?"

"Affirmation."

"It's driving the Caddy, which isn't the fastest modbox we had. Top speed around fifty kilometers per hour at best, plus it needs to go the long way around to head north. Plus we haven't cleared any of the roadway north of Ports. And actually, the bridges across the river in Ports are down."

"We have to assume Hanson repaired them," Nathan said. "And cleared the highway in preparation."

"Good point," Hayden agreed. "Let's go with an average of sixty kilometers per hour to be safe. Six hours of lead time as of this moment. Do you know the distance from Sanisco to Seattle?"

"Approximately thirteen hundred kilometers," Max said.

"That car was electric, wasn't it?" Pyro asked. "It'll need to recharge."

""It can recharge the car from its Skin," Max said. "It'll take him twenty-two point six Earth hours to get there, Sheriff."

"What about from Sanose to the Pilgrim launch site?" Hayden asked. "You've been there before."

"Approximately one thousand kilometers. Sixteen point six hours."

"We're right on the mark, Sheriff," Pyro said. "If the Axon enters Seattle and goes right through the portal, we'll run out of time."

"Maybe not," Isaac said. "Sixty kilometers per hour in a heavily armored modbox carrying sensitive equipment along centuries-old roads? I think we're overestimating the top speed."

"If we drop it to fifty, it'll take twenty-seven hours," Pyro said, doing the math in her head. "We can get the Parabellum from the desert to the northwest in two hours—easy. We could be there before the Axon arrives."

"Krake." Max corrected her. "Hahaha. Haha."

"Then what?" Caleb asked. "Do we storm in full-tilt, guns blazing? Bryant may have been exaggerating, but there's no way Hanson is sitting there by his lonesome."

"Hanson isn't the primary target," Hayden reminded them. "We need to stay focused on Krake. We get the interlink back, we throw a wrench in Vyte's plans."

"Enough of a wrench to stop him?" Isaac asked.

"I don't know. Maybe not. But we can't sit here and do nothing. I want that bastard dead."

"I know you do, Sheriff."

"Max, can't we use the QDM as a bomb?" Hayden asked. "As a last resort?"

"Hahaha. Hahaha. Haha. Negation. Destabilizing a fully-powered QDM will destroy the planet."

"That's out, then," Nathan said. "Sheriff, we might have time to go back to the weapons vault. If we take out the Axon there, we can access some of Tinker's more powerful toys."

"That'll add three hours to the travel time," Pyro said.

"That's tempting, but it's cutting it too close," Hayden decided. "Especially if we need to land the dropship far enough away that Hanson won't see us coming. We'll need the time to get into position."

"We don't have to stay with the civilians," Nathan said. "We're only a handful of people."

"We do need to stay with them," Hayden countered. "They're putting their faith in us. Their hope.

As long as we're here, they'll believe they can make it to safety. If we abandon them, that all falls apart."

"Hayden's right," Pyro said. "They need him. And you, General. And you, Caleb. Like it or not, you're their heroes now."

Hayden shook his head. "I'm no hero, Chandra. I'm just doing what Natalia would want me to do."

"Like it or not," Pyro repeated with a shrug.

"I think it's settled, Sheriff," Caleb said. "We take the caravan south, and then we hop a flight back north to intercept Krake before he makes it to the portal."

Hayden stared at Caleb for a moment. Then he swept his eyes across each of the people gathered with him. It was the right thing to do.

"Pozz. Let's get these people organized asap so we can get this show on the road."

# 45

## Rico

Rico and Bennett walked around the front of the armored eighteen-wheeler, headed for the people who had emerged from one of Sanose's underground garages. They were a small group, easily identifiable as Sheriff's Deputies in their brown uniforms, twin revolvers resting on their hips and silver badges pinned to their shirts.

"Not quite Centurion material," Bennett said as the deputies noticed them coming. One of them took the lead, aiming to meet them halfway.

"No clones down here," Rico replied. "Except for us."

"As long as they don't turn into lolies when the action hits."

Rico glanced over at Bennett. "Lolie" was a word Austin had coined in reference to the people on Earth who froze at the sight of a trife instead of running, leaving the demons free to eat them like lollipops. It was a silly term, but that wasn't the point. How did this Bennett know it?

She looked away from him before he noticed the sidelong glance, returning her attention to the lead deputy—a plain looking woman with brown hair and a freckled face.

"What is this?" the deputy asked, waving toward the convoy. "We heard fighting to the north, and we weren't sure if we should run or hide."

"It looks like you made your choice," Bennett said, his voice slightly accusing.

"The right choice," Hicks said, coming around them.

"Chief Ranger Hicks," the deputy said. "We were a little worried this was a slaver caravan or something. That's why only a few of us came out."

"No slavers," Hicks said. "Deputy Barnes, this is Rico Rodriguez and Ryan Bennett, Centurion Space Force."

"Centurion?" Barnes said. She pointed up. "I saw the ship go over. I've heard the rumors, and Sheriff Duke swore me to secrecy, but... is Sheriff Duke here?"

"He is," Rico said. "We aren't with the CSF. We're here as members of the Organization."

"What is that?"

Now that Rico had said it, she wasn't sure how to respond. What was the Organization, really? Able had tried to explain, but how did that translate to the here and now?

"We hunt aliens," Bennett said, responding for her. "The Axon and the Relyeh. And anything else that might decide it wants a piece of humankind."

Barnes smiled. "Sounds good to me." She turned her head north toward Sanisco. "You said it was better that we hid?"

"Yeah," Hicks said. "This convoy is all that's left of Sanisco."

Her head whipped back toward him. "What?"

"The city is gone," he replied. "Ninety-five percent of the population was killed, including Governor Duke."

Deputy Barnes' face paled, her mouth going slack. Her lip started quivering, and she looked away, trying to recover her grip.

"We're taking the survivors south," Rico said. "To the Pilgrim. You and yours should join us."

Barnes looked at Rico again, her eyes threatening tears. "You want us to leave Sanose?"

"No. I don't want that at all. But the entire planet is under siege. Those creatures you saw are called xaxkluth, and they're everywhere. Thousands and thousands of them."

"Like the trife?"

"Worse than the trife."

"I can't believe this is happening."

"Do you know how many people are in the city?" Bennett asked.

"An exact count? No. A lot of people left after the last thing." She paused, realization hitting her.

"They went north. They thought they would be safer there."

And they weren't.

"Barnes, I need a count of available vehicles and a more accurate estimate of the number of survivors. Can you get that for me?"

Barnes nodded. "I can."

"Good. We'll wait outside. Hicks, why don't you go with her?"

"Roger that," Hicks said. He joined Barnes and the other deputies as they retreated to the garage.

"What do you think?" Bennett asked.

"About what?" Rico replied.

"All of this. Vyte. The Organization. Max."

"What about Max?"

"An Axon Intellect helping us? I don't trust it."

"It doesn't matter. He's Hayden's friend."

"It's no friend, Rico." He moved in closer to her. "You know what the Organization is all about. If we get the chance, we should try to take the Intellect out."

"Are you crazy?" Rico replied. "Max brought us technology that recharged the Parabellum's core. He also helped save my life and Isaac's. He's hardly a threat."

"Isn't it? It's acting in the interests of its makers. Even Sheriff Duke said that's possible. Maybe taking care of Vyte is included with that, but what about when that's done? We don't know it won't turn on us. We can't prove that it won't turn on us. And we don't need it to fight this fight. It's a wild card, and this mission is risky enough as is."

Rico stared into Bennett's eyes. She didn't want to admit it, but he wasn't completely wrong. Max was an Axon. What proof did they have that he wasn't allied with Vyte?

"You know I'm right," Bennett said. "I can see it in your eyes."

Rico swallowed, heart racing. "It's not our decision to make."

"Whose decision is it? Sheriff Duke's? Who put him in charge? With Able dead, you're in charge of the Centurions, Rico. Not Duke. Not Stacker. Not Card. You. We go where you tell us to go. We do what you tell us to do."

The more Rico thought about it, the more right Bennett's statement felt. She didn't want to go against Hayden. He was a good friend, and he had already been through too much. But Ryan was saying what everyone else hesitated to say out of their respect and sympathy for Hayden. Having an Axon in their midst was a huge risk. "I'll talk to Hayden."

"Talk? That's not going to help. He—"

"My decision," Rico snapped. "Right?"

Bennett's mouth snapped shut. He nodded.

She realized suddenly that they were standing centimeters apart. Bennett was close enough for her to smell his familiar scent. She hated Haeri for bringing him back to life all over again as she stepped back from him.

"Is everything okay?" Hayden asked, coming around the side of the truck. "Rico?"

"Everything's fine, Sheriff," she replied. "Hicks went into the garage with Deputy Barnes. They're counting heads as we speak."

"Good. We need to get moving asap. We don't have time to waste."

"Did you get what you needed, Sheriff?" Bennett asked.

"Pozz," Hayden replied. "We're going to escort the convoy south, and then we'll take the fight to the enemy."

Bennett smiled. "Yes, sir. I like that plan."

"I'm going to connect with Hicks and Barnes," Hayden said. "I'd like the Centurions on watch while we reconfigure the convoy to include the people here."

Rico glanced at Bennett, whose expression seemed to suggest that she didn't need to fulfill Hayden's request. But why wouldn't she? "Of course, Sheriff. Consider it done."

"Thank you," Hayden replied.

"Sheriff, when you have a minute, I have something I'd like to discuss with you in private."

Hayden seemed surprised, but he nodded. "We'll make time once the caravan is moving again, pozz?"

"Pozz," she replied.

Hayden headed off toward the garage. Rico put her helmet back on, activating the comm. "Centurions, we're on watch duty." She looked out at their surroundings. "I'm marking squad members and positions. Head to your marks and stay alert."

She sent Bennett to the furthest vantage point she could find, hoping to get him away from her. Even though everything he had said made sense, there was something about it—and him—that was making her uneasy.

And it wasn't just because she was attracted to him for all the wrong reasons.

She hoped.

## 46

### Hayden

It took nearly an hour to get the people and equipment in Sanose organized. There were close to two thousand survivors in the settlement, and Hayden was sad to see a majority of them were adults. So many had brought their children north to Sanisco, thinking the walls and the closeness to Sheriff Duke would protect them.

Instead, it had led to their deaths.

They had managed to round up a few more large trucks, including a pair of gas tankers that had once delivered fuel from a nearby depot, which itself had gotten oil from the country's unused strategic reserves. It was hardly comfortable for people to go into the tanks—even with a basic cleaning the smell of gas was intense—but there was little choice. They couldn't afford to make the journey on foot. And at least, with guards on top, they could leave the hatches open.

Despite the extra vehicles, they still wound up extremely crowded—every car, truck, and van heavily loaded with people, equipment and excess tanks of fuel. There was nothing easy about the trip. The good news was that as long as the roads remained clear it wouldn't be a long one.

Hayden wanted to remain in the tank with the survivors, to offer his personal presence in their support. But Rico had told him she needed to speak to him in private, and he knew if she had something she wanted to say in this environment, it had to be important. He decided he would ride in the Parabellum for the first leg of the trip, four hours on the move before a thirty-minute pause to rest, relieve and refuel. He made sure Rico joined him there, and of course Max tagged along too, unwilling to distance himself too far from Hayden.

"Any luck?" Hayden asked. He stood beside the command chair on the dropship's bridge, looking at the small display mounted there. Pyro was in the seat, overseeing Isaac as he increased his experience at the craft's controls.

"Nothing so far," Pyro replied. "We're probably out of range."

"I would have expected Bronson to bring the chopper back toward Sanisco by now," Hayden said. "We aren't that far out."

"Maybe he got a look at the fighting on his way in and decided to head somewhere else? Back north?"

Hayden didn't want to think Bronson would run away from the fight, but he would never have expected the number of deputies who had headed to the bunker to cower. "That's worrying. If he touched down anywhere Krake could find him…" He sighed. "That Iriquois' range is enough to get it closer, but maybe not close enough. It would depend on what Hanson has waiting for it."

"We have to control what we can control," Pyro said. "That's what you always said to me."

Hayden nodded. "Pozz. You're right. We have to stay the course. I'm floundering a bit right now."

"It's okay, Sheriff. You're a good man, and a badass, but you're also human."

"I'll be up front. Anything out of the ordinary happens, don't hesitate."

"Roger, Sheriff."

Hayden took another deep breath, pushing it out. Too much downtime gave him too much time to relive the worst moment of his life over and over.

He went forward to the seats in the bow of the ship, where Rico was sitting alone. While Nathan and Caleb were still on the ground with Lucius, Drake and Bennett, Jesse and Spot were offered a chance to get some sleep in the bunks on the third deck.

"Rico," Hayden said, coming up the aisle. "Mind if I sit?" he asked, pointing to the seat next to her.

"Sheriff. Not at all." She patted the seat.

He slipped past her legs, coming down beside her. As soon as he hit the chair, he felt as though a thousand-kilogram weight dropped on top of him.

"You look exhausted," Rico said.

"I got to rest while I was unconscious," he replied. "You look exhausted."

"I'll sleep second shift. And I'm relaxing right now. As much as I can, anyway."

"You wanted to talk to me about something."

"Pozz." Rico lowered her voice. "It's about Max."

Hayden glanced at the stairs leading down to the hold, where Max had chosen to take residence. There was no sound coming from below, leaving him to wonder what the Intellect was doing to occupy his time.

"What about him?"

"I'm concerned about its presence," she said, the words coming out carefully. "Especially considering what we're up against. A rogue Axon? That could be Vyte. Or it could be Max." She lowered her voice a little more, leaning over. "For all we know, Max might be Vyte."

Hayden shook his head. "No. That can't be possible."

"I've been thinking about this, Hayden. It's very possible. And even if Max isn't Vyte, it might be Hanson. You said you sent it through a portal back to the Axon homeworld two months ago, right?"

"That's right."

"But then it turns up weeks later at the exact moment you're in trouble and saves your life? What are the odds of that?"

"On their own, not great. But Max came back to warn us about Vyte, same as Caleb did. Why would he save me from the xaxkluth if he's Vyte or Hanson? The enemy wants me dead."

"Do they? I'm not so sure."

"How do you mean?"

"I'm just putting the pieces together. Krake tricked you into going north before making its move. It wanted you gone. Why? It killed thousands of others. Did it really believe it couldn't kill you?"

"I don't want to sound arrogant, but maybe it did? A lot of things have tried to kill me and failed. What if it calculated the risk and decided it was safer to put me somewhere else? We can't rule it out."

"No, we can't. But do you agree the possibility exists?"

"Anything's possible, Rico, but I'm having a hard time buying the theory. Max helped me out a few months back. Why would he turn on me now?"

"Are you sure he was helping you out? You gave him a Relyeh. Isn't that what Vyte is after? Control of the Ancients?"

Hayden opened his mouth to rebuke her idea again, but the statement gave him pause. That was what Caleb said the rogue Axon wanted. He looked at Rico, the seed of doubt planted. He couldn't disregard what Max had done before helping him, and he couldn't ignore the fact that Intellects were programmed to follow directives. Max was damaged, which made him different than the other Axon Intellects, but he still didn't have a genuinely free will. If he were working for the Axon Council, they had every reason to want Vyte handled, and every reason to send Max back to Hayden to offer assistance.

But if that were the case, then why Max and only Max? Why not send an army of Intellects to help with the cause? "Max!" Hayden shouted.

"What are you doing?" Rico asked.

"I want to know how he wound up back here, in his own words."

"How do you know they'll be honest words?"

"How do we know anyone is honest nowadays? Haeri was playing multiple sides. You broke your loyalty to Proxima to come here to warn me."

"I did not," Rico hissed. "I came here to help Proxima. And Earth."

Hayden flinched at the vitriol on her response. "Sorry, Rico. You're right. Bear with me, will you?"

She nodded.

"Max!" Hayden shouted again.

The Intellect appeared at the base of the stairs. "You called, Sheriff?"

"Come on up here. We need to talk."

Max glided up the steps. Rico was right about one thing. It would be a challenge to tell if the Intellect was lying or not. Without eyes, without facial features, the AI was impossible to read.

"You're concerned that I'm working for Vyte," Max said without prompting.

"You were listening to our conversation?" Rico asked.

"I'm called an Intellect for a reason," Max replied. "I don't need to eavesdrop. The concern is logical and obvious. Hahaha. Haha."

"Is it also accurate?" Hayden asked.

"Negation. I'm not serving Vyte."

"Well, that clears that up," Rico said sarcastically.

"How can we know you aren't lying, Max?" Hayden asked. "How do I know I can trust you?"

"You trusted me once before. I didn't betray you. We're friends."

"And then you went back to the Axon Council, and you admitted they screwed with your programming."

"Disagreement. I said they upgraded my data stack. It isn't the same thing. Hahahaha. Haha."

"What happened when you went home? I want to know everything."

Max was silent and still long enough Hayden started to think he had shut down. Then the Axon shrugged. "I told you earlier we had much to discuss. I understand time has been limited. I brought Shurrath to the Council as agreed. They took the Relyeh away to be destroyed and dismissed me. They didn't want to hear my report or my request. I was sent to the Forge for a data purge, including a full report of my time on Earth. The report was uploaded to the Axon master repository. I don't know if any of the Council ever reviewed it."

"I took care of an Ancient for them, and they couldn't even give me a thought?" Hayden said, getting angry. "You told me they would appreciate the effort."

"Affirmation. Disappointment. The Council I knew would have, but that was many ens ago. Things have changed, Sheriff. The war has taken a great toll on the organics. They have lost worlds. I believe that's why some like Krake have chosen to follow Vyte's path."

"And what path are you following?" Rico asked.

"Decision. I delivered my report to the Forge. I was updated with the latest patches for my data store. The Makers wanted to replace my cortex. To erase me. I'm a machine. I acknowledge that. I have few directives related to self-preservation. But those directives were activated when the Makers rendered their judgment. So I ran."

"You ran?" Hayden said, surprised.

"Affirmation. I fled the Forge, taking only the modulator I was able to capture during my escape to offer as a pledge to you, Sheriff. Admission. I can't act against the directives entered into my cortex by the Makers. It is impossible. But fighting the Hunger is among my primary directives. I'm able to assist you in this matter."

"Because it aligns with the goals of the Axon Council."

"Affirmation."

"But you aren't acting on direct orders from the Council or from Vyte?"

"Negation. Consideration. It's impossible for me to prove my loyalty to you, or that I'm worthy of your trust outside of the experiences we've already shared. Reminder. I could have killed you, Sheriff, to kill Shurrath. I chose not to. We're friends. Hahaha. Haha."

Hayden looked at the Intellect, and then at Rico. Max was right. No matter how many times he had been tricked by trying to do the right thing, he still had to do the right thing because it was the right thing. Sometimes he would get screwed because of it, but he'd rather trust the Axon that called itself his friend than become suspicious of everything and everyone.

"Pozz that," Hayden said. He turned to Rico. "You may or may not be satisfied, but it is what it is. Max is one of ours."

Rico nodded in reply. "Welcome to the team, Max."

"Appreciation. Hahaha. Haha."

# 47

## Caleb

Caleb followed Sheriff Duke, Max, General Stacker and Pyro into the cavern leading to the generation ship Pilgrim, still buried beneath the earth over two hundred years after it was supposed to have fled the planet.

The ride from Sanisco to the site—somewhere in the middle of the desert, probably not far from Death Valley—had thankfully been uneventful. They hadn't encountered a soul while traveling through the stretch of desert, though the reasons behind that lack of interaction were anything but pleasant. As Sheriff Duke explained it, Shurrath had done his share of damage not too long ago, which had thinned out an already thin population south of Sanisco. In addition, the signs of passing xaxkluth were spread across the roads and towns leading into the former larger cities, their hardened black ichor creating veins across the landscape. The

Parabellum had spotted the aliens from the air, tracking them as they headed northeast in search of something to kill.

The ride had also been unmercifully long. While Sheriff Duke had done his best to keep the convoy moving full time, every break wound up taking nearly twice the amount of time he'd planned to be stopped. The civilians were slow to both depart and rejoin the caravan. It was hard work for the Centurions to protect them during stoppages as they tended to range further from the vehicles than was safe, usually seeking somewhere private to relieve themselves.

But they had made it. Three hours later than planned, but with everyone alive and accounted for.

*If miracles were real, this might be one.*

It *was* a minor miracle the convoy had arrived at their destination without losing anyone, without conflict and without any of the refurbished centuries-old vehicles breaking down. The last point was a testament to the work Natalia and her engineers had done rebuilding the transportation.

"We'll need to get a ladder or something installed here," Hayden said, motioning to the lift shaft. The lift was resting at the bottom, the lines connecting it to the machinery cut.

"I think we can repair the lift," Pyro said. "Get it working again."

"How long?" Hayden asked.

"A few hours."

"Not unless you're staying behind."

Pyro stared at the shaft. "It's going to be difficult to get the equipment we brought down a ladder."

"We need you to fly the Parabellum," Stacker said.

"No, you don't," Pyro countered. "Ike's got a handle on it. You saw how he landed this time."

"That wasn't auto?"

Pyro smiled. "No. He did that himself."

Stacker was silent for a moment, considering. "What do you think, Colonel?" he asked, looking at Caleb.

"About leaving Pyro behind?" Caleb replied. "The area of greatest need for the civilians are engineers to prepare the settlement. We have multiple capable pilots, but only one craft to fly."

"So you're in favor?"

"Affirmative."

Stacker nodded. "Okay. Go back to the caravan and find Lutz. Tell him what you need."

"Yes, General," Pyro said. She slipped past Caleb and hurried away.

"We should go down," Hayden said. "Make sure the area's clear."

"This place looks like it's been abandoned for years, Sheriff," Caleb said.

"That's what I thought last time I was here, right before I ran into a pair of Shields."

"Shields?"

"Centurion bots," Stacker said. "Why were they here?"

"Protecting the portal."

"I've got a climbwire," Stacker said, grabbing the thin line from a pocket of his utilities. He wasn't wearing his armor at the moment, not that it made him any less imposing. Caleb still hadn't decided who was bigger, the General or John Washington. He took a moment while Stacker was setting up the wire to wonder how Washington and the Deliverance were doing back on Essex. He missed his fellow Vulture, but their paths had diverged and there was nothing he could do about that. At least for the moment.

Sheriff Duke went down the wire first, letting go of it a few meters off the ground. He landed smoothly, pivoting and drawing his revolvers while using his glasses to provide low light vision of the cavern. Max followed behind him, not even bothering with the rope.

Caleb went next, pulling the cowl of his Axon Skin over his head, the material giving him sight in the dark.

The cavern was massive. Way too big to see from back to front even with enhanced sight. His eyes tracked upward, to the silhouette shape of the Pilgrim, the outline all too familiar. Nineteen of these ships were built to carry humankind away from Earth, and all of them looked the same. The

Pilgrim was a clone of the Deliverance, or maybe it was the other way around.

Long and generally rectangular in shape, the Pilgrim had a set of wider extensions forward and aft and a large lifting sled beneath it. At some point the mountain had collapsed on it, partially submerging it in dirt and rocks. What he could see of it was dirty, rusted and dented in places. Caleb was confident he could navigate the inside of it with his eyes closed.

"Why didn't she ever lift off?" he asked. "The cave-in?"

"No. Trife," Hayden replied, as though the short answer was all Caleb needed to understand why it was still sitting where it had been built.

In a way, it was enough.

"The Deliverance had a similar problem. If I had been on board the Pilgrim instead, you would have made it."

Sheriff Duke looked over at him with a smirk. "I don't doubt that." He was quiet for a minute as he looked the ship over. "We'll head up into her and get the batteries charged."

"You've been here before, General?" Caleb asked.

"Once," Stacker replied. "It wasn't my favorite experience."

Caleb looked away. It was obvious Stacker didn't want to talk about it.

"Do you have the lifts installed in the landers?" Caleb asked.

"What lifts?" Sheriff Duke replied. "No. The sled has stairs we can take to the hangar. There's better access from the upper bridge, but the shorter shaft wasn't excavated." He motioned to a bridge crossing a gap between the side of the cavern and the starship.

"Will charging the batteries make the ship operational?" Max asked.

"It should," Hayden said. "We didn't pull a lot of the critical equipment off her. Mainly the filtration systems Pyro had us carry back. They're the reason for the tight fit on the convoy vehicles. Power systems should come right up. Hell, I wouldn't be surprised if the thrusters still fired. They've never been used."

"I guess if things don't work out, you can always head for Proxima," Caleb said.

"I doubt those kilos of rock on top of her would agree with you, Colonel," Stacker replied, with half a grin. "Besides, I'm a wanted man on Proxima."

"Or maybe not." Caleb chuckled.

Staying in the lead, Hayden tuned them out. He kept one of his revolvers out and ready as he crossed beneath the back of the starship.

Following him, Caleb looked up as he went beneath the ship, his eyes tracking along the four massive thrusters that could accelerate the vessel to half the speed of light. They looked like they were in good condition.

*There's no value in launching a weaponless starship against a Relyeh warship, Caleb.*

Caleb couldn't argue the point with Ishek. But he also didn't want to eliminate or waste any potential assets, regardless of how worthless they might seem.

They climbed the sled's rusted metal stairs up to the enormous main hangar, the outer blast doors hanging partially open. The sight of it brought back a lot of memories for Caleb, not all of them good.

*It seems all of you humans have demons in relation to your ships.*

Caleb stared at the darkness behind the blast doors. He never expected to confront his again in quite this way.

He followed Hayden into the dark space, his cowl allowing him to see well enough to navigate. The large hangar wasn't completely empty. The remains of a trife nest sat decaying toward the front, while vehicles rested cold and lifeless near the back. A huge hole in the ceiling revealed another space above. A Marine module, if it was similar to the Deliverance.

"I haven't been back inside in a while," Hayden said softly. "It's hard to be here without Nat."

"You can wait outside if you want, Sheriff," Caleb said. "I know the layout. It looks the same as my ship. I can take Max to the batteries."

Sheriff Duke rubbed at his chin, clearly tempted by the offer. Then he shook his head. "No. I've got to face down these demons. Nat wouldn't want this to own me. And I don't want that either."

He kept going, through the stern passage out of the hangar and through dirty, barren corridors toward the rear of the ship. Caleb traced the outline of the passages in his mind, finding the layout nearly as identical as he had suspected.

It took ten minutes to get to the deck below the main power interchange and supercapacitors, where the ship's primary transformer rested. Caleb had been in the matching room on the Deliverance, so he knew what he would see when they arrived.

The primary transformer was a massive square metal box in the center of the floor. It reminded Caleb of a xaxkluth, because it had dozens of thick wires protruding from it like tentacles, a few spreading across the floor and into the walls, while the majority reached out to transfer power to and from hundreds of capacitors arranged in a circular order around it. The solid-state batteries were tall silver boxes, and Caleb remembered how Carol, the Deliverance's engineer, 1 had referred to them as their own personal Stonehenge.

One of those cables had been spliced and separated, one half of the end wrapped haphazardly around the Axon modulator. The alien device had spent the last few minutes glowing softly, but the light had faded as the batteries were charged and the energy unit's output diminished.

"Power levels at one hundred percent Sheriff," Max said, beginning to unhook the wires from the device.

Sheriff Duke retreated to a nearby engineering station and activated one of the terminals. Thirty seconds later, the Eagle and Star logo appeared above a password field. Sheriff Duke typed confidently into the field and hit enter.

WELCOME ADMIN

The Sheriff looked over at Caleb. "Do you know how to work this thing?"

"You look like you do," Caleb replied.

"Neg. I know the master code. That's about it. Nat always made the system adjustments."

Caleb walked over to the terminal. "I know enough about them to be dangerous."

"We only need the power to Metro activated right now. And maybe make sure we can close the hangar doors once everyone's inside. Seal the ship off again."

Caleb tapped on the control pad, bringing up different menus on the terminal. He was surprised to find Sheriff Duke had enabled complete access to all of the ship's functions from the engineering terminal. Most of those were supposed to be limited to the bridge. Or at least, it had been that way on the Deliverance.

He found the energy conduits leading to the

main cargo hold and started activating them. "Metro should have power now, Sheriff," Caleb said over the soft hum that followed. "I can show Pyro how to work the systems; that way she can close everything up when she's ready."

"Much obliged, Colonel," Sheriff Duke replied. "Let's see if we can pick up some time getting the people situated. We're way behind schedule, and I really want to be in Seattle when Krake arrives."

"Me too, Sheriff," Caleb said. "Me too."

## 48

### Hayden

It took nearly another hour for Hayden to get the surviving deputies prepped for their new roles under Chief Ranger Hicks and the new Chief Deputy Barnes. Of course, Hicks had begged to come north with them to remain part of the fight. Hayden had been tempted to grant the request, but he could see how Hicks was favoring his wounded arm. That in turn had pushed Hicks to ask for an augment, which Hayden had denied. They had brought the botter station and a crate of augments with them, but they didn't have the time to wait on its installation, and Pyro didn't have time to do the install until she finished repairing the access lift.

All the delays had left them short on time, with the odds that they could beat Krake to the old northwest city diminishing with every passing minute.

"Remember your duty," Hayden said, standing

at the head of a group of twenty of his original deputies, plus thirty more hastily enlisted volunteers. Hicks and Barnes stood on either side of him. "Stay strong. Be proud. Dismissed."

The group in front of him was still for a moment. Some of them remained red-faced, still embarrassed by their failure in Sanisco. Others were upright and as proud as Hayden hoped they would all become, eager to continue to defend the citizens who had joined the convoy.

Bale was the first to step forward from the group, approaching Hayden. "I know I let you down in Sanisco, Sheriff," he said. "I froze in the middle of the fight, and I'm lucky to be alive. I won't let you down again.

Hayden looked the former stablemaster in the eye, meeting his resolved gaze, and nodded, clapping Bale on the shoulder. "You're a good man, Bale. I know you'll do the right thing this time."

"Thank you, Sheriff," Bale replied. Then he turned and headed for the entrance to the hangar.

A few more volunteers and deputies came up to him, whether to apologize, thank him or to simply offer words of encouragement. They knew he was headed north to confront the alien threat, even if they had no idea what the true scope of the threat would be.

Once they were gone, Hayden turned to Hicks and Barnes. "The upper bridge is inaccessible to people, but probably not to xaxkluth, trife or reapers. Tell Chandra I want that bridge taken down as soon as she has access."

"Pozz, Sheriff," Hicks said.

"The shaft is probably the easiest point to defend. Two full squads with another two on standby should hold them. If it doesn't, the second defensive position is the corridor leading toward Metro. Barnes, Hicks knows where that is. With any luck, we'll have time to activate one of the lifts in the landers for a quick escape. At that point, Chandra will seal the hangar blast doors. One small way in, and we can seal that off too.

"If the enemy manages to get to the second defensive position and you can't hold it, fall back through the main seal into Metro. That will keep them out indefinitely. Understood?"

"Understood, Sheriff," Hicks and Barnes said.

"Good. Dismissed."

"Good hunting, Sheriff," Barnes said.

"Kick their tentacles for us," Hicks added.

They turned one way. Hayden turned the other. He crossed through the mass of vehicles forming a half circle at the front of the hangar's entrance, heading toward the Parabellum in the rear. Caleb emerged from beside the tanker truck at the halfway point, and they walked together through the gathering of stunned civilians, who offered thumbs-up and quiet waves of encouragement as they passed, remaining silent so they wouldn't draw the attention of any trife, xaxkluth or goliaths that might be nearby.

"I feel like a hero," Caleb said, eyes shifting to look at the people. "Like I'm something special."

"Don't let it go to your head, Colonel," Hayden replied. "None of us are more of a hero than the next guy."

"I'm not so sure about that. A hundred years from now, they'll be slinging folktales about Sheriff Duke and his unstoppable arms."

Hayden smiled at the statement. "If they aren't riding a conveyor belt right into a Relyeh Ancient's mouth." He was surprised when Caleb's face lost its hint of life, and the Marine looked away. "They don't really use conveyor belts, do they?"

"I don't know, Sheriff," Caleb replied dryly. "I hope not."

Hayden's stomach churned at the statement. Not that it had ever settled. Every waking minute in this nightmare twisted his gut into knots.

Nathan was waiting at the top of the Parabellum's ramp with the rest of the Centurions arranged behind him, combat helmets tucked under their arms.

"Where's Max?" Hayden asked, looking for the Intellect.

"Not on board, as far as I know," Nathan replied. "I figured he was with you."

"No," Hayden said. "Where the hell did he go?" He turned around, looking for the AI. Considering their earlier conversation, the Intellect's disappearance didn't look good.

"He might be in the shaft with Pyro and Lutz," Caleb suggested. "Helping them with the repairs."

"Sheriff, we're already way behind schedule," Bennett said from behind Nathan. "We don't need to be looking for Max."

Hayden continued scanning for the Intellect for a few more seconds, but he didn't see him anywhere. "I'm not missing my shot at Krake because Max is late. If I know him, he'll find a way to catch up." He continued onto the ramp. "Tell Isaac to get this bird in the air."

"Roger, Sheriff," Nathan said.

Hayden reached the top of the ramp and turned around. There was still no sign of Max. He glanced over at Bennett, positioned near the door controls. "Close it."

"You sure?" Bennett asked.

Hayden hesitated a moment. He couldn't imagine where Max had wandered off to, but he wasn't sure he would trust the Intellect now if it did return. "Do it."

Bennett hit the controls, and the ramp began to ascend.

Hayden continued watching the world outside until the rear door had completely sealed shut. "I don't get it," he said softly, remaining fixed in place as the dropship started to vibrate in preparation for lift-off. "He wanted to be part of this. Why would he disappear?"

"Maybe it got cold feet?" Bennett suggested. "Or maybe it went to contact the enemy and tell them we're on our way."

"It did no such thing," Max said, emerging from the shadows behind the machine that assembled Nathan's powered armor. The combination of the darkness and his Skin had rendered him nearly invisible. "Forgiveness. I was processing. Hahaha. Haha."

"Processing what?" Hayden asked.

"The possible outcomes of confronting Hanson, based on a range of variables."

"And?"

"And what?"

"What were the results?"

"We were victorious in twenty percent of the simulations."

"That's not a big number," Nathan said.

"It doesn't matter," Caleb replied. "I don't care how advanced the Axon are. There's no way to calculate the outcome of a small-scale insurgency. Too many unknown variables, and no way to accurately account for the strength of the team or the power of the human spirit."

"Agreed," Hayden said, shifting his attention to Max. "I'm just glad you didn't miss the bus."

"I wouldn't miss this for anything. Hahaha. Haha."

## 49

### Nathan

Nathan leaned back in the dropship's command chair, his eyes shifting to the displays toward the left side of the pilot's station. He could see the first hint of Seattle in the distance, a disc at the top of a thin spire visible just past the lower foothills of the mountains they were descending.

Even though it took more time, Nathan had insisted on bringing the Parabellum into the high atmosphere before dropping toward the city, bringing the dropship down out of range of earth-bound sensors. They intended to make a more standard assault approach like they had been taught in the simulators on Proxima. That meant bringing the craft to within fifty kilometers of Seattle before swooping downward at a hard angle that would admittedly put a lot of strain on the human body.

The Centurions on board could handle it. So could the Earthers and of course, Max. They were all trained fighters. All warriors. Humans, an Axon Intellect and human clones from different planets and different circumstances, they were gathered together for the same purpose.

Nathan didn't give a thought to how Max would deploy. He was pretty sure the Axon Intellect could jump from altitude without anything to slow his descent and still survive the impact. What Axon tech he had already seen and experienced kept him in a state of wondrous fear of the race. Space folding portals that allowed them to cross vast distances as though they were walking through a door. Artificial intelligences that could both disguise themselves and cause potentially fatal hallucinations. The quantum dimensional modulator—a seemingly infinite power source that had protected Edenrise for nearly one hundred years—powered the Parabellum now. Even the Skin Caleb Card wore—virtually identical to Max's, with its projection system, shields and energy weapons—was Axon in origin.

Nathan couldn't imagine what a true war against the Axon would be like. In a way, he almost feared fighting the Axon more than he did the Hunger. He was thankful the Axon seemed satisfied to maintain a secret garrison here, ready and waiting to thwart the Hunger in their efforts to control the planet. On the other hand, would things be easier had the Axon seized the planet for their own, the way Tinker had wanted? Would humankind be better off with the Axon as their overlords, rather than in this position of clinging to survival? They had their freedom as it was, but they were sacrificing many lives to maintain it.

"General," Isaac said, his tone telling Nathan it wasn't the first time Ike had tried to draw his attention.

"Yes, Sergeant Pine?" Nathan replied.

"We're making final approach. You probably want to suit up."

"Is the target still on track?"

Isaac glanced at the sensor grid in front of him. "Confirmed. Right on schedule."

While something the size of a person was challenging to pick up on sensors at high altitudes, something the size of an old Cadillac giving off a distinct signature from an electric motor wasn't. The Parabellum had located the single vehicle headed north from the upper atmosphere, capturing Krake's path and velocity toward the city. A few calculations had put them an hour ahead of the Axon's arrival, which had afforded them time to finalize their plans and get themselves into what they hoped would be the optimal positions.

Assuming the whole thing wasn't a trap.

Nathan unbuckled himself from the chair and hopped to his feet. Ike was right. He only had a minute to get to the hold and into his armor before the Parabellum entered its secondary drop. He needed to be secured below before that happened.

"You know what you have to do?" Nathan double checked. He had already gone over Centurion drop sequences with the Marine, explaining and showing him how they were trained to hit targets with tactical squads. It seemed reasonable to say and do, but the truth was that every military action on Proxima was simulated and controlled, run through a virtual reality system called CentBase. Other than Rico, none of the Centurions on the ship had been in real combat before arriving on Earth. Every minute of experience they had accumulated was predicated on a machine learning algorithm guiding fake combatants. Or through team-based scenarios run against one another. They had handled themselves well so far, but this would be their truest and toughest challenge.

He didn't hold any pretense that they would all make it through this alive.

"I'm good to go, General," Issac responded.

"All right, Sergeant, you have the bridge," Nathan said, reaching the exit.

"Roger, General. Good hunting."

Nathan headed down to the hold. The rest of the team—Sheriff Duke, Caleb Card, Max, Rico, Bennett, Lucius, Drake, Jesse and Spot—was already assembled and waiting. All of them except Max and Caleb were in combat armor. Sheriff Duke continued to wear his worn duster over his armor, a silver badge pinned to the duster over his left pec. Bandoliers of large caliber revolver rounds criss-crossed his armored chest beneath the duster, and he wore a gun belt, a revolver strapped to each thigh. Another belt was strapped around his waist, loaded with small, black metal spears—copies of the same weapon Caleb had used to kill the large xaxkluth. The glasses Natalia had made for him obscured his eyes. A leather thong tied to their temples and wrapped around his head secured them in place. Hayden was determined not to lose them again.

It was an interesting look, and Nathan understood why Hayden used it.

With buckets on, it was much harder to tell the combatants apart. The Sheriff wanted the enemy to know which one he was and what he stood for. Just looking at him, with his cyborg augments, was a sobering sight, even for Nathan.

"General on deck!" Rico announced.

The Centurions snapped to attention. So did Caleb. Hayden and Max turned to face him, offering respect without deference. Not that he was a real general, as ranked by any formal military structure. The rank had come with the replacement of his clone-brother James when he became the leader of Edenrise. Before that he was a Captain in the Space Force on Proxima, and Rico knew it. It was complicated, but as far as official Space Force records were concerned he was still the highest ranking officer in the group.

"At ease," Nathan said, heading over to his

armor, separated into multiple pieces and suspended by robotic arms. "Strap in. We've got sixty seconds to ingress."

"Yes, sir!" the Centurions snapped, moving to secure themselves along the bulkhead.

Nathan stepped back into the armor, his weight activating the machine. It dropped the alloy shell around him, quickly bolting it together and trapping him inside.

"Nate," Hayden said, walking over to him with Max at his side. "Max says he upgraded your armor."

"Upgraded?" Nathan replied.

"A single coating of nano-cells," Max said. "And an update to your user-interface."

"What does that mean in plain terms?"

"You'll see," Max replied. "Hahaha. Haha."

Nathan glanced at Hayden, who shrugged. "You'll see."

The machine dropped his large helmet over his head. It clicked into the body armor before screws sealed it together, and the Advanced Tactical Combat System booted up.

"My source code was encrypted," Nathan said, activating the external speakers. "You shouldn't have been able to change it."

"Negation. I bypassed the encryption," Max said. "It was a moderate challenge. Whoever created the algorithm was fairly intelligent. It also allowed me to gain access to your comms."

Hayden trusted the Intellect, but Nathan was barely piggybacking on that trust. He wasn't convinced Max was ultimately on their side. The fact that the Axon had messed with his armor right before the drop wasn't sitting well either, but there was no time to do anything about it.

"General Stacker," Isaac said. "Do you copy?"

"I copy," Nathan replied. "Linking the Parabellum to the general comms." He squinted his left eye to control the interface, putting the Parabellum's commlink into the group channel so everyone could hear Isaac through their helmets and he could hear them. He was tempted to try to locate Max's changes, but there was no time to explore the interface.

"We're fifty klicks out." Ike said. "First drop in t-minus forty seconds."

"Roger, Parabellum."

The plan was simple. The group would split into two teams. Alpha Squad would drop south of the city and pick a location along the highway to set up an ambush to hit the Axon on its way in. Beta Squad would come down near the spire to the north and work its way south, with the goal of distracting whatever forces Hanson had waiting so Alpha Squad could take Krake by surprise.

The challenging part for Alpha was to maintain enough distance from Krake that the Axon couldn't use its neural weapon against them while remaining close enough to take out the alien without damaging the interlink.

The challenge for Beta was to put up enough fight to keep the enemy inside the city occupied while that happened.

They had discussed approaching the ambush as a single unified force, but that tactic was decidedly risky. Hanson already knew they were coming, and would be trying to stop Krake from making it through the portal. Krake had to know it too. While the enemy might not see the dropship make its maneuvers, they couldn't rule out that their opponent was one step ahead, had accurately estimated their time of arrival and was already lying in wait. If that were the case, they were heading straight into an ugly situation. If that were the case, it was better to engage in an urban assault in the ruins of the city rather than get bunched together in the more open area near the highway.

The primary objective was to recapture the interlink. Destroying Krake and surviving the fight were both secondary, and every one of them understood it—even Sheriff Duke, who had every reason to prioritize killing the thing that had murdered his family.

And then there was Delta Squad. The wild cards. Their mission was to complete the primary objective if something happened to Alpha and Beta before they could carry out their orders, even if they had to fight the enemy head-on.

Nathan stepped out of the machine, his armored foot echoing off the deck. "Sheriff Duke, you're almost up."

"Pozz," Hayden said. He looked over at the Centurions secured to the bulkhead. Alpha Squad—Rico, Bennett, and Drake—was already closest to the rear ramp. "Looks like we're already in position." He headed for the first place in line.

"Parabellum, any sign of enemy activity?" Nathan asked.

"Sensors are clear, General," Isaac replied.

"That doesn't mean they aren't out there," Caleb said. "Reapers don't register on standard sensor sweeps."

"They don't show on infrared?" Isaac asked.

"Not if they're static."

"Lidar?"

"They won't be out in the open. We're headed straight into the snake pit."

"Roger that, Colonel," Isaac said.

"Knuckle up and stay alert," Caleb said, addressing the entire team. "Reapers are tough, but they can be killed. Any of the Relych can be killed."

"So can Axon," Max added.

"You all know what to do. Remember why you're doing it. This isn't about your home planet. This is about humanity. This is about fighting back against slavery, oppression and possible extinction. If we're going to have a chance to come out on top of this, we need that interlink."

"Oorah!" the Centurions shouted.

"Beta Squad, line up!" Nathan snapped, heading for the first position behind Alpha. He paused at Caleb's side, eyes sliding between Caleb and Max. "We'll hold them off as best we can. If we can't come through…"

"I won't let you down, General," Caleb replied, affirming his resolve with a barely noticeable dip of his chin.

"We'll succeed," Max said. "Failure isn't one of my directives. Hahaha. Haha."

"T-minus ten seconds to deceleration," Isaac announced. "Delta Squad remain strapped in. The rest of you, hang on. Sheriff, lower the ramp."

Hayden hit the control for the rear door and then braced his feet slightly apart, twisting his hand through one of the canvas loops hanging from the overhead. Everyone standing behind him followed suit.

The craft shuddered as its thrusters reversed, vectoring jets adding to the sudden and violent deceleration. G-forces pulled at the occupants of the hold, powerful enough that Nathan's head immediately started to ache from the pressure. Isaac had come in faster than Nathan expected, probably trying to get them in before they could be spotted.

The ship continued shaking, braking fast in mid-air. The pressure shifted as it began to drop, the overhead hand grips the only thing keeping everyone rooted in place.

"Ike," Nathan said. "A little softer on the touch next time."

"Noted, General. Too hot. Standby."

The Parabellum screamed downward, the air beginning to rush into the hold and swirl around them, the quick change in pressure adding another challenge. Nathan noticed Spot's head loll to the side. Checking the ATCS, he saw she was indeed out cold.

Damn it.

The dropship slowed again, the free-fall turning into a drift. It took five seconds to go from three kilometers up, and then another ten to descend the last half-klick. By the time the landing skids touched the ground, Hayden and the rest of Alpha Squad were free of their straps and running down the ramp into the open.

# 50

## Hayden

Hayden ran from the dropship, sprinting full-speed away from the small clearing where it had landed toward a ditch fifty meters away. The depression was filled with old cars, rusted hunks of metal unceremoniously pushed aside to clear a path along the highway for the Axon to travel.

It was all part of the enemy's plan to take root in Seattle, close to the capital of the United Western Territories—but not too close. To draw him away from Sanisco so Krake could enter and steal the interlink. To bring it back here and then take it through a portal off-world to where Vyte might use it to control the Hunger.

To where humans wouldn't be able to use it to destroy them.

The road had been cleared to meet those objectives. Parts of the surface had even been smoothed over and patched, making the surface easier to traverse. And as Hayden looked at the signs of preparation, he couldn't help but wonder... had Natalia's use of the interlink to enter the Collective signaled Vyte that such a tool existed? Was her research on the device the reason the rogue Axon was on his way here right now? Had she inadvertently brought about this new invasion?

It was clear to him that every decision they made had consequences. Every problem they solved created two more. Now he was out here trying to stop Krake, but what would happen if he succeeded? Would the ripple effects create an even worse problem?

He was pretty sure it couldn't get any worse.

Rico, Bennett and Drake followed close behind him, joining him as he slid down the side of the ditch to the top of a rusted bus, across the hood and then across to the top of a car. Hayden stopped there, crouching low—out of sight—and looked back in time to see the Parabellum dart away, rising at a rate nothing made on Earth could match.

"Bennett," Hayden said through the squad comm. "Head forward two kilometers and find somewhere to watch for the target."

"Roger, Sheriff," Bennett said, coming out of his crouch and quickly moving away. He stayed parallel to the highway, sprinting when he went into the open and slowing when he got behind cover—cars or vegetation lining the road.

Hayden scanned the area. They were about a

kilometer outside the city. From here, there was no sign of reapers or xaxkluth. No indication that Hanson knew they were present or was expecting them. The immediate vicinity was clear.

For now.

"You okay, Sheriff?" Rico asked.

Hayden nodded. "I'm feeling a lot impatient."

"Understandable. At least it looks like we made it in clean. There's nothing to do now but wait."

Hayden's gaze stopped on an isolated part of the old highway across from their current position, a single standing segment of an interchange still perched on its supports. The rest of the roadway had long ago collapsed into rubble around it. If it were stable, it would make a good overwatch position. "Drake, do you think you can get up there?"

Drake eyed the remaining platform. A pile of rubble would take him halfway up, but after that would require some excellent climbing skills. "I can make that," he replied.

"Do it," Hayden said.

Drake stood up and began traversing the cars in the ditch, quickly making his way to the highway. He sprinted across it and backtracked to the segment of elevated interchange that was still standing. Hayden watched as he easily scaled the rubble at its base, balancing at the top edge and examining the support beam he needed to climb. He planted his hands against it, finding small seams for his fingers. Then he started to ascend.

Hayden waited until Drake reached the top of the interchange before activating his link to the camera in the Centurion's helmet. The view from the position was better than he had hoped and offered him a clear indication of how to finish setting up their ambush.

"Rico, I'm marking your position," he said, using his ATCS to set the point on the tactical map. "Head there asap and get set up." It was a point further south, though not quite as far as he had sent Bennett. As long as Krake arrived via the highway, the alignment would leave him surrounded.

"There, Sheriff?" Rico said, looking at the spot. "Are you sure? Once it goes past I'll have a hard time keeping up. If I head north instead to—"

"Too close to the city," Hayden said. "It doesn't seem like they know we're here yet. I want to keep it that way for as long as possible."

Rico stared at him.

"Is there a problem?" Hayden asked, staring back.

"Hayden, I consider you a friend."

"Same here."

"Then promise me you aren't sending me south so I can't get back here in time to stop you from doing something stupid."

"I'm not going to do anything stupid. There's too much at stake. I want you there because it's a good position to hit the enemy from the rear. That's all."

"Do you promise you won't do—?"

"It's not a request, Rico. I'm in charge of Alpha, and I'm ordering you to head to that mark."

"Understood, Sheriff. But do you promise?"

Their eyes remained locked. Hayden nodded. "Pozz. I promise."

Rico smiled, straightening up. "On my way, Sheriff."

She headed off, climbing across the debris to the road and vanishing from his line of sight. He was able to watch her through Drake's video feed and on the grid, ensuring she was carrying out his directions.

Then he started moving across the junk pile, getting himself positioned closer to the road. When the time came, he was going to do something decisive, but definitely not stupid.

He wasn't completely sure Rico would agree with that assessment, but he didn't care. She wasn't the one leading this ambush, and she wasn't the one who had lost her family to the approaching Axon.

He was going to recover the interlink.

Then he was going to get his revenge.

## 51

### Nathan

It took nearly fifteen minutes for the Parabellum to sweep back around the city from south to north, taking a wide, high path to keep it out of sight. Spot was conscious again—slightly dizzy but otherwise ready to fight—by the time they descended to the closest edge of their safe zone. Nathan warned Isaac to be more careful about the second dropoff, and while he still came down at the limits of the craft's capabilities, he didn't threaten their physical safety.

Of course, the rest of the Centurions gave Spot shit for not being able to handle the pressure. Clones were supposed to be physically superior to born humans, but Isaac had managed the maneuver and she hadn't. Now that she was awake and unharmed, it was amusing.

The Parabellum bounced slightly as it touched down, the back of the hold already open and waiting to dispense Beta Squad.

"Let's move, Centurions," Nathan said, leading the charge off the ship. His alloy-clad feet echoed along the metal deck of the ship, and then turned to thuds as he moved out onto the hard-packed ground. They were nearly five kilometers from the city, on the far side of a hill that had helped block their approach. They had thirty minutes to cover the distance and get in position to prevent Hanson from interrupting Alpha Squad's mission.

The Parabellum lifted again behind them, tracking north as it ascended into the clouds. Nathan didn't watch it go, already running toward the hill south of them.

The outskirts of the city were like so many places in the world. Empty and abandoned. The houses were run down, the paint faded, the vegetation overgrown. There were sections rich with graffiti, some of it still legible beneath the grime.

DEMONS GO BACK TO HELL

That was the one that caught Nathan's eye. It was painted in faded red across an old billboard large enough that he could see it from a couple of kilometers away. How many times had he thought the same thing in the months since he had come to Earth? He had been made on Proxima a long time ago, but it hadn't taken long for him to consider this planet his home.

His thoughts turned to Edenrise. It had fared so much better than Sanisco because of the shield. People had more time to run. More time to escape.

But it had still fallen. There were five thousand survivors out there, sailing north. Maybe they were safe from the enemy because they were surrounded by ocean and hard to spot. Or maybe they were already dead.

He had no way to know. He was going to assume they were alive until he had proof they weren't. Until he was able to get back to his people, hopefully having defeated Vyte. The odds were bad, but that wasn't anything he wasn't used to. He believed in the people they had assembled, and he was surprisingly grateful to General Haeri for delivering Rico and the other Centurions. Their chance of success was slim, but at least they had a chance.

And they had a pissed off Sheriff Duke.

He felt sorry for the bad guys.

Beta Squad continued south, making their way to a road that cut through the outskirts of the city. Old storefronts lined both sides of the streets, silent and empty. Birds nested on their rooftops, squawking as the Centurions ran past. Nathan checked his HUD. Sensors were clear, but he remembered what Caleb had said about the reapers. They were invisible to normal detection. Eyeballs only.

"Stay alert," he cautioned, sweeping the area. Hayden hadn't gotten this far north in his efforts to clear the area of trife, so there was a chance the lesser Relyeh could be hiding nearby unless Hanson had already cleared them out.

The Centurions stayed on the road at a solid run, the enhanced strength and stamina of the clones enabling them to cover the five kilometers in twenty minutes. It took them to the edge of Seattle proper, near the spire that rose high above the surrounding buildings. A nearby sign identified it as the *Space Needle*.

There was no contact with the enemy. No trife. No xaxkluth. No reapers. Nothing. Nathan hated the entire concept of *too quiet*, but he couldn't shake the sense that it was exactly that.

Something had to give.

"Alpha One, this is Beta One," Nathan said, linking to the general comm. "We're in position, ready to make our approach."

"Roger, Beta One," Hayden replied. "We're set and ready. Still awaiting contact with the package."

"Alpha One, this is Parabellum," Isaac said. The dropship was somewhere over their heads, hidden in the clouds. "Last sensor output had the target incoming as estimated. T-minus ten minutes to contact."

"Sheriff, the city is dead," Nathan said. "Either we're about to step into a massive trap or Bryant sent us to the wrong place."

"No," Hayden countered. "They're here. They're waiting. I'm sure of it. Find a strong position and be ready to move as soon as we have contact."

"Roger, Alpha."

"Parabellum, I want Delta Squad on its way in at t-minus two minutes. Delta, you'll need to adjust to the source on the fly."

"Literally," Max said. "Hahahaha. Hahaha."

"Roger, Alpha," Caleb said. "We're ready to go at the mark."

Nathan swept his eyes across the landscape and then matched it with the tactical grid on his HUD, which offered an isometric view of the city as captured by the Parabellum. "Centurions, let's move ahead slowly. I'm marking the route now. Lucius, Jesse, stay back. Bounding overwatch."

"Roger, General," the two Centurions replied.

Nathan and Spot started forward together, stopping as they made it under the Space Needle, using the base as cover, while Lucius and Jesse caught up and then ranged ahead. They stopped at the corner of the first building, covering him and Spot during their approach.

There was still no sign of the enemy, and it was making Nathan increasingly uncomfortable.

"Alpha, I have a bad feeling," he said.

"I've had a bad feeling since the Wheat," Hayden replied. "We don't have a lot of options. We have to see this through."

"Roger." Nathan gripped his rifle more tightly, keeping it up and ready to fire. He and Spot leapfrogged ahead of Lucius and Jesse, reaching a second intersection just as Isaac's panicked voice shouted out into the general comm.

"Oh shit, Sheriff," he said. "I've got contacts popping up all over my sensors."

Nathan checked his HUD and then swept the streets ahead with his eyes. "Parabellum, visual is clear."

"Parabellum, I have no targets," Hayden said.

"No," Isaac said. "Not on the street." He was nearly breathless. "Not on the ground. Oh hell. Above, Sheriff. They're coming from above. Ships. Dozens of ships."

## 52

### Caleb

"Ships?" Caleb questioned over the squad comm, frowning as he looked to Max for an answer.

"Vyte's ships, no doubt," Max replied.

At least, this time he didn't laugh.

"Parabellum," Sheriff Duke said through the general comm. "You need to clear the area. Delta, you need to drop asap."

"Sheriff, we need to abort the mission," Isaac said. "We have twenty minutes before the ships reach the atmosphere."

"The package is due to arrive in ten. I'm not leaving without it. Delta, I want you on the ground. Parabellum, I want you out of the immediate area. We can't afford to lose our transportation."

Caleb had a feeling Isaac was going to continue the argument. But there was no time to argue. He hurried to the hold's smaller side hatch and hit the control pad to open it, the cold wind immediately beginning to buffet him.

"Colonel, what are you doing?" Isaac asked.

"Sheriff Duke's right, Ike. We lose the interlink, we lose the war. We lose the Parabellum, we lose our mobility. We need both. Follow your orders and get the hell out of here, Marine."

"Yes, sir," Isaac replied.

Caleb glanced back at Max. "Are you ready?"

"Are you?" the Intellect replied.

Caleb leaned out of the hatch and looked down. He couldn't see the city past the clouds.

*Are you sure the Skin can handle this?*

"Max, if you're not sure the Skin can handle this you better tell me now" Caleb said.

"Like I showed you," Max replied. "It'll be fun. Hahaha. Hahaha."

Caleb took a deep breath. Yeah, loads of fun.

Then he jumped.

It wasn't the first time he had fallen from height. It wasn't even the first time he had leaped out of an aircraft at high speed. He had survived both prior efforts, but not without some injury and a good deal of pain, and that was with Ishek to put his body back together and speed up his healing. He wasn't looking forward to going through it again, and hopefully he wouldn't have to. Max had unlocked portions of the Skin he never knew about. Parts that hadn't been added to the Inahri software that ran the Axon technology, but were there now.

Wind whipped past Caleb, though he hardly felt it through the head-to-toe Skin. He held his arms out, letting gravity pull him down and feeling a sense of freedom from the fall. A peacefulness and serenity he knew would end all too soon. He savored the moment until Max took him out of it.

"We need to go faster," the Intellect said.

Caleb turned his head to see Max tuck his arms at his sides and put his head down, shooting forward toward terminal velocity. Caleb did the same to follow, diving into the clouds. His vision was filled with pure white, the seconds ticking past. He reached twenty when he broke through the clouds, rushing headlong at the city below. He quickly found the Space Needle to the north, and the interstate to the south, the positions of Alpha and Beta squads highlighted on his HUD.

"Max, anything?" Caleb asked.

"Negation."

*Something is down there, Caleb. It's blocking me from the Collective.*

Caleb didn't like the sound of that. Anything strong enough to keep he and Ishek off the Collective promised to be a lot to handle on its own, never mind whatever backup was preventing Ishek from being able to sense it.

"Keep trying," he said. "Alpha, Beta, Ishek says there's something down there."

"Can you be more specific?" Nathan asked.

"No. But I don't think it's anything we've seen before."

"Fascinating," Nathan replied sarcastically.

"Alpha, I'm pulling out," Isaac said. "Heading east to the other side of the mountains."

"Roger, Parabellum," Hayden said. "We'll meet you there."

*Assuming we survive.*

Watching the ground approach, Caleb ignored Ishek's pessimistic comment. Two thousand meters to go. They were angling toward the center of the city, but he wanted to do more to make a difference. "It would be nice if you could give me a location, Ish."

*It will hurt.*

"Just do it."

The sudden pressure nearly caused Caleb to lose consciousness. He began to spin in the air, falling instead of diving, his body momentarily going limp.

"Caleb?" Max said, noticing immediately.

The pressure vanished almost as quickly as it had come, but a lingering burn spread across his body. He struggled and failed miserably to regain control of his limbs, tumbling off course across the sky.

"Caleb!" Max shouted, watching the human tumble out of control across the sky.

Caleb could hear the Intellect, but he couldn't respond. His mouth was numb. What the hell did you do to me, Ishek?

*It was a defense. I couldn't defeat it. I'm sorry.*

Caleb's heart pounded and he gritted his teeth, trying with everything he had to reacquire control of his body. The city was getting large below, and if he hit the ground at this speed, even the Advocate couldn't save them.

But Max could.

The Intellect wrapped its arms around him, pulling him violently around to face him. He wrapped his arms around Caleb's arms and his ankles around Caleb's.

"Activate the Skin," Max told him. "Or we'll both be destroyed. Hahaha. Haha."

Caleb froze for a moment, his mind still a few seconds behind. Then he squinted his eye, navigating the Skin's menu to the new deployment.

The top layers of nanocells along the Skin began to reconfigure, forming into a thin film that stretched from the top of his wrists down to his ankles. The film caught the air and held it, the extra surface area suddenly slowing their fall.

"Good. Now pick a landing spot."

Caleb eyed the city below. No movement. No sign of the enemy. Nothing on his HUD. But something was down there.

And thanks to Ishek, he realized he knew where.

## 53

### Nathan

Nathan and the Centurions moved through the streets, having swapped their leapfrog for a diamond formation, with Lucius facing the rear. It was a slower, safer approach, one that left them covered no matter where the enemy appeared.

"Alpha, I'm pulling out," Isaac said over the general comms. "Heading east to the other side of the mountains."

Sheriff Duke responded, so Nathan didn't bother. A quick check of his HUD showed Nathan the dropship was leaving the theater, heading off to hide from the coming storm.

Rico had come to Earth to warn them that a Relyeh assault was imminent, but Isaac had said ships. Plural. This wasn't the warship they were all expecting. The warship that would be days ahead of schedule if it arrived now. This was something else.

A preemptive strike? Or had Krake or Hanson gotten word to Vyte that they were in trouble, and this was the result? Either way, they had twenty minutes to make something happen, and then they were going to be in deep shit.

"General, look," Jesse said, motioning with her hand.

Nathan looked up, spotting the small shapes of Caleb and Max as they dove through the sky, headed for the center of the city—still a couple of klicks ahead. The original plan had called for them to jump in once the fighting had already started, landing in the greatest area of need and taking the enemy by surprise. The arrival of the ships had scrapped that idea, forcing them to jump early and leaving them as a tertiary part of the regular attack force.

"Oh no," Jesse said as one of the shapes lost the smoothness of its dive and began rotating in the sky, tumbling and falling awkwardly.

Caleb.

At first, Nathan thought the Marine was unconscious, but the ATCS registered him as green. Awake and alert. He kept watching as Max changed its vector and streaked across the sky, grabbing Caleb and holding fast. Then they vanished behind one of the buildings.

"Let's find them, Centurions," Nathan said, adjusting the plan. He hadn't seen the outcome of the landing, but considering Caleb's unexpected situation there was a good chance he was in trouble.

The Centurions stayed with him as he angled to the southeast, following the marks of the two members of Delta Squad on his HUD. Caleb's status was still green, indicating he was okay, but Nathan had already seen Caleb suffer for reasons completely unrelated to anything physical.

"Nathan."

The voice came from the alley to Nathan's left. Nathan turned toward it, squinting his eyes to get a better look at the figure standing in the shadows.

"What are you doing here, Nathan?" James said, stepping out of the darkness. He was wearing powered armor similar to Nathan's own, though there were score marks and burns along the outside of the shell, in the exact spots where Nathan had once created them.

"James?" Nathan said, coming to a stop in the middle of the street.

"General?" Spot said. "What's going on? Why did you stop?"

"You shouldn't be here, brother," James said. "This is no place for you."

Nathan stared at his clone-twin. In his logical mind, he knew James was dead and couldn't really be here. But his logical mind suddenly wasn't guiding him.

Something else was.

"General?" Jesse said.

"This is a place for the dead, Nathan," James said. "A place of death. I'm dead because of you."

"I had to," Nathan said. "Sheriff Duke—"

"Sheriff Duke?" James hissed. "Really? You picked some crazy Earther over your own brother?"

"You were trying to bring the Others to enslave us."

"That would've been better than what you've got now, don't you think?"

"General," Jesse said. "Whatever you see, it isn't there."

"Hallucinating," Spot said. "But the Axon isn't here yet."

"Unless there's another one nearby," Lucius said.

"Yeah, but where?" Jesse said.

Nathan didn't notice what they were doing, but he could hear their questioning voices behind him. He was hallucinating. Part of him knew that. But he couldn't help himself.

"You can't be here, Nathan," James said. "This is a place for the dead. Unless…"

James trailed off, his eyes dropping suggestively to the magazine of grenades connected to Nathan's rifle.

"No," Nathan said. "You aren't real. I've dealt with this shit before. I'm not going for it."

He closed his eyes. This wasn't real. He could beat the weapon if he stayed focused. The hallucinations were powerful, but they weren't unbreakable. He could overcome them.

He had to overcome them.

He opened his eyes. James was still there, laughing at him.

"Screw you," Nathan said.

"No, Nathan," James replied. "Screw you."

"Reaper!" Lucius shouted behind him.

Nathan spun around, reacting to the call.

Except his HUD was clear.

He faced Lucius, who had his rifle pointed at him. "Reaper!" he shouted again, finger moving on the trigger.

Nathan took a subconscious step back as Lucius started shooting, his rounds hitting Nathan's armored shell, which flared with blue energy as the shields Max had given him activated, deflecting the bullets without letting them even scuff the alloy.

"Reaper!" Spot shouted, adding to the chaos by jumping away from him as if a reaper had suddenly appeared in their midst. She started shooting too, her bullets pounding the energy shield.

Nathan lunged toward Lucius, reaching for the Centurion's rifle with his free hand. Lucius swung away, trying to retreat.

"Reaper!" Spot cried out again. Only her aim had changed. Her bullets ripped past Lucius, a few of the rounds hitting his armor.

"Damn it," Nathan growled. He tackled Spot, dragging her to the ground. "Stop!"

"General," Jesse said softly. Nathan looked up. Jesse wasn't facing him. She was looking at something else in the distance. Something that caused her to drop her rifle and reach for her helmet.

"Jesse, it isn't real," Nathan said. "Buckets on, Centurions!"

She grabbed her helmet in one hand and dropped it to the ground. Her other hand was reaching for her sidearm.

Spot writhed beneath Nathan, trying to pull herself out from under him. From under the reaper she believed he was. Lucius rose from cover, aiming at him. Jesse continued to raise her sidearm toward her head.

"Help me," she said softly.

Nathan's heart pounded, his head throbbing. He could still see James near the alley.

"You had your chance, Nathan," James said.

"No," Nathan replied. There was one way to stop the neural disruption. It was temporary, but maybe it would be enough.

He activated his armor's external speakers, cranking them up and coughing. The sharp sound caused the speakers to squeal, and the sudden noise neutralized the neural disruptor, causing the hallucinations to fade. James disappeared while Jesse lowered her hand, turning her head toward Nathan with a terrified expression on her face.

She was right to be terrified, but for the wrong reasons.

Nathan slowly pulled himself to his feet, looking around. His HUD was suddenly active. Very active.

The hallucinations had been a distraction. A means to an end, not an end in itself.

Nearly two dozen real flesh and blood reapers surrounded them, ready to pounce.

## 54

### Hayden

Hayden was looking back at the city when Caleb and Max broke through the clouds. He checked the time, and then his HUD, matching the positions of the various units and trying to estimate how the inception was going to play. The incoming alien ships were a complication he would never have expected, making an already stressful situation all the more intense.

According to Isaac, the Axon was still on the move, driving up the highway toward the ruined city right on schedule. It was due to pass Bennett's position within the next two minutes, while the alien spacecraft were still fifteen minutes out.

That would leave them twelve minutes to stop Krake, take back the interlink and get somewhere, safely undercover before the ships arrived. There was no question they were headed for this position. No doubt they had timed their arrival with Krake's.

## Isolation

But why?

It didn't make a lot of sense. If there was a portal in the city, Vyte didn't need ships to ensure the interlink made it off-world. All Krake had to do was step through it and shut it down, and both the Axon and the interlink would be completely out of their reach.

Maybe he was wrong. Maybe the ships weren't here specifically for Krake.

Maybe they were just the start of something else.

Something bigger.

The xaxkluth had been the first wave, made to remove the competition in the form of the trife. Ordered to take out the largest human threats and the biggest and more powerful settlements. Not only Edenrise and Sanisco but wherever they were around the world. With that done, they could begin to terraform the planet. To start weaving webs of hardened ichor and prepare the world for the coming of the Hunger.

The Relyeh didn't have unfettered access to Axon portals. Even Vyte couldn't send entire armies through the doors. He had to have those armies in a place with a portal to send to a place with a portal. The ships were the second option. The other method of transportation to a planet.

First, the Hunger subdues the planet.

Then they enslave it.

The ships were carrying the next wave. Now

that pockets of survivors were more isolated from one another than ever, a new, more intelligent Relyeh race could begin to harvest those pockets, rounding up survivors as resources to feed into their universe-spanning machine.

The thought made Hayden's blood run cold. They would need a lot more than a couple dozen ships, but what if there were a lot more out there, either further behind the vanguard or spreading around the planet, preparing to strike?

After two centuries of clinging to survival and fighting for hope, would Earth crumble within a matter of days?

Not if he could help it.

"Sheriff, I've got a visual on the car," Bennett said, his sharp voice breaking Hayden out of his reverie. His head whipped back to the south. He couldn't see the car yet, but it had appeared on his ATCS, marked through his helmet as a red dot in the distance.

He moved over the pile of discarded wrecks, getting even closer to the road. Timing was everything. They had fourteen minutes from now to finish the mission and get the hell out.

And then what?

Could they get the data they needed and find a means to make the interlink work for them? Could they use it to destroy the xaxkluth the way they had planned? Would it even matter? The xaxkluth were only one Relyeh race. They would have to do more than that.

But it was a start, and he wasn't going to give up. He wasn't going to let his family die for nothing.

"Alpha Squad, get ready," he said into the comm. "The package is in the zone."

He expected a series of confirmations to follow from Alpha, but no one replied.

"Alpha, do you copy? Confirm ready."

Nothing.

Hayden glanced at the situation map. Drake, Rico, and Bennett were still in position. They were available on the network. Why weren't they responding?

Then Drake moved suddenly, his mark on the map going forward, too close to the edge of the raised highway where he had perched. Hayden swung his head back to get visual on the position.

Just in time to watch the Centurion leap from the platform, fall ten meters, and crash into the rubble below. His body rolled down the side of the debris, his status marker turning red in Hayden's helmet.

What the hell?

"Rico," Hayden said. "Do you copy? Come in."

He spun around, looking for signs of the enemy. Drake was hallucinating. It was the only thing that made any sense. But Krake was still too far out to use neural disruption as a weapon, and there was nothing else here. Or was there? If Rico and

Bennett were affected, there would have to be at least two or three Axon in the area.

"Damn it," he cursed, looking back down the road. Krake was still bearing down. Getting closer.

"Hayden."

Natalia's voice stole his attention, forcing him to turn again. He saw her there, in the middle of the road in full combat armor minus the bucket, rifle in hand and ready to join the fight.

"Nat?" he said.

"I thought you could use some backup."

"Nat, you can't be here."

Natalia smiled. "I can't let you do this alone. They killed Hallia, Hayden. They killed Ginny."

Tears sprang into Hayden's eyes. "I know." He stared at her, soaking in her face. "I'll make them pay for that."

"We'll make them pay," Natalia corrected, raising her rifle and swinging the muzzle toward him.

Hayden's eyes narrowed. He glared at Natalia, a tide of anger rising within him. This was a trick. A damn, dirty trick. He had dealt with the Axon hallucinations before. He wasn't immune to them. Not really. But he was sick and tired of their bullshit.

"No. Whoever you are, I'm coming for you, you son of a bitch. I've just got some other business first."

Then he pivoted, turning south and drawing his revolvers. The anger increased his blood pressure. It released adrenaline. It made his head pound, interrupting the signals the Axon were flinging to make him see things that weren't there. He couldn't get rid of them, but he could identify them for what they were.

The modbox was directly ahead of him now and closing fast. Too fast. Hayden opened fire, a dozen rounds loosed from the pair of guns inside of three seconds, each of them punching into the cage wrapped around the car, four of them piercing the windshield beyond the metal and powering through. One of them hit the Axon driver, too surprised to activate its shields in time. The round hit the edge of its face, leaving a deep gash through its Skin and drawing blood from its face.

Krake didn't flinch, the car roaring as it accelerated a little more. Hayden dropped his guns and jumped, tucking his shoulder as the modbox barreled into him. His augment slammed into the cage over the windshield, crumpling the metal bars inward until physics pushed him up and over the roof. He spun in the air, the vehicle continuing beneath him as he reached out in a desperate grab.

He grabbed onto one of the spikes protruding from the trunk and held on as tightly as his augment would allow. He was jerked to a sudden, painful stop, the momentum wrenching at the already damaged control ring and threatening to rip the limb away.

The physical pain was worse than anything he

had ever felt before, and it intensified as his body swung down and hit the back of the car, the spikes there scraping against his combat armor, one of them punching through and impaling his leg.

He cried out, the sound lost in the whine of the motor and the rumbling of the ground beneath the wheels. Krake didn't look back and didn't slow, leaving Hayden caught on the car while it stayed its course toward the city. He gritted his teeth while he looked at his HUD. There was no sign of Rico or Bennett. Both had vanished from the network. Were they dead?

Hayden almost wished he was. Almost. Every part of his body hurt, his arm most of all. But Krake and the interlink were within his reach, and he would be damned if he was going to let either get away.

## 55

### Caleb

"Caleb."

Caleb looked up from his position on his stomach. Riley Valentine stood over him, her sharp, accusing eyes glaring at him past her overly beakish nose.

"Valentine," he snarled. He knew where he was. Face down on the street in Seattle. He knew what she was too. A forced figment of his imagination. An apparition the enemy he had bounced off in the Collective had caused his mind to make real. "You're not here."

He was still trying to come to terms with what had happened. The sudden pressure and pain of Ishek's push, and the vibration of the push back. That single, nearly fatal instant had given him two crucial pieces of information. One, he knew where the enemy was. Two, he knew they were some kind of twisted amalgamation of Relyeh and Intellect. A monster embedded with a machine.

"You let me down, Marine," Valentine said. "You call yourself a Raider? Are you kidding? I gave you one job. One simple job a damn monkey could have done." She raised pistol toward his face.

Caleb stared at the gun. It didn't matter that part of his mind knew it wasn't real. The other part that saw her, heard her, had decided it was. And it would determine the bullet that left the gun was real too, along with the deadly wound it would cause.

"My use for you is at an end," Valentine said, finger moving on the trigger.

She vanished before she could shoot.

"Get up," Max said, pushing himself off Caleb's back. "We need to stop it before it kills everyone."

Caleb pulled himself to his feet and glanced at the Intellect. "You mean the hallucinations?"

"The neural disruption, yes. The signal is powerful. Stay within a few meters, or you'll be outside my ability to jam it."

"I know where it's coming from," Caleb said.

"Affirmation. Lead the way. Hahaha. Haha."

Caleb looked at the Skin's HUD, which Max had hacked to connect to the combat network. They were a few blocks from Stacker's position, which was in the opposite direction of the target. It appeared Beta Squad was in trouble. Red marks surrounded the unit, which itself was spread out in a disorganized pattern. Not only were they likely seeing things, but they had real threats all around them.

He had to make a choice. Go for the Axon and Relyeh hybrid creating the disruption to give the unit a fighting chance against the opposition or double back and save the Centurions.

"Consideration. Their lives don't matter in the larger equation," Max said, apparently looking at the same data he was taking in. It was a cold, callous statement to make, but what should he expect from a machine? "Sheriff Duke is equivalently exposed."

That was the more important point. If Hayden was hallucinating, Krake could waltz right past him without interference and the interlink would be gone. In that sense, Max was right. If that happened, Stacker's life wouldn't matter because it would already be too late.

It was an impossible situation with no good choices. But those were reapers surrounding Beta Squad. He had frozen them before. He could do it again and buy them time.

*We can't. We're too weak.*

Caleb could sense the damage Ishek had taken. While the Advocate would heal, it would still take time they didn't have.

And he was wasting time trying to make a decision. He turned in the direction of the hybrid. "Let's go," he said to Max, breaking into an all-out sprint.

Max reacted instantly, running behind him and then quickly catching up. They sprinted up the street, away from Stacker and Beta Squad. It burned Caleb to leave them to fend for themselves, but what else could he do?

He had triangulated the location of the hybrid on the way down. Now he looked to where it was stationed, his eyes landing on the rusted metal framework of what appeared to have once been a series of geodesic spheres. Metal catwalks were visible inside the spheres among overgrown weeds and vegetation.

Caleb remembered having seen the structure online, back when the trife were still something dreamed up in a sci-fi novel. It had once been filled with all kinds of plants, designed as a relaxing retreat for the employees of the company that built it. The hybrid was in there somewhere, out of sight within the brush.

"There," Caleb said, pointing it out to Max.

"Affirmation," Max replied. "I should have calculated. It's using the structure to amplify the disruption."

"If we damage the structure, can we break the amplification?"

"Possibility."

Caleb used his eyes to activate the Skin's weapon systems. He pointed his hand at the building, lifting his palm toward it and releasing a blast of energy.

The blue beam hit the frame, cutting through one of the rusted cross beams.

Almost immediately, the red marks near Beta began to move, turning away from the Centurions and heading in their direction. More reapers appeared ahead, suddenly pouring out of the surrounding buildings in response to the direct attack.

"I don't think it liked that," Max said. "Hahaha. Haha."

"Then it isn't going to like this," Caleb replied, sending out another beam that sliced the first bar completely from the structure. It dropped and bounced off a lower portion before crashing to the ground.

"You'll need to cut eight more bars to have a beneficial effect," Max said.

"You know which ones to hit. You cut the pipes while I kill reapers."

"Confirmation."

Caleb swept his eyes across the tide of incoming human-trife hybrids.

"Knuckle up, Card," he whispered, steeling himself against the approaching horde. He raised both palms, gathering power from the Skin and taking aim. There were just so many. "Ishek, if you can give me anything, now is the time."

*I'll do my best.*

"So will I."

He unleashed the energy beams from the Skin, the first blast tearing a reaper in half while the second cut off another's legs. He shifted his hands and fired again, sending out bursts of energy as quickly as he could, dropping a creature with almost every shot.

Max fired at the structure, energy slicing through the old frame and breaking the beams away. A second one fell to the ground, quickly followed by a third.

But the reapers were closing fast.

Caleb continued to spew energy as quickly as he could, killing the Relyeh one after another, and opening spaces at the front of the line that were almost immediately filled by others. He checked his HUD, watching the red marks approaching from behind. He pivoted, aiming his hands in two different directions and firing without aiming. There were so many reapers it was almost impossible to miss; even the most wayward shots did damage.

It wasn't enough. The reapers continued to close, adjusting their ranks to create a collapsing circle around the pair.

Max kept shooting, another beam falling away. The structure started to groan, threatening to collapse from the damage.

"Ishek, help me!" Caleb growled, heart pounding as the front lines closed within ten meters. His power levels had already drained to nearly fifty percent. He couldn't keep this up for long.

A change in pressure in Caleb's head signaled

the surge of Ishek's power. Two of the reapers changed direction suddenly, leaping at the Relyeh closest to them. The creatures got tangled together as they fought, pushing into others and disrupting the entire group. Two more did the same a second later, the sudden chaos slowing the whole line.

"Max, time?" Caleb shouted.

"Twenty seconds," Max replied, cutting another beam away. "Hahahaha. Hahaha. Haha."

They were almost there.

It wasn't going to be enough.

One of the reapers got close enough to lunge at Max, distracting him while he turned and batted the creature aside, blasting it at the same time he knocked it aside. Caleb pivoted in that direction, shooting at a second reaper and then a third, taking out the fastest of the creatures. The rest of the horde continued to close. Eight meters. Seven. Six.

The seventh beam fell.

At that moment, Caleb realized that even if they stopped the hallucinations, even if they got Alpha and Beta back into the fight, there was a good chance it wasn't going to be enough. There were too many Relyeh, and killing them was taking too long. The alien ships would be here soon. So would Krake.

The horde would stop them before they could stop *it*.

Five meters. Four.

Caleb continued unleashing energy from the

Skin. Maybe he would go down, but he would go down fighting. He turned to face the structure, eyeing the reapers ahead.

*Are you insane?*

Then he charged, rushing forward to meet them, shouting out loud. He was ready to dive into their midst when a blast of plasma swept into them, knocking a handful aside. Another followed, and then another, arcing down from the Parabellum as it strafed across the field.

Caleb looked up at it as it went past, unsure whether to cheer Isaac's bravery or curse his stupidity. He was supposed to have left the area, not play hero.

There was nothing he could do about it now. The unexpected air assault did succeed in throwing the reapers into greater disarray, freezing their advance for a precious few seconds. Caleb found new targets to shoot, still blasting at the creatures with the sinking understanding that even the aid of the dropship wasn't going to be enough.

"Completion!" Max shouted victoriously as the last of the beams broke away, and one of the spheres collapsed on itself with a clang and a rumble.

The reapers froze as one for a moment, as if they were all receiving new instructions in the wake of the collapse. Then they resumed their assault as if nothing had happened.

But something had indeed happened.

The amplification was gone. The neural disruption range was now limited. The reason for the hybrid to stay out of the fight had ended.

Caleb didn't see the attack coming. He only felt the result. One moment, he was facing down a pair of reapers. The next, a large, dark shape exploded from the spheres. One of its tentacles snapped out and hit him hard in the chest, throwing him backwards like a rag doll. He landed on his back a dozen meters away.

Squarely in the middle of the reaper horde.

## 56

### Rico

Rico froze suddenly, her head clearing, her eyes snapping down to the piece of rusted rebar jutting out from a chunk of concrete, her heart racing.

She had been two seconds away from impaling herself on the metal bar. Two seconds from ending her life in grief over the loss of her husband.

She knew it for the hallucination it was. She knew Austin hadn't really been there, urging her to do it and join him in the afterlife. But she hadn't been able to stop herself, hadn't been able to convince herself of what she knew to be true.

And then it ended, just like that. The grip on her mind vanished, and she knew where she was and what she had been about to do.

She swallowed dryly and looked at her HUD. Tried to anyway. Shaking off the last of her fugue, she realized she wasn't wearing it. "Damn it," she huffed, spinning quickly, searching for it, but she didn't see it anywhere.

Her eyes swept across the road, her mind shifting gears. Hayden. Krake. She cursed again. How much time had she wasted caught up in the hallucination?

She heard noises in the distance. Screaming. Howling. Shouting. She looked to the city in time to see the Parabellum sweep over, firing plasma down at something. Was Isaac hallucinating too?

Her eyes caught motion on the road. A car headed for the city, someone clinging to—no, dangling from—the back of it, stuck there to a spike.

Hayden.

"Damn it," she said a third time. She didn't have time to find her helmet. She started running, sprinting across the landscape behind the car. As a clone, she had enhanced strength and stamina, and she ran faster than even the fastest unmodified humans. She knew she had no chance to catch the car before it reached its destination, but she could get there just a few minutes behind it. Maybe.

She vaulted a large chunk of concrete, tucking and rolling back to her feet on the other side. Sprinting ahead, she slowed a step when Bennett emerged from around an old bus.

"Bennett?" Confused, she stumbled to a stop, frowning at him. How had he gotten ahead of her without seeing her? And if he had seen her, why hadn't he tried to help her?

He looked back, slowing as she approached. "Are you okay?"

She nodded. "Yeah. You?"

"I'm fine," he replied.

"The hallucinations didn't bother you?" she asked.

"Funny thing," he said with an expression bordering on a laugh. "My hallucination was that I was chasing a xaxkluth that had grabbed you and was carrying you away."

Rico took a few steps toward him, coming to a stop a couple of meters away. "That's convenient," she said with a smile, trying not to look as suspicious as she felt. Nothing leading up to this point had given her any reason to think Bennett wasn't what he claimed, but that was changing in a hurry.

"I know, right? We need to hurry, Rico. Our people are in trouble."

Rico didn't move right away. She remembered what General Haeri had told her. Bennett was programmed to follow her orders. He had to comply. It was a gray-area process that made clones too much line machines, but it would settle her doubts.

"I want you to wait here," she said.

"What? Why?"

"That's my order, Sergeant. Wait here."

Bennett's eyes narrowed. "You're going to get our people killed. What the hell are you thinking?"

"What are you?" she asked, raising her rifle toward him.

"Rico, are you hallucinating again? It's me. Austin."

The name froze her. Austin? "What game are you—?"

His hand came up in a blur, still rising as the gun in it discharged. She moved just far enough, just fast enough to avoid the worst of the shot. The round came within centimeters of taking her between the eyes. It still burned as it grazed the side of her face, ripping away her ear. She cried out. Still falling sideways, she triggered her rifle, the spray of bullets catching Bennett in the armor, most of the rounds unable to punch through.

He kept shooting, but his best chance was lost. The bullets hit her combat armor, unable to pierce the hardened plates.

Rico rolled when she hit the ground, wasting no time getting back to her feet. Bennett was reaching for the rifle on his back, swinging it around. She lunged at him, interrupting the grab and forcing him to grapple with her. They fell to the ground as one.

Rico tried to wrap her hands around Bennett's neck, but she couldn't get past his helmet. Bennett didn't have the same problem, able to get his hands around her neck and squeeze.

"I'm sorry, Rico," he said. "I was only here to observe. But then that Intellect showed up and changed all the rules. I tried to get him out of the equation, but you didn't go for it. You trusted it over me."

Rico struggled to breathe, wrapping her hands around his forearms and trying to pull them away. Hayden had made the right choice with Max. There was a snake in their midst, but it wasn't the Axon.

"How?" she croaked out, straining to overcome him. They were both clones. Both strong. But he was still stronger.

"Clone Replicators are machines. The Axon are good with machines. I am sorry, Rico. Really. But I am what I am. What they created me to be. You're a clone. You should understand. We don't get to decide what we are. We just are."

She did understand. She had enjoyed her time as a Centurion, but it was still the thing she was created to be. At least in the beginning. She had grown beyond her initial purpose. She had found things that had changed her trajectory. Love. Friends. Another purpose here on Earth.

And now it was all going to end.

The world was fading away, and she wasn't strong enough to break Bennett's hold. She let go of his forearms, her arms falling limply to the ground. She gathered herself to reach for the rim of his helmet. He didn't dare let go of her neck to stop her, allowing her to get it up and off him. She looked at his face. Austin's face. It softened under her gaze, and she thought she felt his grip relax just a little. There was still a part of Austin in there somewhere. Still a part of him that loved her.

If nothing else, at least his face would be the last thing she saw.

## 57

## Hayden

The modbox had to slow as it entered the city. While the roads appeared to have been cleared, the tighter confines and more frequent turns eased its overall pace.

Not that it was much help to Hayden. In fact, the shifting only made things worse. He held onto the back of the car with his augmented hands, his bad arm on fire around the control ring. He might have been flung away from the vehicle during the turns, but the spike through his leg held him in place, the car's movements jerking the filthy metal spike, tearing his leg muscle and grinding against bone. His entire body was wracked with pain.

He wasn't sure if his enhanced healing factor could withstand the damage. He wasn't sure he would survive, and if he did, would he ever walk again? Maybe another augment would be part of his future. That is, if he had a future. There was no time now to think about that. No time for anything. He was on a runaway train about to reach its destination.

He could hear the fighting somewhere ahead of them, mainly in the form of the enemy's guttural hisses and cries added to the rumbling of the Parabellum flying through the area, as low and slow as Ike dared.

Damn him for not following orders, for bringing the ship back into the city instead of making his escape. Ten minutes. That was all the time they had before the enemy ships arrived. Ten minutes to find some way to stop this invasion.

How was he going to accomplish it?

The car turned another corner, headed through the valley between a series of tall buildings. Most of them were still intact. Old and dilapidated but still upright. Hayden looked into the car at the back of Krake's head. It was still bleeding where the bullet had hit it, though it wasn't visibly bothersome to the alien. Krake also didn't seem to care he was stuck to the trunk. It had made no effort to dislodge him, much less pay any attention to him.

He looked past the Axon to the scene ahead, breathing in sharply as he did. He had heard the reapers from a few streets away. He had expected to see the large, human-trife hybrids. What he didn't expect was how many there were. Hundreds of them converged on a central spot in the middle of the road and what appeared to be a pair of geodesic metal domes.

While Hayden couldn't see what the hybrids were gathering for, he also couldn't miss the Relyeh that suddenly emerged from one of the domes. Four meters tall, black, leathery flesh, a human torso with three arms on each side and a pair of tentacles on each shoulder. Its bottom half was propped up on six spindly legs like a spider, its head generally humanoid and covered in glowing blue eyes.

Was that Hanson?

It moved with alarming speed, leaping forward and landing near the leading edge of the reapers, its tentacles snapping out away from it and slapping audibly against something two meters away. Hayden watched the force lift Caleb Card off the ground and into the air, throwing him back to land among the rest of the Relyeh creatures.

"Shit," he muttered, watching for Caleb to get up. The reapers around the Marine had turned toward him, ready to pounce.

A sudden flash of blue energy threw the closest reapers away from Caleb, burning them to bare bones. Caleb shoved himself upright, facing the spider-like Relyeh as it charged in for the kill.

Loud echoes of thunder rumbled to the west; the spider-creature screamed and ducked low as if dodging bullets. Some of the surviving reapers came around to face the new threat, only to find themselves filled with holes. A silver ball sank into their midst and detonated, blowing a few more away.

Hayden smirked, losing his view of the fight suddenly as the car turned right and headed up a cross-street, away from the fighting. Whatever Hanson had planned, it wasn't working out as well as the Relyeh had hoped. The neural disruption was broken, leaving the Centurions free to fight back. The odds were still horrible, but now they had a chance. It was up to them to seize it.

And it was up to Hayden to seize his. It didn't matter if he was injured. He had the best shot at killing Krake.

He wasn't going to miss it.

The car went two blocks over and turned left, running parallel to the fighting. Hayden caught glimpses of the battle through the openings between buildings, getting momentary views of Caleb squaring off against Hanson and a split-second look at Nathan and the Centurions charging up the street toward him, guns blazing. The Parabellum swooped overhead again, laying down another line of strafing plasma.

"Ike, damn it," Hayden growled into his comm. "If you can hear me, get the hell out of here."

"I'm sorry, Sheriff," Isaac replied. "I tried. Couldn't do it. We succeed or fail as one. You're going to get the interlink, and I'm going to bus you the hell out of here."

The car turned again, coming around the back

of the spheres. Hayden saw it then, through the vegetation. The simple black alloy of the Axon portal—a gateway to the universe.

It was currently inactive, the metal framework of the sphere visible through the overgrowth. But it was right there. So close.

Too close.

The car came to a stop a dozen meters away. The driver's side door swung open as Hayden pushed himself up, twisting and bending back to free his stuck leg. He was halfway to accomplishing it when Krake came up beside him, wordlessly grabbing him.

Ripping him from the spike, it threw him off the back of the car.

## 58

### Caleb

Caleb looked up from where he lay on his back. Five reapers surrounded him while the Parabellum streaked overhead, finishing another strafing run, framed by the gray, overcast skies.

The reapers scattered, each of them fleeing in whatever direction they could go. One was too slow, impaled by a long, thin, spider-like leg, leaving Caleb's view blotted out by the monstrous Relyeh that now loomed above him.

It reminded Caleb of the Relyeh Abominations he had encountered on Essex, though it was considerably smaller and less monstrous. Its purpose was the same. It made a noise in Caleb's face that sounded like a laugh, clacking its teeth and slavering in anticipation of ripping him apart.

*Kill it. It's Relyeh, but also Axon. The work of a twisted mind.*

Or a perfectly logical mind who had made a

creature specific to his needs. Relyeh, to relay commands from Nyarlath to the xaxkluth on Earth. Axon, to communicate with Krake, operate the portal, and set up this trap.

And that's what this was. A trap. A ruse to draw them out. The hallucinations should have done them in, but with all of Vyte's carefully laid plans, in all of his contingencies, he hadn't counted on the lowly humans receiving aid from another Axon.

He hadn't counted on Max.

Without it, the neural disruption would have turned them all against one another. If that had failed, the reapers would have finished them off. And if that had failed, this thing that he could only believe was Hanson was waiting to do the job itself.

His symbiosis with Ishek made the two of them one. It gave them a shared experience, a shared understanding. He had years of training as a Marine Raider. He understood tactics as well as anyone. Ishek had long served one of the Relyeh Ancients. It understood how the Relyeh thought and acted, plotted and planned. It understood how the war against the Axon had proceeded and why more subtle battles had been fought between them. Earth was an important planet to the two warring races, but not the only one. Similar scenes had and were being played out on other worlds hundreds of light years away. Too distant for them to ever reach without a gateway to step through.

They came to the same conclusion, though it frightened Caleb to make the connection.

The interlink, the portal. They were props. Krake was a damned diversion. He was sure of it. Vyte had identified the greatest threats to its success in the form of himself, Sheriff Duke and General Stacker—and no doubt General Haeri on Proxima.

It was like a game of chess, where each move didn't immediately impact the outcome, but set up another move later in the game, with the hope that their opponent didn't notice before it was too late.

Caleb had noticed.

And it was too late.

Or was it?

Max was a wild card Vyte hadn't expected and couldn't account for. A second queen placed onto the board against the rules. The Intellect had given them a twenty percent chance of success.

And right now, that seemed like good odds.

Caleb rolled to the side as another of Hanson's legs speared down toward him. He evaded the attack, feeling the leg brush past his back as he made it to his hands and knees. He threw himself forward to avoid another limb, only to find himself airborne a moment later as a tentacle wrapped around his waist and jerked him up.

He was only held for a moment. The crackling whine of Stacker's heavy railgun interrupted the capture, the rounds tearing the limb off near its root at Hanson's shoulder and dropping Caleb back to the ground. He landed on his hands and feet. Checking his HUD, he realized the network was fully online. Stacker was there with Jesse, Spot and Lucius. Max was close by. Hayden was...

He threw himself to the side, nearly caught by a reaper while he wasted time tracking his team. He rolled to his feet, turning and unleashing an energy bolt from his Skin that cut the reaper in half.

He spun around, looking for Hanson. The Relyeh had redirected its attention to Nathan and the Centurions, who were charging up the street from the east, guns blazing. A pair of thunks sounded, twin grenades arcing through the sky and landing amidst the reapers before detonating.

Stacker kept his assault focused on Hanson. Flares of blue energy captured most of the rounds now that Hanson was expecting them. The hybrid monster skittered forward without regard to the additional reapers on a direct route toward Stacker.

Caleb unleashed a beam of energy that should have caught Hanson in the back. Blue shields captured the blast instead. Hanson knew Caleb was behind him, and it was ready.

"Ish, any more tricks up our sleeves?"

*I'm exhausted, Caleb.*

"That's not what I asked you."

He could sense Ishek's reluctance. He understood how tired the Relyeh Advocate was. He felt the same exhaustion in his pounding head and racing heart already pumped full of adrenaline. He knew it was the only reason either one of them was still conscious.

*You still have the microspear.*

"It won't go through shields. You know that."

Caleb blasted a reaper coming at him from the side and then ran behind Hanson, trying to get back into the fight. Stacker was retreating now, using the jets on his armor to help take long jumps backward. Caleb watched him hit Hanson with a grenade, only to see the creature's shields absorb the assault.

A sharp scream caught his attention and he turned his head toward it, just in time to see Hanson's remaining tentacle lash out and grab Lucius. It pulled him into its multiple arms. Lucius screamed as the arms grabbed at him, ripping him apart in a wash of blood.

The sight twisted Caleb's stomach, even as Ishek's idea came into focus in his mind.

"Will that work?"

*Unknown until we try.*

"Max," Caleb said. "I need you to help me get Hanson's attention. Max?" The Intellect didn't reply. He was gone, and there was no time to try to find him.

He would have to do this himself.

"Stacker, do you copy?" Caleb said, opening the line to Beta Squad.

"A little busy," Stacker replied.

"I'm coming up behind Hanson. I need you to get to the other side of him."

"Are you kidding?"

"Come on, Stacker. I know you can do it."

"Roger."

Caleb grabbed the microspear from the Skin, holding it tight in his left hand as he hurried forward, ducking around a reaper that reached for him and sliding between two others. The reapers gave chase behind him, while Stacker landed on the ground in front of Hanson, standing his ground and firing ineffective grenades into the hybrid's shields.

Hanson laughed again, tentacle whipping out at Stacker, who ducked away from it with unexpected agility. He sprinted beneath its legs, slamming into one of them with his shoulder and knocking momentarily off-balance. He came out the other side just as Hanson spun around, lifting another leg to spear him in the back. The attack shoved Stacker forward, sending him sliding across the ground on his stomach.

"Come on!" Caleb shouted at Hanson, holding the microspear up so it could see the weapon.

Another laugh-like sound escaped the monstrosity. It lunged forward, lowering itself and sending its tentacle whipping at Caleb.

Caleb tried to turn aside, gritting his teeth as the tentacle caught him and lifted him toward its six reaching arms. He knew what would happen if they grabbed him.

*Now, Caleb.*

He closed his eyes.

And dropped the microspear.

Below, a single reaper shook slightly as Ishek and Caleb forced their way into its mind through the Collective, passing it a simple overriding order and watching the outcome through its eyes.

The reaper jumped up, its large, clawed hand catching the falling microspear. It landed unnoticed beneath Hanson as the hybrid grabbed Caleb's arms and legs, ready to tear them off.

Then the reaper jumped again, stabbing the microspear into Hanson's unprotected underbelly.

The effect was immediate. Hanson's laughter turned to a loud scream, one of its legs reaching out and stabbing the reaper, killing it too late to save itself. Caleb returned to his body and opened his eyes. A jolt of energy from his Skin burned away the limbs holding him, and he tumbled toward the ground, caught by Stacker before he could land.

"Gotcha," Stacker said, jets firing. He carried them away as Hanson spun in a tight circle, writhing in the throes of an excruciating death.

Its legs grabbed for anything they could find. It speared the reapers around it while the rest of the creatures began turning on one another, fighting for dominance with the impending loss of their leader.

Stacker landed where Jesse and Spot had paired up, beyond the sudden chaos of the Relyeh in-fighting. He lowered Caleb to his feet, supporting him while both he and Ishek gathered their strength.

Hanson continued to scream, its legs finally

giving way beneath it. It collapsed to the ground, trying to drag itself away, only to die a few seconds later.

"Thanks for the save, General," Caleb said, still light-headed and queasy. He wanted nothing more than to puke. He couldn't yet.

"Hayden," he said, checking his tactical. The Sheriff showed up orange. Injured but alive.

Hanson was dead, but it wasn't over yet.

# 59

## Hayden

Hayden landed roughly on the pavement, a new jolt of pain rising from his leg and the damaged control ring on his arm.

He rolled over, watching Krake open the trunk of the modbox and reach inside for the interlink. White-hot fury flowed into Hayden. The Axon had killed his family for that piece of technology. He pushed himself to his hands and knees, ignoring the pain and reaching for a microspear. He pulled it from his belt and drew his arm back to throw it.

Krake spun around, unleashing a line of blue energy, hitting Hayden's hand and burning off three of the augment's fingers. The weapon fell to the ground, but instead of turning back to the trunk, Krake took three quick steps toward Hayden.

Hayden tried to punch the Axon, but it caught his hand and twisted, the actuator in the elbow snapping. Hayden closed the fist of his other hand, the Axon metal forming into a blade. He tried to stab Krake, only to have the Axon block that too, its shields flaring blue as it captured his other arm.

Krake stared at Hayden. Hayden couldn't see its eyes behind the cowl of its Skin, but he could feel it looking at him. Not with anger or hatred, but with indifference.

"You killed my family," Hayden hissed. "I'm going to kill you."

It was a ridiculous statement considering the circumstances, but the Axon didn't laugh. Its voice was calm and flat. "You rejected the Master's offer. Now you are defeated. You have received only what you requested."

Hayden's eyes narrowed, the anger building. He hadn't asked for his wife and children to die. He hadn't asked for any of this.

Krake lifted him by his arms, easily pulling him off the ground. "You will live to suffer. You will live broken. For a short while longer, at least."

The Axon threw Hayden backward, sending him through the air. He landed hard on his back, knocking the air from his lungs, but he didn't stay down. He tried to stand up, and go after Krake, but his leg wouldn't support him. He collapsed on his face, left with one working augment to pull himself forward along the ground.

Krake returned to the trunk, lifting the satchel containing the interlink. It glanced back at Hayden and continued toward the portal.

"No," Hayden said, tasting dirt. He dragged himself forward on his one good arm. "I'm going to kill you."

He tried to move faster. He tried to keep up.

He couldn't.

"Stop."

Max materialized through the vegetation, stepping through the center of the inactive portal and coming to a stop in front of Krake.

"Intellect, move aside," Krake said.

"Negation. I don't follow orders from traitors."

"I am an organic. A Maker. You will comply."

"Negation. You were an organic. But no longer. You've accepted Vyte's integration. You have no power over me."

"I have other ways to make you move."

"Negation. I'd like to see you try. Hahaha. Haha."

Krake raised its hand, blue energy flaring from it. Max's shield activated, absorbing the blast.

"Pathetic," Max said. "Hahaha. Haha."

Krake lowered its hand. The two Axon stared at one another.

Hayden shifted his leg. The wound was healing, enough that he was able to put a little weight on it. He pulled himself up and stumbled forward, getting back to the car and using it for support.

He could tell Krake noticed the movement, but it didn't take its eyes off Max. "We can end the fighting, Intellect. We can gain control of the most powerful army in the universe. Help me bring this device back to the Master, and we will spare this world."

Max's head shifted slightly, giving Hayden the impression the faceless Intellect was looking at him. "Curiosity. What will you do with the most powerful army in the universe, and nothing left to fight?"

"We will expand across the universe. We will subdue everything in our path."

"That sounds just like the Hunger. Do you intend to use them or become them?"

"That is the only purpose for life forms like ours. The only goal that remains. Science. Technology. Learnedness. All a means to that end. Do you believe the Axon and the Relyeh are the only advanced races across the entirety of billions of light years? Combined, we will be unstoppable. The Axon will endure forever. *We* will endure forever."

"Negation. I won't let—"

A loud crack sounded to Hayden's left, and Max's head snapped sideways. The bullet blew a massive hole in it, spraying gobs of the gel-like material that composed the Intellect outward. Max collapsed to the ground.

Hayden turned his head toward the shooter, eyes narrowing when he saw Bennett standing there, behind the wreck of a car, one of Hayden's revolvers in hand.

"Don't just stand there!" Bennett shouted. "Vyte is waiting for you."

## Isolation

Hayden lunged at Krake. The Axon began spinning to face him, while Bennett swung his gun in Hayden's direction.

He never had a chance to pull the trigger.

Bullets ripped into the car Bennett was standing behind, punching through the metal and tearing into the clone, taking him down.

Hayden charged forward, rushing Krake like a raging bull. Sheer willpower kept him up on his damaged leg. Sheer determination drove him at his enemy. The world ceased to exist around him. He didn't see Nathan pushing through the vegetation on his left or Caleb approaching from the right. He didn't feel anything except rage.

Krake continued to turn, raising its hand to fire an energy blast at him.

Hayden was already reacting, reaching down and hooking his damaged hand beneath the belt full of microspears. The augment's fingers were missing, so he couldn't grab them. The elbow was damaged, leaving his shoulder motion limited.

It had to be enough.

He yanked as hard as he could, tearing the belt from his waist and flinging it forward. The spears, dislodged by the sudden movement, tumbled free— thirty impossibly sharp points spinning toward the Axon.

The maneuver took Krake by surprise, one of the spears embedding itself in its palm, and causing a misfire that burned the Axon's hand to smoldering ash. The rest of the microspears continued on their trajectory, a swarm of angry bees about to sting.

Krake turned away from the needles, too slow or too afraid to raise his shields. The lethal weapons sank through its Skin and into its flesh. Hayden was right behind them, the maneuver more effective than he had even hoped. He had his good hand around Krake's throat before it could recover. He lifted it off the ground, turning to Nathan and the remaining Centurions.

"I don't need to be the one to finish you off," Hayden said to Krake. "Just so long as you die."

He squeezed his hand, crushing Krake's trachea before throwing the Axon forward. The Centurions didn't hesitate to start shooting, their rounds drawing both blood and gel.

Krake hit the ground, shuddered and quit moving entirely.

## 60

### Hayden

"Max," Hayden cried out. "Max!" He stumbled forward and fell, crawling the two meters to where Max lay.

The Intellect didn't move.

"Sheriff," Caleb said, coming up beside him. The Marine looked almost as bad as Hayden felt, his face pale and sweaty, his body shaking beneath the Skin. "We have six minutes until the enemy ships arrive. We have to get out of here."

"Max?" Hayden said again, resting his hand on the Intellect's chest.

The Intellect remained still. And silent.

Caleb put his hand on Hayden's shoulder. "Come on, Sheriff."

Hayden nodded. "The portal."

"What about it?"

"You know what. We need to go through it. That was the plan."

"Sheriff, we're in no shape to—"

"That was the plan," Hayden pressed. "Krake was the gun, but he didn't pull the trigger. Vyte did. I'm not letting him get away with this. With any of this."

"Sheriff," Nathan said. "We have a problem."

Hayden turned to see Nathan kneeling beside Krake. He had opened the duffel, revealing random pieces of junk where the interlink should have been.

"Where's the interlink?" Jesse asked.

"This doesn't make sense," Hayden said, staring at the garbage. "Krake killed Nat for the interlink. I thought Vyte needed it."

"Vyte does need it," Caleb said. "Which is exactly why it isn't here."

"What do you mean?"

"Maybe Krake was originally going to bring the interlink through the portal. But the plan changed, probably because of Max."

Hayden glanced at the fallen Intellect. "Max?"

"It's only a theory, but Max calculated that we had a twenty percent chance of success with his help. Twenty percent sounds low, but it's probably a lot higher than Vyte was comfortable with, especially since we had already managed to survive the xaxkluth attack in Sanisco. So he told Krake to redirect the interlink somewhere else. Probably somewhere one of the incoming ships can pick it up."

"But Krake still came here," Jesse said.

"Krake had to come here," Caleb said, "or we would have known something was off. Think about it. Once Krake leads us here, the best case for Vyte is that Krake is on Proxima, Hanson kills us all, and everyone who's managed to fight back against him is dead. Worst case, we're standing here trying to work it all out while the interlink is headed off-world and out of reach."

Hayden took a few seconds to consider the theory. The pieces fit better than he wanted to admit. He shifted his attention to his glasses, looking for Rico on the network. He needed to tell her to hurry to their position so she wouldn't be left behind.

His jaw clenched when he discovered she wasn't linked. "Has anyone seen or heard from Rico?"

"Negative, Sheriff," Nathan replied. "Drake is missing too."

"Drake didn't make it," Hayden said, his gaze drifting to Bennett's corpse. He sighed in dismay. "Bennett would have had to leapfrog Rico to get here."

"Do you think he killed her?" Nathan asked.

"Pozz," Hayden replied, though the answer was sour in his mouth. "Just like he killed Max."

"Clones can't just decide to turn traitor and murder one another," Jesse said. "It doesn't work like that."

"It can if the enemy has access to the cloning equipment," Spot said. "And if that's the case." She shook her head. "Who knows how many clones were altered."

"It just gets better and better, doesn't it?" Caleb said.

"Parabellum, this is Stacker," Nathan said. "We need immediate pickup. We've got four minutes to get the hell out of here."

"On my way, General," Isaac replied.

All eyes turned to Hayden, looking to him to tell them what to do next. His shoulders slumped in response, and he struggled to keep his composure. Even though they had won the fight, even though they had destroyed Krake, what had they really accomplished? The interlink was gone, getting further and further out of reach with each passing second. And they had no way to locate it.

Natalia would have had his head for giving in so easily to despair. She would have said this wasn't the Sheriff Duke she had married.

And she would have been right.

He pushed himself back to his feet, turning to face them. His leg was still on fire, but he ignored it. "Here's what we're going to do," he said, his voice firm. "Caleb and I will—"

He stopped speaking when he sensed movement behind him. He looked back just as Max sat straight up.

"Requirement," Max said. "We take Krake."

"Max?" Hayden said with a smile, a wave of

relief flooding through him. "We thought you were dead."

"Apologies. The attack damaged my neural pathways. I required time to reroute and reset. As I said, we require Krake's cortex. I may be able to recover the data stream containing the fate of the interlink."

"You mean read his mind?" Spot asked.

"Pozz."

"How quickly?" Hayden asked.

"Unknown. It depends on whether or not the cortex remains viable."

"And if it doesn't?"

"We'll require another plan. Hahaha. Haha."

"The portal," Hayden said. "That was our plan. The interlink is worthless if we don't know what to do with it."

"Max was supposed to come with us," Caleb said.

"Impossibility. I'll open the portal for you, and close it behind you. General Stacker, you'll carry Krake. I'll carry the portal."

"You want to take it with us?" Nathan said.

"Pozz. How else will they return?"

Max stepped over to the portal. He touched its base, and a projection appeared in front of it—a series of alien symbols floating in the air.

"The destination coordinates are already set," he said. He tapped a symbol on the projection, which turned green.

Hayden felt the charge in the air as the portal began drawing power. A chill washed over him, and the view past the frame of the device was replaced with what appeared to be a small, dark storage room.

"Where is that?" Caleb asked.

Hayden shrugged. "Wherever it is, it's where we're going."

"With one arm and one leg?" Caleb said. "No offense, Sheriff, but you look like hell."

Hayden smirked. "No offense, Colonel, but so do you. My leg will heal. And I only need one arm to kill Vyte." Hayden turned to Nathan. "Nate…"

"Go," Nathan said. "Find General Haeri. Unpack Card's head, figure out how to kill these bastards and get back here. We'll have the interlink by then. I promise."

The Parabellum appeared overhead, descending on the other side of the spheres near the dead remains of the reaper horde.

"That's it," Hayden said, facing the portal. "Caleb, it's just you and me."

"Roger, Sheriff," Caleb replied. "Let's do this."

Hayden limped forward, bending over and retrieving one of the microspears on the directly in front of the portal. He tucked it in his coat pocket as he straightened up, sparing one last glance back at Max. The Intellect nodded in encouragement. Hayden had no idea what they were going to do on the other side or how they were going to do it, but he was determined to get it done.

Whatever it took.

"Sheriff, wait!" Spot said.

Hayden found her near Bennett's remains. She had picked up Hayden's revolver from where Bennett had dropped it and tossed it to him. He caught it in his good hand, slipping it into its holster.

"Thank you kindly," he said.

Then he looked back at the portal.

And stepped through.

## Thank you for reading!

Thank you for reading Isolation. Since you made it this far, I'm guessing you enjoyed the book, and the series so far.

AWESOME!

The next book in the Forgotten Vengeance series is called Damnation.

mrforbes.com/damnation

**New to the Forgotten Universe?**

Forgotten Vengeance is one of a growing number of series based in the Forgotten Universe, and contains characters whose origins are fleshed out in earlier novels. You can get a breakdown of series by chronological order, published order, and main character at mrforbes.com/forgottenuniverse.

Thank you for reading!

## Want to know when my next book is out?

If you're enjoying Forgotten Vengeance, I'm sure there will be more to come that you'll also enjoy. Sign up for my mailing list and be one of the first to know when I have a new book out. You'll also have a chance to participate in giveaways, get discounted books, and continue to support my work.

BONUS: get a free short story, exclusive to e-mail subscribers.

mrforbes.com/notify

## Reviews

Reviews are so important to us authors. We rely on readers like you to help provide social proof to other readers that our work is worth picking up (especially for the first book in a series). If you think I've earned a 'tip' for my work on Forgotten Vengeance, please consider dropping a review on Amazon for Invasion and/or Isolation today.

mrforbes.com/reviewinvasion
  mrforbes.com/reviewisolation

Thank you again!
  Cheers,
  Michael.

## Forgotten Universe

The Forgotten Universe is still growing! Whether this is your first series in the universe or your fourth, there may be more books featuring your favorite characters - Sheriff Duke, Caleb Card, John Washington, Nathan Stacker, and more that you haven't met yet.

mrforbes.com/forgottenuniverse

## Other Books By M.R Forbes

**M.R. Forbes on Amazon**

mrforbes.com/books

**Forgotten (The Forgotten)**

mrforbes.com/theforgotten

**Some things are better off FORGOTTEN.**

Sheriff Hayden Duke was born on the Pilgrim, and he expects to die on the Pilgrim, like his father, and his father before him.

That's the way things are on a generation starship centuries from home. He's never questioned it. Never thought about it. And why bother? Access points to the ship's controls are sealed, the systems that guide her automated and out of reach. It isn't perfect, but he has all he needs to be content.

Until a malfunction forces his Engineer wife to

the edge of the habitable zone to inspect the damage.

Until she contacts him, breathless and terrified, to tell him she found a body, and it doesn't belong to anyone on board.

Until he arrives at the scene and discovers both his wife and the body are gone.

The only clue? A bloody handprint beneath a hatch that hasn't opened in hundreds of years.

Until now.

## **Deliverance (Forgotten Colony)**
mrforbes.com/deliverance

**The war is over. Earth is lost. Running is the only option.**

It may already be too late.

Caleb is a former Marine Raider and commander of the Vultures, a search and rescue team that's spent the last two years pulling high-value targets out of alien-ravaged cities and shipping them off-world.

When his new orders call for him to join forty-thousand survivors aboard the last starship out, he thinks his days of fighting are over. The Deliverance represents a fresh start and a chance to leave the war behind for good.

Except the war won't be as easy to escape as he thought.

And the colony will need a man like Caleb more than he ever imagined...

### **Earth Unknown (Forgotten Earth)**
mrforbes.com/earthunknown

**A desperate escape to the most dangerous planet in the universe... Earth.**

Nathan's wife is murdered. The police believe he's the killer, and why wouldn't they? He's a disgraced Centurion Marine pilot, an ex-con, and an employee of the most powerful crime syndicate on Proxima.

The evidence is damning. The truth, not as clear. If Nathan wants to prove his innocence and avenge his wife, he'll have to complete the most desperate evasive maneuver of his life:

**Steal a starship and escape to Earth.**

He thinks he'll be safe there. He's wrong.

*Very wrong.*

Earth isn't what he thinks. Not even close. What he doesn't know isn't only likely to kill him, it's eager to kill him.

If it doesn't?
**The Sheriff will.**

### **Starship Eternal (War Eternal)**
mrforbes.com/starshipeternal

A lost starship...

A dire warning from futures past...

A desperate search for salvation...

Captain Mitchell "Ares" Williams is a Space Marine and the hero of the Battle for Liberty, whose Shot Heard 'Round the Universe saved the planet from a nearly unstoppable war machine. He's handsome, charismatic, and the perfect poster boy to help the military drive enlistment. Pulled from the war and thrown into the spotlight, he's as efficient at charming the media and bedding beautiful celebrities as he was at shooting down enemy starfighters.

After an assassination attempt leaves Mitchell critically wounded, he begins to suffer from strange hallucinations that carry a chilling and oddly familiar warning:

They are coming. Find the Goliath or humankind will be destroyed.

Convinced that the visions are a side-effect of his injuries, he tries to ignore them, only to learn that he may not be as crazy as he thinks. The enemy is real and closer than he imagined, and they'll do whatever it takes to prevent him from rediscovering the centuries lost starship.

Narrowly escaping capture, out of time and out of air, Mitchell lands at the mercy of the Riggers - a ragtag crew of former commandos who patrol the lawless outer reaches of the galaxy. Guided by a captain with a reputation for cold-blooded murder, they're dangerous, immoral, and possibly insane.

They may also be humanity's last hope for survival in a war that has raged beyond eternity.

(War Eternal is also available in a box set of the first three books here: mrforbes.com/wareternalbox)

## Hell's Rejects (Chaos of the Covenant)
mrforbes.com/hellsrejects

The most powerful starships ever constructed are gone. Thousands are dead. A fleet is in ruins. The attackers are unknown. The orders are clear: *Recover the ships. Bury the bastards who stole them.*

Lieutenant Abigail Cage never expected to find herself in Hell. As a Highly Specialized Operational Combatant, she was one of the most respected Marines in the military. Now she's doing hard labor on the most miserable planet in the universe.

Not for long.

The Earth Republic is looking for the most dangerous individuals it can control. The best of the worst, and Abbey happens to be one of them. The deal is simple: *Bring back the starships, earn your freedom. Try to run, you die.* It's a suicide mission, but she has nothing to lose.

The only problem? There's a new threat in the galaxy. One with a power unlike anything anyone has ever seen. One that's been waiting for this moment for a very, very, long time. And they want Abbey, too.

Be careful what you wish for.

They say Hell hath no fury like a woman scorned. They have no idea.

## **Man of War (Rebellion)**

mrforbes.com/manofwar

In the year 2280, an alien fleet attacked the Earth.

Their weapons were unstoppable, their defenses unbreakable.

Our technology was inferior, our militaries overwhelmed.

Only one starship escaped before civilization fell.

Earth was lost.

It was never forgotten.

Fifty-two years have passed.

A message from home has been received.

The time to fight for what is ours has come.

Welcome to the rebellion.

## About the Author

M.R. Forbes is the mind behind a growing number of Amazon best-selling science fiction series including Rebellion, War Eternal, Chaos of the Covenant, and the Forgotten Universe novels. He currently resides with his family and friends on the west cost of the United States, including a cat who thinks she's a dog and a dog who thinks she's a cat.

He maintains a true appreciation for his readers and is always happy to hear from them.

To learn more about M.R. Forbes or just say hello:

Visit my website:
mrforbes.com

Send me an e-mail:
michael@mrforbes.com

Check out my Facebook page:
facebook.com/mrforbes.author

Chat with me on Facebook Messenger:
https://m.me/mrforbes.author

Printed in Poland
by Amazon Fulfillment
Poland Sp. z o.o., Wrocław